THE FIRST MISSION

But the biggest thing that doesn't compute for me is this: Day has never killed anyone before. That's another reason why I don't think he's connected to the Patriots. In one of his past crimes, he crept into a quarantine zone by tying up a street policeman. The policeman didn't have a scratch on him (except a black eye). Another time, he broke into a bank vault but left the four security guards at its back entrance untouched—although a bit stupefied. He once torched a whole squadron of fighter jets on an empty airfield in the middle of the night and has on two occasions grounded airships by crippling their engines. He once vandalized the side of a military building. He's stolen money, food, and goods. But he doesn't set roadside bombs. He doesn't shoot soldiers. He doesn't attempt assassinations. He doesn't *kill.*

So why Metias? Day could've made his escape without killing him. Did Day hold some sort of grudge? Had my brother done something to him in the past? It couldn't have been accidental—that knife went straight through Metias's heart.

Straight through his intelligent, stupid, stubborn, overprotective heart.

Day's exploits used to fascinate me. But now he is my matched enemy—my target. My first mission.

OTHER BOOKS YOU MAY ENJOY

Champion	Marie Lu
Crossed	Ally Condie
Fire	Kristin Cashore
Incarceron	Catherine Fisher
The Madness Underneath	Maureen Johnson
Matched	Ally Condie
The Name of the Star	Maureen Johnson
Nightshade	Andrea Cremer
Prodigy	Marie Lu
Reached	Ally Condie
Sapphique	Catherine Fisher
Wolfsbane	Andrea Cremer
The Young Elites	Marie Lu

LEGEND

MARIE LU

speak
An Imprint of Penguin Group (USA)

For My Mother

SPEAK
Published by the Penguin Group
Penguin Group (USA) LLC
375 Hudson Street
New York, New York 10014

USA * Canada * UK * Ireland * Australia
New Zealand * India * South Africa * China

penguin.com
A Penguin Random House Company

First published in the United States of America by G. P. Putnam's Sons,
a division of Penguin Young Readers Group, 2011
Published by Speak, an imprint of Penguin Group (USA) Inc., 2013

THE LIBRARY OF CONGRESS HAS CATALOGED THE G. P. PUTNAM'S SONS EDITION AS FOLLOWS:
Lu, Marie, date.
Legend / Marie Lu. p. cm.
Summary: In a dark future, when North America has split into two warring nations, fifteen-year-olds Day, a famous criminal, and prodigy June, the brilliant soldier hired to capture him, discover they have a common enemy.
[1. Fugitives from justice—Fiction. 2. Criminals—Fiction. 3. Soldiers—Fiction. 4. War—Fiction. 5. Brothers and sisters—Fiction. 6. Government, Resistance to—Fiction. 7. Plague—Fiction.] I. Title.
PZ7.L96768Leg 2011 [Fic]—dc22 2011002003

Speak ISBN 978-0-14-242207-6

Design by Marikka Tamura

Printed in the United States of America

15 17 19 20 18 16 14

LEGEND

LOS ANGELES, CALIFORNIA

REPUBLIC OF AMERICA

POPULATION: 20,174,282

PART ONE

★★★

THE BOY WHO WALKS IN THE LIGHT

MY MOTHER THINKS I'M DEAD.

Obviously I'm *not* dead, but it's safer for her to think so.

At least twice a month, I see my Wanted poster flashed on the JumboTrons scattered throughout downtown Los Angeles. It looks out of place up there. Most of the pictures on the screens are of happy things: smiling children standing under a bright blue sky, tourists posing before the Golden Gate Ruins, Republic commercials in neon colors. There's also anti-Colonies propaganda. *"The Colonies want our land,"* the ads declare. *"They want what they don't have. Don't let them conquer your homes! Support the cause!"*

Then there's my criminal report. It lights up the JumboTrons in all its multicolored glory:

WANTED BY THE REPUBLIC

FILE NO: 462178-3233 "DAY"

WANTED FOR ASSAULT, ARSON, THEFT,
DESTRUCTION OF MILITARY PROPERTY,
AND HINDERING THE WAR EFFORT
200,000 REPUBLIC NOTES FOR
INFORMATION LEADING TO ARREST

They always have a different photo running alongside the report. One time it was a boy with glasses and a head full of thick copper curls. Another time it was a boy with black eyes and no hair at all. Sometimes I'm black, sometimes white, sometimes olive or brown or yellow or red or whatever else they can think of.

In other words, the Republic has no idea what I look like. They don't seem to know much of *anything* about me, except that I'm young and that when they run my fingerprints they don't find a match in their databases. That's why they hate me, why I'm not the most *dangerous* criminal in the country, but the most *wanted*. I make them look bad.

It's early evening, but it's already pitch-black outside, and the JumboTrons' reflections are visible in the street's puddles. I sit on a crumbling window ledge three stories up, hidden from view behind rusted steel beams. This used to be an apartment complex, but it's fallen into disrepair. Broken lanterns and glass shards litter the floor of this room, and paint is peeling from every wall. In one corner, an old portrait of the Elector Primo lies faceup on the ground. I wonder who used to live here—no one's cracked enough to let their portrait of the Elector sit discarded on the floor like that.

My hair, as usual, is tucked inside an old newsboy cap. My eyes are fixed on the small one-story house across the road. My hands fiddle with the pendant tied around my neck.

Tess leans against the room's other window, watching me closely. I'm restless tonight and, as always, she can sense it.

The plague has hit the Lake sector hard. In the glow of the

JumboTrons, Tess and I can see the soldiers at the end of the street as they inspect each home, their black capes shiny and worn loose in the heat. Each of them wears a gas mask. Sometimes when they emerge, they mark a house by painting a big red *X* on the front door. No one enters or leaves the home after that—at least, not when anyone's looking.

"Still don't see them?" Tess whispers. Shadows conceal her expression.

In an attempt to distract myself, I'm piecing together a makeshift slingshot out of old PVC pipes. "They haven't eaten dinner. They haven't sat down by the table in hours." I shift and stretch out my bad knee.

"Maybe they're not home?"

I shoot Tess an irritated glance. She's trying to console me, but I'm not in the mood. "A lamp's lit. Look at those candles. Mom would never waste candles if no one was home."

Tess moves closer. "We should leave the city for a couple weeks, yeah?" She tries to keep her voice calm, but the fear is there. "Soon the plague will have blown through, and you can come back to visit. We have more than enough money for two train tickets."

I shake my head. "One night a week, remember? Just let me check up on them one night a week."

"Yeah. You've been coming here *every* night this week."

"I just want to make sure they're okay."

"What if you get sick?"

"I'll take my chances. And you didn't have to come with me. You could've waited for me back in Alta."

Tess shrugs. "*Somebody* has to keep an eye on you." Two years younger than me—although sometimes she sounds old enough to be my caretaker.

We look on in silence as the soldiers draw closer to my family's house. Every time they stop at a home, one soldier pounds on the door while a second stands next to him with his gun drawn. If no one opens the door within ten seconds, the first soldier kicks it in. I can't see them once they rush inside, but I know the drill: a soldier will draw a blood sample from each family member, then plug it into a handheld reader and check for the plague. The whole process takes ten minutes.

I count the houses between where the soldiers are now and where my family lives. I'll have to wait another hour before I know their fate.

A shriek echoes from the other end of the street. My eyes dart toward the sound and my hand whips to the knife sheathed at my belt. Tess sucks in her breath.

It's a plague victim. She must've been deteriorating for months, because her skin is cracked and bleeding everywhere, and I find myself wondering how the soldiers could have missed this one during previous inspections. She stumbles around for a while, disoriented, then charges forward, only to trip and fall to her knees. I glance back toward the soldiers. They see her now. The soldier with the drawn weapon approaches, while the eleven others stay where they are and look on. One plague victim isn't much of a threat. The soldier lifts his gun and aims. A volley of sparks engulfs the infected woman.

She collapses, then goes still. The soldier rejoins his comrades.

I wish we could get our hands on one of the soldiers' guns. A pretty weapon like that doesn't cost much on the market—480 Notes, less than a stove. Like all guns, it has precision, guided by magnets and electric currents, and can accurately shoot a target three blocks away. It's tech stolen from the Colonies, Dad once said, although of course the Republic would never tell you that. Tess and I could buy five of them if we wanted. . . . Over the years we've learned to stockpile the extra money we steal and stash it away for emergencies. But the real problem with having a gun isn't the expense. It's that it's so easy to trace back to you. Each gun has a sensor on it that reports its user's hand shape, thumbprints, and location. If that didn't give me away, nothing would. So I'm left with my homemade weapons, PVC pipe slingshots, and other trinkets.

"They found another one," Tess says. She squints to get a better look.

I look down and see the soldiers spill from another house. One of them shakes a can of spray paint and draws a giant red *X* on the door. I know that house. The family that lives there once had a little girl my age. My brothers and I played with her when we were younger—freeze tag and street hockey with iron pokers and crumpled paper.

Tess tries to distract me by nodding at the cloth bundle near my feet. "What'd you bring them?"

I smile, then reach down to untie the cloth. "Some of the stuff we saved up this week. It'll make for a nice celebration once they pass the inspection." I dig through the little pile of goodies inside the bundle, then hold up a used pair of goggles. I check them again to make sure there are no cracks in the glass. "For John. An early birthday gift." My older brother turns nineteen later this week. He works fourteen-hour shifts in the neighborhood plant's friction stoves and always comes home rubbing his eyes from the smoke. These goggles were a lucky steal from a military supply shipment.

I put them down and shuffle through the rest of the stuff. It's mostly tins of meat and potato hash I stole from an airship's cafeteria, and an old pair of shoes with intact soles. I wish I could be in the room with all of them when I deliver this stuff. But John's the only one who knows I'm alive, and he's promised not to tell Mom or Eden.

Eden turns ten in two months, which means that in two months he'll have to take the Trial. I failed my own Trial when I was ten. That's why I worry about Eden, because even though he's easily the smartest of us three boys, he thinks a lot like I do. When I finished my Trial, I felt so sure of my answers that I didn't even bother to watch them grade it. But then the admins ushered me into a corner of the Trial stadium with a bunch of other kids. They stamped something on my test and stuffed me onto a train headed downtown. I didn't get to take anything except the pendant I wore around my neck. I didn't even get to say good-bye.

Several different things could happen after you take the Trial.

You get a perfect score—1500 points. No one's *ever* gotten this—well, except for some kid a few years ago who the military made a goddy fuss over. Who knows what happens to someone with a score that high? Probably lots of money and power, yeah?

You score between a 1450 and a 1499. Pat yourself on the back because you'll get instant access to six years of high school and then four at the top universities in the Republic: Drake, Stanford, and Brenan. Then Congress hires you and you make lots of money. Joy and happiness follow. At least according to the Republic.

You get a good score, somewhere between 1250 and 1449 points. You get to continue on to high school, and then you're assigned to a college. Not bad.

You squeak by with a score between 1000 and 1249. Congress bars you from high school. You join the poor, like my family. You'll probably either drown while working the water turbines or get steamed to death in the power plants.

You fail.

It's almost always the slum-sector kids who fail. If you're in this unlucky category, the Republic sends officials to your family's home. They make your parents sign a contract giving the government full custody over you. They say that you've been sent away to the Republic's labor camps and that your family will not see you again. Your parents have to nod and agree. A few even celebrate, because the Republic gives them one thousand Notes as a condolence gift. Money and one less mouth to feed? What a thoughtful government.

Except this is all a lie. An inferior child with bad genes is no use to the country. If you're lucky, Congress will let you die without first sending you to the labs to be examined for imperfections.

Five houses remain. Tess sees the worry in my eyes and puts a hand on my forehead. "One of your headaches coming on?"

"No. I'm okay." I peer in the open window at my mother's house, then catch my first glimpse of a familiar face. Eden walks by, then peeks out the window at the approaching soldiers and points some handmade metal contraption at them. Then he ducks back inside and disappears from view. His curls flash white-blond in the flickering lamplight. Knowing him, he probably built that gadget to measure how far away someone is, or something like that.

"He looks thinner," I mutter.

"He's alive and walking around," Tess replies. "I'd say that's a win."

Minutes later, we see John and my mother wander past the window, deep in conversation. John and I look pretty similar, although he's grown a little stockier from long days at the plant. His hair, like most who live in our sector, hangs down past his shoulders and is tied back into a simple tail. His vest is smudged with red clay. I can tell Mom's scolding him for something or other, probably for letting Eden peek out the window. She bats John's hand away when a bout of her chronic coughing hits her. I let out a breath. So. At least all three of them are healthy enough to walk. Even if one of them is infected, it's early enough that they'll still have a chance to recover.

I can't stop imagining what will happen if the soldiers mark my mother's door. My family will stand frozen in our living room long after the soldiers have left. Then Mom will put on her usual brave face, only to sit up through the night, quietly wiping tears away. In the morning, they'll start receiving small rations of food and water and simply wait to recover. Or die.

My mind wanders to the stash of stolen money that Tess and I have hidden. Twenty-five hundred Notes. Enough to feed us for months . . . but not enough to buy my family vials of plague medicine.

The minutes drag on. I tuck my slingshot away and play a few rounds of Rock, Paper, Scissors with Tess. (I don't know why, but she's crazy good at this game.) I glance several times at my mother's window, but don't see anyone. They must have gathered near the door, ready to open it as soon as they hear a fist against the wood.

And then the time comes. I lean forward on the ledge, so far that Tess grips my arm to make sure I don't topple to the ground. The soldiers pound on the door. My mother opens it immediately, lets the soldiers in, and then closes it. I strain to hear voices, footsteps, anything that might come from my house. The sooner this is all over, the sooner I can sneak my gifts to John.

The silence drags on. Tess whispers, "No news is good news, right?"

"Very funny."

I count off the seconds in my head. One minute passes. Then two, then four, and then finally, ten minutes.

Then fifteen minutes. Twenty minutes.

I look at Tess. She just shrugs. "Maybe their reader's broken," she suggests.

Thirty minutes pass. I don't dare move from my vigil. I'm afraid something will happen so quickly that I'll miss it if I blink. My fingers tap rhythmically against the hilt of my knife.

Forty minutes. Fifty minutes. An hour.

"Something's wrong," I whisper.

Tess purses her lips. "You don't know that."

"Yes I do. What could possibly take this long?"

Tess opens her mouth to reply, but before she can say anything, the soldiers are exiting my house, single file, expressionless. Finally, the last soldier shuts the door behind him and reaches for something tucked at his waist. I suddenly feel dizzy. I know what's coming.

The soldier reaches up and sprays one long, red, diagonal line on our door. Then he sprays another line, making an *X*.

I curse silently under my breath and start to turn away—

—but then the soldier does something unexpected, something I've never seen before.

He sprays a third, vertical line on my mother's door, cutting the *X* in half.

1347 HOURS.
DRAKE UNIVERSITY, BATALLA SECTOR.
72°F INDOORS.

I'M SITTING IN MY DEAN SECRETARY'S OFFICE. AGAIN. On the other side of the frosted glass door, I can see a bunch of my classmates (seniors, all at least four years older than me) hanging around in an attempt to hear what's going on. Several of them saw me being yanked out of our afternoon drill class (today's lesson: how to load and unload the XM-621 rifle) by a menacing pair of guards. And whenever that happens, the news spreads all over campus.

The Republic's favorite little prodigy is in trouble again.

The office is quiet except for the faint hum coming from the dean secretary's computer. I've memorized every detail of this room (hand-cut marble floors imported from Dakota, 324 plastic square ceiling tiles, twenty feet of gray drapes hanging to either side of the glorious Elector's portrait on the office's back wall, a thirty-inch screen on the side wall, with the sound muted and a headline that reads: "TRAITOROUS 'PATRIOTS' GROUP BOMBS LOCAL MILITARY STATION, KILLS FIVE" followed by "REPUBLIC DEFEATS COLONIES IN BATTLE FOR HILLSBORO"). Arisna Whitaker, the dean secretary herself, is seated behind her desk, tapping on its glass—no doubt typing up my report.

This will be my eighth report this quarter. I'm willing to bet I'm the only Drake student who's ever managed to get eight reports in one quarter without being expelled.

"Injured your hand yesterday, Ms. Whitaker?" I say after a while.

She stops typing to glare at me. "What makes you think that, Ms. Iparis?"

"The pauses in your keystrokes are off. You're favoring your left hand."

Ms. Whitaker sighs and leans back in her chair. "Yes, June. I twisted my wrist yesterday in a game of kivaball."

"Sorry to hear it. You should try to swing more from your arm and not from your wrist."

I'd meant this simply to be a statement of fact, but it sounded sort of taunting and doesn't seem to have made her any happier. "Let's get something straight, Ms. Iparis," she says. "You may think you're very smart. You may think your perfect grades earn you some sort of special treatment. You may even think you have fans at this school, what with all *this* nonsense." She gestures at the students gathered outside the door. "But *I've* grown incredibly tired of our get-togethers in my office. And believe me, when you graduate and get assigned to whatever post this country chooses for you, your antics won't impress your superiors there. Do you understand me?"

I nod, because that's what she wants me to do. But she's wrong. I don't just *think* I'm smart. I'm the only person in the entire Republic with a perfect 1500 score on her Trial. I was assigned here, to the country's top university, at twelve, four years ahead of schedule. Then I skipped my sophomore year. I've earned perfect grades at Drake for three years. I *am* smart. I have what the Republic considers *good* genes—and better genes make for better soldiers make for better chance of victory against the Colonies, my professors always say. And if I feel like my afternoon drills aren't teaching me enough about how to climb walls while carrying weapons, then . . . well, it wasn't *my* fault I had to scale the side of a nineteen-story building with a XM-621 gun strapped to my back. It was self-improvement, for the sake of my country.

Rumor has it that Day once scaled five stories in less than eight seconds. If the Republic's most-wanted criminal can pull that off, then how are we ever going to catch him if we're not just as fast? And if we can't even catch *him*, how are we going to win the war?

Ms. Whitaker's desk beeps three times. She holds down a button. "Yes?"

"Captain Metias Iparis is outside the gate," a voice replies. "He's here for his sister."

"Good. Send him in." She releases the button and points a finger at me. "I hope that brother of yours starts doing a better job of minding you, because if you end up in my office one more time this quarter—"

"Metias is doing a better job than our dead parents," I reply, maybe more sharply than I intended.

We fall into an uncomfortable silence.

Finally, after what seems like an eternity, I hear a commotion out in the hall. The students pressed against the door's glass abruptly disperse, and their shadows move aside to make room for a tall silhouette. My brother.

As Metias opens the door and steps inside, I can see some girls out in the hall stifling smiles behind their hands. But Metias fixes his full attention on me. We have the same eyes, black with a gold glint, the same long lashes and dark hair. The long lashes work particularly well for Metias. Even with the door closed behind him, I can still hear the whispers and giggles from outside. It looks like he came from his patrol duties straight to my campus. He's decked out in his full uniform: black officer coat with double rows of gold buttons, gloves (neoprene, spectra lining, captain rank embroidery), shining epaulettes on his shoulders, formal military hat, black trousers, polished boots. My eyes meet his.

He's furious.

Ms. Whitaker gives Metias a brilliant smile. "Ah, Captain!" she exclaims. "It's a pleasure to see you."

Metias taps the edge of his hat in a polite salute. "It's unfortunate it's under these circumstances again," he replies. "My apologies."

"Not a problem, Captain." The dean secretary waves her hand dismissively. What a brownnoser—especially after what she'd just said about Metias. "It's hardly your fault. Your sister was caught scaling a high-rise during her lunch hour today. She'd wandered two blocks off campus to do it. As you know, students are to use only the climbing walls on campus for physical training, and leaving the campus in the middle of the day is forbidden—"

"Yes, I'm aware of that," Metias interrupts, looking at me out of the corner of his eye. "I saw the helicopters over Drake at noon and had a . . . . *suspicion* June might've been involved."

There'd been *three* helicopters. They couldn't get me off the side of the building by scaling it themselves, so they pulled me off with a net.

"Thank you for your help," Metias says to the dean secretary. He snaps his fingers at me, my cue to get up. "When June returns to campus, she'll be on her best behavior."

I ignore Ms. Whitaker's false smile as I follow my brother out of the office and into the hall. Immediately students hurry over. "June," a boy named Dorian says as he tags alongside us. He'd asked me (unsuccessfully) to the annual Drake ball two years in a row. "Is it true? How high up did you get?"

Metias cuts him off with a stern look. "June's heading home." Then he puts a hand firmly on my shoulder and guides me away from my classmates. I glance behind me and manage a smile for them.

"Fourteen floors," I call back. That gets them buzzing again. Somehow, this has become the closest relationship I have with the other Drake students. I am respected, discussed, gossiped about. Not really talked *to.*

Such is the life of a fifteen-year-old senior in a university meant for sixteen and up.

Metias doesn't say another word as we make our way down the corridors, past the manicured lawns of the central quad and the glorious Elector's statue, and finally through one of the indoor gyms. We pass by the afternoon drills I'm supposed to be participating in. I watch my classmates run along a giant track surrounded by a 360-degree screen simulating some desolate warfront road. They're holding their rifles out in front of them, attempting to load and unload as fast as they can while running. At most other universities, there wouldn't be so many student soldiers, but at Drake, almost all of us are well on our way to career assignments in the Republic's military. A few others are tapped for politics and Congress, and some are chosen to stay behind and teach. But Drake is the Republic's best university, and seeing as how the best are always assigned to the military, our drill room is packed with students.

By the time we reach one of Drake's outer streets and I climb into the backseat of our waiting military jeep, Metias can barely contain his anger. "Suspended for a week? Do you want to explain this to me?" he demands. "I get back from a morning of dealing with the Patriot rebels and what do I hear about? Helicopters two blocks from Drake. A girl scaling a skyscraper."

I exchange a friendly look with Thomas, the soldier in the driver's seat. "Sorry," I mutter.

Metias turns around from his place in the passenger seat and narrows his eyes at me. "What the hell were you thinking? Did you know you'd wandered right off campus?"

"Yes."

"Of course. You're *fifteen*. You went fourteen floors up a—" He takes a deep breath, closes his eyes, and steadies himself. "For once, I'd appreciate it if you would let me do my daily tours of duty without worrying myself sick over what you're up to."

I try to meet Thomas's eyes again in the rearview mirror, but he keeps his gaze on the road. Of course, I shouldn't expect any help from him. He looks as tidy as ever, with his perfectly slicked hair and perfectly ironed uniform. Not a strand or thread out of place. Thomas might be several years younger than Metias and a subordinate on his patrol, but he's more disciplined than anyone I know. Sometimes I wish I had that much discipline. He probably disapproves of my stunts even more than Metias does.

We leave downtown Los Angeles behind and travel up the winding highway in silence. The scenery changes from inner Batalla sector's hundred-floor skyscrapers to densely packed barrack towers and civilian complexes, each one only twenty to thirty stories high, with red guiding lights blinking on their roofs, most with all their paint stripped off after this year's rash of storms. Metal support beams crisscross their walls. I hope they get to upgrade those supports soon. The war's been intense lately, and with several decades of infrastructure funding diverted to supplying the warfront, I don't know if these buildings would hold up well in another earthquake.

After a few minutes, Metias continues in a calmer voice. "You really scared me today," he says. "I was afraid they'd mistake you for Day and shoot at you."

I know he doesn't mean this as a compliment, but I can't help smiling. I lean forward to rest my arms on top of his seat. "Hey," I say, tugging his ear the way I did when I was a kid, "I'm sorry I made you worry."

He lets out a scornful chuckle, but I can tell his anger is already fading. "Yeah. That's what you say every time, Junebug. Is Drake not keeping your brain busy enough? If not, then I don't know what will."

"You *know* . . . if you'd just take me along on some of your missions, I'd probably learn a lot more and stay out of trouble."

"Nice try. You're not going anywhere until you graduate and get assigned to your own patrol."

I bite my tongue. Metias did pick me once—*once*—for a mission last year, when all third-year Drake students had to shadow an assigned military branch. His commander sent him to kill a runaway prisoner of war from the Colonies. So Metias brought me along with him, and together we chased the POW deeper and deeper into our territory, away from the dividing fences and the strip of land running from Dakota to West Texas that separates the Republic and the Colonies, away from the warfront where airships dot the sky. I tracked him into an alley in Yellowstone City, Montana, and Metias shot him.

During the chase, I broke three ribs and had a knife buried in my leg. Now Metias refuses to take me anywhere.

When Metias finally speaks again, he sounds grudgingly curious. "So, tell me," he whispers. "How fast did you climb those fourteen stories?"

Thomas makes a disapproving sound in his throat, but I break into a grin. Storm's past. Metias loves me again. "Six minutes," I whisper back to my brother. "And forty-four seconds. How do you like *that*?"

"That must be some sort of record. Not that, you know, you're supposed to do it."

Thomas stops the jeep right behind the lines at a red light and gives Metias an exasperated look. "Come on, Captain," he says. "June—ah—Ms. Iparis won't learn a thing if you keep praising her for breaking the rules."

"Cheer up, Thomas." Metias reaches over and claps him on the back. "Surely breaking a rule once in a while is tolerable, especially if you're doing it to beef up your skills for the Republic's sake. Victory against the Colonies. Right?"

The light blinks green. Thomas turns his eyes back to the road (he seems to count to three in his head before letting the jeep go forward). "Right," he mutters. "You should still be careful what you're encouraging Ms. Iparis to do, especially with your parents gone."

Metias's mouth tightens into a line, and a familiar, strained look appears in his eyes.

No matter how sharp my intuition is, no matter how well I do at Drake or how perfectly I score in defense and target practice and hand-to-hand combat, Metias's eyes always hold that fear. He's afraid something might happen to me one day—like the car crash that took our parents. That fear never leaves his face. And Thomas knows it.

I didn't know our parents long enough to miss them in the same way Metias does. Whenever I cry over losing them, I cry because I *don't* have any memories of them. Just hazy recollections of long, adult legs shuffling around our apartment and hands lifting me from my high chair. That's it. Every other memory from my childhood—looking out into the auditorium as I receive an award, or having soup made for me when I'm sick, or being scolded, or tucked into bed—those are with Metias.

We drive past half of Batalla sector and through a few poor blocks. (Can't these street beggars stay a little farther from our jeep?) Finally we reach the gleaming, terraced high-rises of Ruby, and we're home. Metias gets out first. As I follow, Thomas gives me a small smile.

"See you later, Ms. Iparis," he says, tipping his hat.

I stopped trying to convince him to call me June—he'll never change. Still, it's not so bad being called something proper. Maybe when I'm older and Metias doesn't faint at the idea of me dating . . .

"Bye, Thomas. Thanks for the ride." I smile back at him before stepping out of the jeep.

Metias waits until the door has slammed shut before turning to me and lowering his voice. "I'll be home late tonight," he says. There's that tension in his eyes again. "Don't go out alone. News from the warfront is they're cutting power to residences tonight to save energy for the airfield bases. So stay put, okay? The streets'll be darker than usual."

My heart sinks. I wish the Republic would hurry up and win this war already so that for once we might actually get a whole month of nonstop electricity. "Where are you going? Can I come with you?"

"I'm overseeing the lab at Los Angeles Central. They're delivering vials of some mutated virus there—it shouldn't take all night. And I already told you *no. No missions.*" Metias hesitates. "I'll be home as early as I can. We have a lot to talk about." He puts his hands on my shoulders, ignores my puzzled look, and gives me a quick kiss on my forehead. "Love you, Junebug," he says, his trademark good-bye. He turns to climb back into the jeep.

"I'm not going to wait up for you," I call after him, but by now he's already inside and the jeep's pulling away with him inside of it. "Be careful," I murmur.

But it's pointless to say now. Metias is too far away to hear me.

WHEN I WAS SEVEN YEARS OLD, MY FATHER CAME home from the warfront for a week's leave. His job was to clean up after the Republic's soldiers, so he was usually gone, and Mom was left to raise us boys on her own. When he came home that time, the city patrols did a routine inspection of our house, then dragged Dad off to the local police headquarters for questioning. They'd found something suspicious, I guess.

The police brought him back with two broken arms, his face bloody and bruised.

Several nights later, I dipped a ball of crushed ice into a can of gasoline, let the oil coat the ice in a thick layer, and lit it. Then I launched it with a slingshot through the window of our local police headquarters. I remember the fire trucks that came whizzing around the corner shortly thereafter, and the charred remains of the police building's west wing. They never found out who did it, and I never came forward. There was, after all, no evidence. I had committed my first perfect crime.

My mother used to hope that I would rise up from my humble roots. Become someone successful, or even famous.

I'm famous all right, but I don't think it's what she had in mind.

★★★

It's nightfall again, a good forty-eight hours since the soldiers marked my mother's door.

I wait in the shadows of a back alley one block from the Los Angeles Central Hospital and watch its staff spill in and out of the main entrance. It's a cloudy night with no moon, and I can't even make out the crumbling Bank Tower sign at the top of the building. Electric lights shine from each floor—a luxury only government buildings and the elite's homes can afford. Military jeeps stack up along the street as they wait for approval to enter the underground parking lots. Someone checks them for proper IDs. I keep still, my eyes fixed on the entrance.

I look pretty awesome tonight. I'm wearing my good pair of shoes—boots made of dark leather worn soft over time, with strong laces and steel toes. Bought them with 150 Notes from our stash. I've hidden a knife flat against the sole of each boot. When I shift my feet, I can feel the cool metal against my skin. My black trousers are tucked into my boots and I carry a pair of gloves and a black handkerchief in my pockets. A dark, long-sleeved shirt is tied around my waist. My hair hangs loose down my shoulders. This time I've sprayed my white-blond strands a deep black, as if I'd dipped them in crude oil. Earlier in the day, Tess had traded five Notes for a bucket of pygmy pig's blood from the back alley of a kitchen. My arms, stomach, and face are smeared with it. I've also streaked mud on my cheeks, for good measure.

The hospital spans the first twelve floors of the building, but I'm only interested in the one without windows. That's the third floor, a laboratory, where the blood samples and medicines will be. From the outside, the third floor is completely hidden behind elaborate stone carvings and worn Republic flags. Behind the facade lies a vast floor with no halls and no doors—just a gigantic room, doctors and nurses behind white masks, test tubes and pipettes, incubators and gurneys. I know this because I've been there before. I was there the day I failed my Trial, the day I was supposed to die.

My eyes scan the side of the tower. Sometimes I can break into a building by running it from the outside, if there are balconies to leap from and window ledges to balance on. I once scaled a four-story building in less than five seconds. But this tower is too smooth, with no footholds. I'll have to reach the lab from inside. I shiver a little even in the warmth and wish I'd asked Tess to come with me. But two trespassers are easier to catch than one. Besides, it's not *her* family who needs medicine. I check to make sure I've tucked my pendant beneath my shirt.

A lone medic truck pulls up behind the military jeeps. Several soldiers climb out and greet the nurses while others unpack the truck's boxes. The leader of the group is a young, dark-haired man dressed all in black, except for two rows of silver buttons that line his officer jacket. I strain to hear what he's saying to one of the nurses.

"—from around the lake's edge." The man tightens his gloves. I catch a glimpse of the gun at his belt. "My men will be at the entrances tonight."

"Yes, Captain," the nurse says.

The man tips his cap to her. "My name's Metias. If you have any questions, come see me."

I wait until the soldiers have spread out around the hospital's perimeter and the man named Metias has immersed himself in conversation with two of his men. Several more medic trucks come and go, dropping off soldiers, some with broken limbs, some with gashes on their heads or lacerations on their legs. I take a deep breath, then step out of the shadows and stumble toward the hospital's entrance.

A nurse spots me first, just outside the main doors. Her eyes dart to the blood on my arms and face. "Can I be admitted, cousin?" I call to her. I wince in imaginary pain. "Is there still room tonight? I can pay."

She looks at me without pity before she returns to scribbling on a notepad. Guess she doesn't appreciate the "cousin" affection. An ID tag dangles from her neck. "What happened?" she asks.

I double over when I reach her and lean on my knees. "Was in a fight," I say, panting. "I think I got stabbed."

The nurse doesn't look at me again. She finishes writing and then nods at one of the guards. "Pat him down."

I stay where I am as two soldiers check me for weapons. I yelp on cue when they touch my arms or stomach. They don't find the knives tucked in my boots. They *do* take the little pouch of Notes tied to my belt, my payment for entering the hospital. Of course.

If I was a goddy rich sector boy, I'd be admitted without charge. Or they'd send a doctor for free straight up to where I live.

When the soldiers give the nurse a thumbs-up, she points me toward the entrance. "Waiting room's on the left. Have a seat."

I thank her and stumble toward the sliding doors. The man named Metias watches me as I pass. He's listening patiently to one of his soldiers, but I see him study my face as if out of habit. I make a mental note of his face too.

The hospital is ghostly white on the inside. To my left I see the waiting room, just like the nurse said, a huge space packed with people sporting injuries of all shapes and sizes. Many of them moan in pain—one person lies unmoving on the floor. I don't want to guess how long some of them have been here, or how much they had to pay to get in. I note where all the soldiers are standing—two by the secretary's window, two by the doctor's door far in the distance, several near the elevators, each wearing ID tags—and then I drop my eyes to the floor. I shuffle to the closest chair and sit. For once, my bad knee helps my disguise. I keep my hands pressed against my side for good measure.

I count ten minutes off in my head, long enough so that new patients have arrived in the waiting room and the soldiers are less interested in me. Then I stand up, pretend to stumble, and lurch toward the closest soldier. His hand reflexively moves to his gun.

"Sit back down," he says.

I trip and fall against him. "I need the bathroom," I whisper, my voice hoarse. My hands tremble as I grab his black robes for balance. The soldier looks at me in disgust while some of the others snicker. I see his fingers creep closer to his gun's trigger, but one of the other soldiers shakes his head. No shooting in the hospital. The soldier pushes me away and points toward the end of the hall with his gun.

"Over there," he snaps. "Wipe some of that filth off your face. And if you touch me again, I'll fill you with bullets."

I release him and nearly fall to my knees. Then I turn and stagger toward the restroom. My leather boots squeak against the floor tiles. I can feel the soldiers' eyes on me as I enter the bathroom and lock the door.

No matter. They'll forget about me in a couple of minutes. And it'll take several more minutes before the soldier I'd grabbed realizes that his ID tag is missing.

Once in the bathroom, I abandon my sick routine. I splash water on my face and scrub until most of the pig's blood and mud have come off. I unzip my boots and tear open the inner soles to reveal my knives, then tuck them into my belt. My boots go back on my feet. Then I untie the black collared shirt from around my waist and put it on, buttoning it up all the way to my neck and clipping my suspenders over it. I pull my hair back into a tight ponytail and tuck the tail into the shirt so it's pressed flat against my back.

Finally, I pull my gloves on and tie a black handkerchief around my mouth and nose. If someone catches me now, I'll be forced to run anyway. Might as well hide my face.

When I finish, I use the tip of one of my knives to unscrew the cover to the bathroom's ventilation shaft. Then I take out the soldier's ID tag, clip it to my pendant necklace, and stuff myself headfirst into the shaft's tunnel.

The air in the shaft smells strange, and I'm grateful for the handkerchief around my face. I inch along as fast as I can. The shaft can't be more than two feet wide in any direction. Each time I pull myself forward, I have to close my eyes and remind myself to breathe, that the metal walls around me are not closing in. I don't have to go far—none of these shafts will lead to the third floor. I only need to get far enough to pop out into one of the hospital's stairwells, away from the soldiers on the first floor. I press forward. I think of Eden's face, of the medicine he and John and my mother will need, and of the strange red *X* with the line through it.

After several minutes, the shaft dead-ends. I look through the vent, and in the slivers of light I can see pieces of a curved stairwell. The floor is an immaculate white, almost beautiful, and—most important—empty. I count to three in my head, then bring my arms as far back as I can and give the shaft cover a mighty shove. The cover flies off. I get one good glimpse of the stairwell, a large, cylindrical chamber with tall plaster walls and tiny windows. One enormous, spiraling set of stairs.

Now I'm moving with all speed and no stealth. *Run it.* I squeeze out of the shaft and dart up the steps. Halfway up, I grab the railing and fling myself to the next highest curve.

The security cameras must be focused on me. An alarm will sound any minute now. Second floor, third floor. I'm running out of time. As I approach the third-floor door, I tear the ID tag off my necklace and pause long enough to swipe it against the door's reader. The security cameras haven't triggered an alarm in time to lock down the stairwell. The handle clicks—I'm in. I throw open the door.

I'm in a huge room filled with rows of gurneys and chemicals boiling under metal hoods. Doctors and soldiers look up at me with startled faces.

I grab the first person I see—a young doctor standing close to the door. Before any of the soldiers can point a gun in our direction, I whip out one of my knives and hold it close to the man's throat. The other doctors and nurses freeze. Several of them scream.

"Shoot, and you'll hit him instead," I call out to the soldiers from beneath my handkerchief. Their guns are focused on me now. The doctor trembles in my grasp.

I press my knife harder against his neck, careful not to cut him. "I won't hurt you," I whisper in his ear. "Tell me where to get the plague cures."

He lets out a strangled whimper, and I can feel him sweating under my grip. He gestures toward the refrigerators. The soldiers are still hesitating—but one of them calls out to me.

"Release the doctor!" he shouts. "Put your hands up."

I want to laugh. The soldier must be a new recruit. I cross the room with the doctor, then stop at the refrigerators.

"Show me." The doctor lifts a trembling hand and pulls the fridge door open. A gust of freezing air hits us. I wonder if the doctor can feel how fast my heart is beating.

"There," he whispers. I turn away from the soldiers long enough to see the doctor pointing at the top shelf in the fridge. Half of the vials on the shelf are labeled with the three-lined *X: T. Filoviridae Virus Mutations.* The other half of the vials are labeled *11.30 Cures.* But all the vials are empty. They've run out. I curse under my breath. My eyes skim other shelves—they only have plague suppressants and various painkillers. I curse again. Too late to turn back now.

"I'm letting go," I whisper to the doctor. "Duck." I release my grip and shove him hard enough to make him fall to his knees.

The soldiers open fire. But I'm ready for them—I hide behind the open fridge door as bullets ricochet off it. I grab several bottles of suppressants and shove them into my shirt. I bolt. One of the stray bullets scrapes me and searing pain shoots up my arm. I'm almost at the exit.

An alarm goes off as I burst through the stairwell door. There's a chorus of clicks as all the doors in the stairwell lock from the inside. I'm trapped. The soldiers can still come through any door, but I won't be able to get out. Shouts and footsteps echo from inside the laboratory. A voice yells out, "He's hit!"

My eyes jump to the tiny windows in the stairwell's plaster walls. They're too far away for me to reach from the stairs themselves. I grit my teeth and pull out my second knife so that I now have one in each hand. I pray the plaster is soft enough, then leap off the stairs and throw myself toward the wall.

I stab one knife straight into the plaster. My wounded arm gushes blood, and I scream from the effort. I'm dangling halfway between my launching place and the window. I rock back and forth as hard as I can.

The plaster is giving way.

Behind me I hear the laboratory door burst open and soldiers spill out. Bullets spark all around me. I swing toward the window and let go of the knife buried in the wall.

The window shatters, and I'm suddenly out in the night again and falling, falling, falling like a star to the first floor. I rip open my long-sleeved shirt and let it billow out behind me as thoughts zip through my head. Knees bent. Feetfirst. Relax muscles. Hit with balls of feet. Roll. The ground rushes up at me. I brace myself.

The impact knocks the wind out of me. I roll four times and crash into the wall on the other side of the street. For a moment I lie there blinded, completely helpless. Above me I can hear furious voices coming from the third-floor window as the soldiers realize they're going to have to double back into the laboratory to disable the alarm. My senses gradually sharpen—now I'm very aware of the pain in my side and arm. I use my good arm to prop myself up and wince. My chest throbs. I think I've cracked a rib. When I try to stand,

I realize that I've sprained one of my ankles, too. I can't tell if adrenaline is keeping me from feeling other effects of my fall.

Shouts come from around the building's corner. I force myself to think. I'm now near the rear of the building, and several alleys branch off behind me into the darkness. I limp into the shadows.

When I look over my shoulder, I see a small group of soldiers rush to where I'd fallen, pointing out the broken glass and blood. One of the soldiers is the young captain I saw earlier, the man named Metias. He orders his men to spread out. I quicken my pace and try to ignore the pain. I hunch my shoulders so that the black of my outfit and hair help me melt into the darkness. My eyes stay down. I need to find a sewer cover.

The edges of my vision are blurring now. I push one hand against my ear and feel for blood. Nothing yet, a good sign. Moments later, I catch sight of a sewer cap on the street. I heave a sigh, readjust the black handkerchief covering my face, and bend down to lift the cover.

"Freeze. Stay where you are."

I whirl around to see Metias, the young captain from the hospital's entrance, facing me. He has a gun pointed straight at my chest, but to my surprise, he doesn't fire it. I tighten my grip on my remaining knife. Something changes in his eyes, and I know he recognizes me, the boy who had pretended to stagger into the hospital. I smile—I have plenty of wounds for the hospital to treat now.

Metias narrows his eyes. "Hands up. You're under arrest for theft, vandalism, and trespassing."

"You're not going to take me in alive."

"I'd be happy to take you in dead, if you prefer."

What happens next is a blur. I see Metias tense up to fire his gun. I throw my knife at him with all my strength. Before he can fire, my knife hits him hard in the shoulder and he falls backward with a thud. I don't wait to see him get up. I bend down and heave the manhole cover up, then lower myself down the ladder and into the blackness. I pull the sewer cover back in place.

My injuries are catching up to me now. I stumble along in the sewers, my vision going in and out of focus, one of my hands pressed hard against my side. I'm careful not to touch the walls. Every breath hurts. I *must've* cracked a rib. I'm alert enough to think about which direction I'm moving in and concentrate on heading toward the Lake sector. Tess will be there. She'll find me and help me to safety. I think I can hear the rumble of footsteps overhead, the shouts of soldiers. No doubt someone has discovered Metias by now, and they might even have headed down into the sewers, too. They could be hot on my trail with a pack of dogs. I make a point to take several turns and walk in the filthy sewer water. Behind me, I hear splashes and the sounds of echoing voices. I take more turns. The voices get a little closer, then farther. I keep my original direction planted firmly in my mind.

It would be something—wouldn't it?—to escape the hospital only to die down here, lost in a goddy maze of sewers.

I count off the minutes to keep myself from passing out. Five minutes, ten minutes, thirty minutes, an hour. The footsteps behind me sound far away now, as if they are on a different path than I am. Sometimes I hear strange sounds, something like a bubbling test tube and a sigh of steam pipes, a breath of air. It comes and goes. Two hours. Two and a half hours. When I see the next ladder leading up to the surface, I take my chances and pull myself up. I'm in real danger of fainting now. It takes all my remaining strength to drag myself onto the street. I'm in a dark alley. When I've caught my breath, I blink away my fuzzy vision and study my surroundings.

I can see Union Station several blocks away. I'm not far now. Tess will be there, waiting for me.

Three more blocks. Two more blocks.

I have one more block. I can't hold on any longer. I find a dark spot in the alley and collapse. The last thing I see is the silhouette of a girl off in the distance. Maybe she's walking toward me. I curl up and begin to fade away.

Before I black out, I realize that my pendant is no longer looped around my neck.

JUNE

I STILL REMEMBER THE DAY THAT MY BROTHER MISSED HIS induction ceremony into the Republic military.

A Sunday afternoon. Hot and mucky. Brown clouds covered the sky. I was seven years old, and Metias was nineteen. My white shepherd puppy, Ollie, was asleep on our apartment's cool marble floor. I lay feverishly in bed while Metias sat by my side, his brow furrowed with worry. We could hear the loudspeakers outside playing the Republic's national pledge. When they got to the part mentioning our president, Metias stood and saluted in the direction of the capital. Our illustrious Elector Primo had just accepted another four-year presidential term. That would make this his eleventh term.

"You don't have to sit here with me, you know," I said to him after the pledge finished. "Go to your induction. I'll be sick either way."

Metias ignored me and placed another cool towel on my head. "I'll be *inducted* either way," he said. He fed me a purple slice of orange. I remember watching him peel that orange for me; he cut one long, efficient line in the fruit's peel, then removed it all in one piece.

"But it's Commander Jameson." I blinked through swollen eyes. "She did you a favor by not assigning you to the warfront. . . . She'll be upset you're skipping. Won't she mark it on your record? You don't want to be kicked out like some street con."

Metias tapped my nose disapprovingly. "Don't call people that, Junebug. It's rude. And she can't kick me off her patrol for missing the ceremony. Besides," he added with a wink, "I can always hack into their database and wipe my record clean."

I grinned. Someday I wanted to be inducted into the military too, draped in the Republic's dark robes. Maybe I'd even be lucky enough to get assigned to a renowned commander like Metias did. I opened my mouth so he could feed me another piece of orange. "You should skip going to Batalla more often. Maybe you'd have time to get a girlfriend."

Metias laughed. "I don't need girlfriends. I've got a baby sister to take care of."

"Come on. You're going to get a girlfriend *someday.*"

"We'll see. Guess I'm picky like that."

I stopped to look my brother directly in the eyes. "Metias, did our mother take care of me when I was sick? Did she do things like this?"

Metias reached over to push sweaty strands of my hair away from my face. "Don't be stupid, Junebug. Of course Mom took care of you. And she was much better at it than I am."

"No. *You* take care of me the best," I murmured. My eyelids were growing heavy.

My brother smiled. "Nice of you to say so."

"You're not going to leave me too, are you? You'll stay with me longer than Mom and Dad did?"

Metias kissed me on my forehead. "Forever and ever, kid, until you're sick and tired of seeing me."

★★★

0001 HOURS.
RUBY SECTOR.
72°F INDOORS.

I know something has gone wrong the instant Thomas shows up at our door. The lights in all residential buildings have gone off, just as Metias had said they would, and nothing but oil lamps light the apartment. Ollie is barking up a storm. I'm dressed in my training uniform and a black and red vest with my boots laced and my hair tied back in a tight ponytail. For a brief moment, I'm actually glad that Metias isn't the one waiting at the door. He'd see my getup and know that I'm headed out to the track. Defying him again.

When I open the door, Thomas coughs nervously at the surprised look on my face and pretends to smile. (There is a streak of black grease on his forehead, probably from his own index finger. Which means he just finished polishing his rifle earlier in the evening, and his patrol's inspection is tomorrow.) I cross my arms. He touches the edge of his cap politely.

"Hello, Ms. Iparis," he says.

I take a deep breath. "I'm heading out to the track. Where's Metias?"

"Commander Jameson has requested that you come with me to the hospital as soon as possible." Thomas hesitates for a second. "It's more of an order than a request."

There's a hollow feeling in the pit of my stomach. "Why didn't she just call me?" I ask.

"She prefers for me to escort you."

"Why?" My voice starts to rise. "Where's my brother?"

Now Thomas takes a deep breath. I already know what he's going to say. "I'm sorry. Metias has been killed."

That's when the world around me goes silent.

As if from a great distance, I can see that Thomas is still speaking, gesturing with his hands, pulling me to him for a hug. I hug him back without realizing what I'm doing. I feel nothing. I nod when he steadies me and asks me to do something. To follow him. He keeps an arm around my shoulders. A dog's wet nose nudges my hand. Ollie follows me out of the apartment, and I tell him to stay close. I lock the door and stuff the key into my pocket and let Thomas guide us through the darkness to the stairs. He's talking the whole time, but I can't hear him. I stare straight ahead at the reflective metal decorations lining the stairwell, at the distorted reflections of Ollie and me.

I can't make out my expression. I'm not sure I even have one.

Metias should have taken me with him. This is my first coherent thought as we reach the bottom floor of our high-rise and climb into a waiting jeep. Ollie jumps into the backseat and sticks his head out the window. The car smells damp (like rubber and metal and fresh sweat—a group of people must've ridden in here recently). Thomas sits in the driver's seat and makes sure my seat belt is buckled. Such a small, stupid thing.

Metias should have taken me with him.

I run this thought over and over again in my head. Thomas doesn't say anything else. He lets me stare out at the darkened city as we go, occasionally shooting me a hesitant glance. Some small part of me makes a mental note to apologize to him later.

My eyes glaze over at the familiar buildings we pass. People (mostly workers hired from the slums) pack the first-floor stands even with the lights out, hunched over bowls of cheap food in the ground level cafés. Clouds of steam float high in the distance. JumboTrons, always on, regardless of power shortages, display the latest warnings about floods and quarantines. A few are about the Patriots—this time for another bombing up in Sacramento that killed half a dozen soldiers. A few cadets, eleven-year-olds with yellow stripes on their sleeves, linger on the steps outside an academy, the old and worn *Walt Disney Concert Hall* letters almost completely faded. Several other military jeeps cross our intersection, and I see the blank faces of their soldiers. Some of them have black goggles on so I can't see their eyes at all.

The sky looks more overcast than usual—signs of a rainstorm. I pull my hood over my head in case I forget when we finally get out of the car.

When I turn my attention back to the window, I see the part of downtown that sits inside Batalla. All the lights in this military sector are on. The hospital's tower looms just a few blocks away.

Thomas notices me craning my neck for a better view. "Almost there," he says.

As we draw near, I can see the crisscrossed lines of yellow tape surrounding the bottom of the tower, the clusters of city patrol soldiers (red stripes on their sleeves, like Metias), as well as some photographers and street police, the black vans and medic trucks. Ollie lets out a whine.

"I'm guessing they didn't catch the person," I say to Thomas.

"How do you know?"

I nod toward the building. "That's really something," I continue. "Whoever it was survived a two-and-a-half-story jump and still had enough strength to escape."

Thomas looks toward the tower and tries to see what I see—the broken third-floor stairwell window, the taped-off section right below it, the soldiers searching alleyways, the lack of ambulances. "We haven't caught the guy," he admits after a moment. The rifle grease on his forehead gives him a bewildered look. "But that doesn't mean we won't find his body later."

"You won't find it if you haven't found it yet."

Thomas opens his mouth to say something, then decides against it and goes back to concentrating on the road. When the jeep finally rolls to a stop, Commander Jameson breaks away from the group of guards she's standing with and marches over to my car door.

"I'm sorry," Thomas says abruptly to me. I feel a brief pang of guilt for my coldness and decide to nod back at him. His father had been a janitor for our apartment high-rise before he died, his late mother a cook at my grade school. Metias had been the one to recommend Thomas (who had a high Trial score) to be assigned to the prestigious city patrols, despite his humble background. So he must feel just as numb as I do.

Commander Jameson walks up to my car door and raps twice on the window to get my attention. Her thin lips are painted an angry stroke of red, and in the night her auburn hair looks dark brown—almost black.

"Move it, Iparis. Time is of the essence." Her eyes flicker to Ollie in the backseat. "That's not a police dog, kid." Even now, her demeanor is unflinching.

I step out of the jeep and give her a quick salute. Ollie jumps down next to me. "You called for me, Commander," I say.

Commander Jameson doesn't bother to return my gesture. She starts walking away, and I'm forced to hurry along beside her, struggling to fall into step. "Your brother, Metias, is dead," she says. Her tone doesn't change. "I'm of the understanding that you are almost done with your training as an agent, correct? That you've already finished your courses on tracking?"

I fight hard to breathe. A second confirmation of Metias's death. "Yes, Commander," I manage to say.

We head into the hospital. (Waiting room is empty; they've cleared out all patients; guards are clustered near the stairwell entrance; that's probably where the crime scene starts.) Commander Jameson keeps her eyes forward and her hands behind her back. "What was your Trial score?"

"Fifteen hundred, Commander." Everyone in the military knows my score. But Commander Jameson likes to pretend not to know or care.

She doesn't stop walking. "Ah, that's right," she says, as if it is the first time she's heard it. "Maybe you'll be of use after all. I've called ahead to Drake and told them that you are dismissed from further training. You were almost done with your coursework anyway."

I frown. "Commander?"

"I received a full history of your grades there. Perfect scores—you've already finished most of your courses in half the number of years, yes? They also say you're quite a troublemaker. Is this true?"

I can't understand what she wants from me. "Sometimes, Commander. Am I in trouble? Did they expel me?"

Commander Jameson smiles. "Hardly. They've graduated you early. Follow me—there's something I want you to see."

I want to ask about Metias, about what happened here. But her icy demeanor stops me.

We walk down a first-floor hall until we reach an emergency exit door at the very end of it. There, Commander Jameson waves away the soldiers guarding it and ushers me through. A low growl rumbles in Ollie's throat. We step out into open air, this time at the back of the building. I realize that we are now inside the yellow tape. Dozens of soldiers stand in clusters around us.

"Hurry up," Commander Jameson snaps at me. I quicken my pace.

A moment later, I realize what she wants to show me and where we are walking. Not far ahead is an object covered in a white sheet. (Six feet long, human; feet and limbs look intact under the cloth; definitely didn't fall naturally like that, so someone had to lay him out.) I start to tremble. When I look down at Ollie, I see that the fur on his back is standing up.

I call to him several times, but he refuses to walk any closer, so I'm forced to follow Commander Jameson and leave him behind.

Metias kissed me on my forehead. "Forever and ever, kid, until you're sick and tired of seeing me."

Commander Jameson halts in front of the white sheet, then bends down and throws it aside. I stare down at the dead body of a soldier clad in military black, a knife still protruding from his chest. Dark blood stains his shirt, his shoulder, his hands, the grooves of the knife hilt. His eyes are closed now. I kneel before him and smooth strands of his dark hair away from his face. It's odd. I don't take in any details of the scene. I still feel nothing but that deep numbness.

"Tell me about what might have happened here, cadet," Commander Jameson demands. "Consider this a pop quiz. This soldier's identity should motivate you to get it right."

I don't even flinch from the sting of her words. The details rush in, and I start talking. "Whoever hit him with this knife either stabbed him from close range or has an incredibly strong throwing arm. Right-handed." I run my fingers along the blood-caked handle. "Impressive aim. The knife is one of a pair, correct? See this pattern painted on the bottom of the blade? It cuts off abruptly."

Commander Jameson nods. "The second knife is stuck in the wall of the stairwell."

I look toward the dark alley that my brother's feet point to and notice the sewer cover several yards away. "That's where he made his getaway," I say. I estimate the direction the sewer cap is turned in. "He's also left-handed. Interesting. He's ambidextrous."

"Please continue."

"From here, the sewers will take him deeper into the city or west to the ocean. He'll choose the city—he's probably too wounded to do otherwise. But it's impossible to track him accurately now. If he has any sense, he'll have taken half a dozen turns down there and done it in the sewer water too. He wouldn't have touched the walls. He'll give us nothing to track."

"I'm going to leave you here for a bit, so you can collect your thoughts. Meet me in two minutes in the third-floor stairwell so you can give the photographers some room." She glances once at Metias's body before she turns away—for a brief second, her face softens. "What a waste of a good soldier." Then she shakes her head and leaves.

I watch her go. The others around me stay a good distance away, apparently eager to avoid an awkward conversation. I look down at my brother's face again. To my surprise, he appears peaceful. His skin looks tan, not pale like I'd assumed it would. I half expect his eyes to flutter, his mouth to smile. Bits of dried blood flake off onto my hands. When I try to brush them off, they stick to my skin. I don't know if this is what sets off my anger. My hands start shaking so hard that I press them against Metias's clothes in an attempt to steady them. I'm supposed to be analyzing the crime scene . . . but I can't concentrate.

"You should have taken me with you," I whisper to him. Then I lean my head against his and begin to cry. In my mind, I make a silent promise to my brother's killer.

I will hunt you down. I will scour the streets of Los Angeles for you. Search every street in the Republic if I have to. I will trick you and deceive you, lie, cheat, and steal to find you, tempt you out of your hiding place, and chase you until you have nowhere else to run. I make you this promise: your life is mine.

Too soon, soldiers come to take Metias to the morgue.

0317 HOURS.
MY APARTMENT.
SAME NIGHT.
THE RAIN HAS STARTED.

I lie on the couch with my arm draped over Ollie. The spot where Metias usually sits is empty. Stacks of old photo albums and Metias's journals clutter up the coffee table. He'd always loved our parents' old-fashioned ways, and kept handwritten journals just like how they'd kept all these paper photos. "You can't trace or tag them online," he always said. Ironic coming from an expert hacker.

Was it just this afternoon that he'd picked me up from Drake? He'd wanted to talk to me about something important, right before he left. But now I'll never know what he had to say. Papers and reports cover my stomach. One of my hands clutches a pendant necklace, a piece of evidence I've been studying for a while now. I squint at its smooth surface, its lack of patterns. Then I drop my hand with a sigh. My head hurts.

I learned earlier why Commander Jameson pulled me out of Drake. She's had her eye on me for a long time. Now she suddenly has one less in Metias's patrol, and she's looking to add an agent. A perfect time to nab me before other recruiters do. Starting tomorrow, Thomas is taking over Metias's position for the time being—and I'm entering the patrol as a detective agent in training.

My first tracking mission: Day.

"We've tried a variety of tactics to catch Day in the past, but none of them have worked," Jameson told me just before she sent me home. "So. Here's what we'll do. I'll continue with my patrol's projects. For you, let's test out your skills with a practice run. Show me how you'd track Day. Maybe you'll get somewhere. Maybe not. But you're a set of fresh young eyes, and if you impress me, I'll promote you to be a full agent on this patrol. I'll make you famous—the youngest agent out there."

I close my eyes and try to think.

Day killed my brother. I know this because we found a stolen ID tag lying halfway up the third-floor stairwell, which led us to the soldier pictured on the tag, who stammered out a description of what the boy looked like. His description didn't match anything we have on file for Day—but the truth is, we know little about what he looks like, except that he's young, like the kid at the hospital tonight. The fingerprints on the ID tag are the same prints found just last month at a crime scene linked to Day, prints that don't match any civilian the Republic has on record.

Day was there, in the hospital. He was also careless enough to leave the ID tag behind.

Which makes me wonder. Day broke into the laboratory for medicine as part of a desperate, last-minute, poorly thought-out plan. He must have stolen plague suppressants and painkillers because he couldn't find anything stronger. He himself certainly doesn't have the plague, not with the way he was able to escape. But someone else he knows must, someone he cares enough about to risk his life for. Someone living in Blueridge or Lake or Winter or Alta, sectors all recently affected by the plague. If this is true, Day won't be leaving the city anytime soon. He's bound here by this connection, motivated by emotions.

Day could also have a sponsor who hired him to pull this stunt. But the hospital is a dangerous place, and a sponsor would've had to pay Day a great deal of money. And if that much money was involved, he certainly would have planned more thoroughly and known when the laboratory's next shipment of plague medicine would arrive. Besides, Day wasn't a mercenary in any of his past crimes. He's attacked the Republic's military assets on his own, slowed down shipments to the warfront, and destroyed our warfront-bound airships and fighter jets. He has some sort of agenda to stop us from winning against the Colonies. For a while we thought he might work for the Colonies—but his jobs are crude, without high-tech equipment or noticeable funding behind them. Not really what you'd expect from our enemy. He's *never* taken jobs for hire as far as I know, and it's unlikely he'd start now. Who would hire an untested mercenary? Another possible sponsor is the Patriots—but if Day had been working for them on this job, one of the Patriots would've drawn their signature flag (thirteen red and white stripes, with fifty white dots on a blue rectangle) on a wall somewhere near the crime scene by now. They'd never miss a chance to claim victory.

But the biggest thing that doesn't compute for me is this: Day has never killed anyone before. That's another reason why I don't think he's connected to the Patriots. In one of his past crimes, he crept into a quarantine zone by tying up a street policeman. The policeman didn't have a scratch on him (except a black eye). Another time, he broke into a bank vault but left the four security guards at its back entrance untouched—although a bit stupefied. He once torched a whole squadron of fighter jets on an empty airfield in the middle of the night and has on two occasions grounded airships by crippling their engines. He once vandalized the side of a military building. He's stolen money, food, and goods. But he doesn't set roadside bombs. He doesn't shoot soldiers. He doesn't attempt assassinations. He doesn't *kill*.

So why Metias? Day could've made his escape without killing him. Did Day hold some sort of grudge? Had my brother done something to him in the past? It couldn't have been accidental—that knife went straight through Metias's heart.

Straight through his intelligent, stupid, stubborn, overprotective heart.

I open my eyes, then lift my hand and study the pendant necklace again. It belongs to Day—fingerprints told us that much. It's a circular disk with nothing engraved on it, something we found lying on the floor of the hospital's stairwell along with the stolen ID. It's not from any religion I know of. It's worth nothing in terms of money—cheap nickel and copper, the necklace part made of plastic. Which means he probably didn't steal it, and it has a different meaning for him and is worth carrying around with the risk of losing or dropping it. Maybe it's a good luck charm. Maybe it was given to him by someone he has emotional ties with. Maybe this is the same person he tried to steal plague medicine for. It has a secret; I just don't know what.

Day's exploits used to fascinate me. But now he is my matched enemy—my target. My first mission.

I gather my thoughts for two days. On the third day, I call Commander Jameson. I have a plan.

DAY

I'M DREAMING THAT I'M HOME AGAIN. EDEN SITS on the floor, drawing some sort of loopy shape on the floorboards. He's about four or five years old, with cheeks still round with baby fat. Every few minutes he gets up and asks me to critique his art. John and I are crouched together on the sofa, trying in vain to fix the radio that we've had in our family for years. I can still remember when Dad brought it home. *It'll tell us which quarters have plague,* he'd said. But now its screws and dials sit worn and lifeless in our laps. I ask Eden for help, but he just giggles and tells us to do it ourselves.

Mom stands alone in our tiny kitchen, trying to cook dinner. This is a scene I know well. Both her hands are wrapped in thick bandages—she must've cut herself on broken bottles or empty tins while cleaning out the trash cans around Union Station today. She winces as she breaks up some frozen corn kernels with the flat edge of a knife. Her injured hands tremble.

Stop, Mom. I'll help you. I try to get up, but my feet feel glued to the ground.

After a while, I lift my head to see what Eden's drawing now. At first I can't make out what the shapes are—they seem jumbled, littered in random patterns under his busy hand.

When I look closer, I realize that he's drawing soldiers breaking into our home. He's drawing them with a bloodred crayon.

I wake with a start. Dim streaks of light, gray and waning, are filtering in through a nearby window. I hear the faint sound of rain. I'm in what looks like a child's abandoned bedroom. The wallpaper is blue and yellow, and peeling at the corners. Two candles light the room. I can feel my feet hanging off the end of a bed. There's a pillow under my head. When I shift, I let out a moan and close my eyes.

Tess's voice drifts over to me. "Can you hear me?" she says.

"Not so loud, cousin." My voice comes out in a whisper through dry lips. My head throbs with a blinding, stabbing headache. Tess recognizes the pain on my face and stays quiet while I keep my eyes closed and wait it out. The pain goes on, like a pick slamming repeatedly into the back of my head.

After an eternity, the headache finally starts to fade. I open my eyes. "Where am I? Are you all right?"

Tess's face comes into focus. She has her hair pulled back in a short braid, and her lips are pink and smiling. "Am *I* all right?" she says. "You've been knocked out for over two days. How are *you* feeling?"

Pain hits me in waves, this time from the wounds that must cover me. "Fantastic."

Tess's smile fades. "You pulled a close one there—closest one yet. If I hadn't found someone to take us in, I don't think you would've made it."

Suddenly everything comes rushing back to me. I remember the hospital entrance, the stolen ID tag and the stairwell and the laboratory, the long fall, my knife thrown at the captain, the sewers. The medicine.

The medicine. I try to sit up, but I move too fast and have to bite my lip from the pain. My hand flies to my neck—there's no pendant to grab. Something aches in my chest. *I lost it.* My father had given me that pendant, and now I'd been careless enough to *lose* it.

Tess tries to calm me. "Easy, there."

"Is my family okay? Did some of the medicine survive my fall?"

"Some of it." Tess helps me back down before leaning her elbows on my bed. "I guess suppressants are better than nothing. I've dropped it off at your mother's home already, along with your gift bundle. I went through the back and handed them all off to John. He says to tell you thanks."

"You didn't tell John what happened, did you?"

Tess rolls her eyes. "You think I can keep that from him? Everyone's heard about the break-in at the hospital by now, and John knows you're hurt. He's pretty angry about it."

"Did he say who's sick? Is it Eden? Mom?"

Tess bites her lip. "It's Eden. John says everyone else is fine for now. But Eden can talk and seems alert enough. He tried to get out of bed and help your mother fix the leak under your sink, to prove he felt strong, but of course she sent him back to bed. She ripped up two of her shirts to use as cool cloths for Eden's fever, so John said if you find any more clothes that fit Mom, he'd be happy to take them."

I let out a deep breath. Eden. Of course it's Eden—still acting like a little engineer even with the plague. At least I managed to get some medicine. *Everything's going to work out.* Eden will be okay for a while, and I don't mind dealing with John's lectures. As for my lost pendant, well . . . for an instant I'm glad that my mother can't find out about this, because it would break her heart.

"I couldn't find any cures, and I didn't have time to do a search."

"It's okay," Tess replies. She prepares a fresh bandage for my arm. I see my worn old cap hanging on the back of her chair. "Your family has some time. We'll get another chance."

"Whose house are we in?"

As soon as I ask this question, I hear a door close, then footsteps in the room next to ours. I look at Tess in alarm. She just nods quietly at me and tells me to relax.

A man walks in, shaking dirty drops of rain from an umbrella. He carries a brown paper bag in his hands. "You're awake," he says to me. "That's good." I study his face. He's very pale and a little chubby, with bushy eyebrows and kindly eyes. "Girl," he says, looking at Tess, "do you think he can leave by tomorrow night?"

"We'll be on our way by then." Tess picks up a bottle of something clear—alcohol, I guess—and wets the edge of the bandage with it. I flinch when she touches it to where a bullet had grazed my arm. It feels like a match lit against my skin. "Thank you again, sir, for letting us stay here."

The man grunts, his expression uncertain, and awkwardly nods his head. He looks around the room as if searching for something he's lost. "I'm afraid that's as long as I can keep you. The plague patrol's going to do another sweep soon." He hesitates. Then he pulls two cans from the paper bag and sets them down on a dresser. "Some chili for you. It's not the best, but it'll fill you up. I'll bring you some bread, too." Before either of us can say anything, he hurries out of the room with the rest of his groceries.

For the first time, I look down at my body. I'm clothed in a brown pair of army trousers, and my bare chest and arm are bandaged. So is one of my legs. "Why's he helping us?" I ask Tess in a low voice.

She looks up from wrapping the fresh bandage around my arm. "Don't be so suspicious. He had a son who worked at the warfront. He died of the plague a few years ago." I yelp when Tess ties a finishing knot on the bandage. "Breathe in for me." I do as she says. Several sharp pains stab me as she presses her fingers delicately against different parts of my chest. Her cheeks turn pink as she works. "You might have a crack in one of your ribs, but definitely no breaks. You should heal quickly enough. Anyway, the man didn't ask our names and so I didn't ask his. Best not to know. I told him why you got yourself injured like this. I think it reminded him of his son."

I lay my head back down on the pillow. My body hurts all over. "I lost both my knives," I mutter, so that the man doesn't hear me. "They were good knives."

"Sorry to hear it, Day," Tess says. She brushes a stray hair from her face and leans over me. She holds up a clear plastic bag with three silver bullets inside. "I found these caught in the folds of your clothes and figured you might want them for your slingshot or something." She stuffs the bag into one of my pockets.

I smile. When I first met Tess three years ago, she was a skinny ten-year-old orphan rummaging through trash bins in the Nima sector. She'd needed my help so much in those early years that I sometimes forget just how much I rely on her now.

"Thanks, cousin," I say. She murmurs something I can't understand, and looks away.

After a while, I fall back into a deep sleep. When I wake up again, I don't know how much time has passed. The headache is gone and it's dark outside. It might be the same day, although I feel like I've slept far too long for that. No soldiers, no police. We're still alive. I lie unmoving for a moment, wide-awake in the darkness. Looks like our caretaker hasn't reported us. Yet.

Tess is dozing on the edge of the bed with her head tucked into her arms. Sometimes I wish I could find her a good home, some kind family willing to take her in. But every time I have this thought, I push it away—because Tess would be back on the Republic's grid if she ever joined a real family. And she'd be forced to take the Trial because she never took it before. Or worse, they'd learn about her affiliation with me and interrogate her. I shake my head. Too naive, too easily manipulated. I wouldn't trust her with anyone else. Besides . . . I'd miss her. The first two years I'd spent wandering the streets by myself were lonely ones.

I gingerly move my ankle in a circle. It's a little stiff, but otherwise pretty painless—no torn muscles, no serious swelling. My bullet wound still burns and my ribs ache something fierce, but this time I'm strong enough to sit up without too much trouble. My hands go automatically up to my hair, which is loose and hanging past my shoulders. With one hand, I pull it into a messy tail and twist it into a tight knot. Then I lean over Tess, grab my beaten newsboy cap from the chair, and pull it on. My arms burn from the effort.

I smell chili and bread. There's a bowl with some steam rising from it on the dresser next to the bed and a small loaf of bread balanced on the bowl's edge. I think back to the two cans our caretaker had placed on the dresser.

My stomach growls. I devour it all.

As I'm licking the last of the chili off my fingers, I hear a door close somewhere in the house and, moments later, footsteps rushing toward our room. I tense up. Next to me, Tess jerks awake and grabs my arm.

"What was that?" she blurts out. I hold a finger to my lips.

Our caretaker hurries into the room, a tattered robe draped over his pajamas. "You should leave now," he whispers. Sweat beads on his forehead. "I just heard about a man who's been looking for you."

I stare levelly at him. Tess gives me a panicked look. "How do you know?" I ask.

The man starts cleaning up the room, grabbing my empty bowl and wiping down the dresser. "He's telling people that he has plague cures for someone who needs it. He says he knows that you're injured. He never gave a name, but he must be talking about you."

I sit up straight and swing my legs over the side of the bed. There's no choice now. "He's talking about me," I agree. Tess snatches up a few clean bandages and stuffs them under her shirt. "It's a trap. We'll leave immediately."

The man nods once. "You can get out through the back door. Straight into the hall, on your left."

I take a moment to meet his eyes. In that instant, I realize that he knows exactly who I am. He won't say it out loud, though. Like other people in our sector who have realized who I am and helped me in the past, he doesn't exactly *disapprove* of the trouble I cause for the Republic. "We're very grateful," I say.

He says nothing in return. I grab Tess's hand and we make our way out of the bedroom, down the hall and through the back door. The night's humidity is thick. My eyes water from the pain of my wounds.

We make our way through silent back alleys for six blocks until we finally slow down. My injuries are screaming now. I reach up to touch my pendant necklace for comfort, but then I remember that it's no longer around my neck. A sick feeling rises in my stomach. What if the Republic figures out what it is? Will they destroy it? What if they trace it back to my family?

Tess slumps to the ground and rests her head against the alley wall. "We need to leave the city," she says. "It's too dangerous here, Day. You know it is. Arizona or Colorado would be safer—or come on, even Barstow. I don't mind the outskirts."

Yeah, yeah. I know. I look down. "I want to leave too."

"But you won't. I can see it on your face."

We're silent for a while. If it were up to me, I'd cross the whole country alone and escape into the Colonies first chance I got. I don't mind risking my *own* life. But there are a dozen reasons I can't go, and Tess knows it. It's not like John and Mom can just pick up and leave their assigned jobs to flee with me, not without raising an alert. It's not like Eden can just withdraw from his assigned school. Not unless they want to become fugitives like me.

"We'll see," I finally say.

Tess gives me a tragic smile. "Who do you think is looking for you?" she asks after a while. "How do they know we're in the Lake sector?"

"I don't know. Could be a dealer who heard about the hospital break-in. Maybe they think we have a lot of money or something. Could be a soldier. Even a spy. I lost my pendant at the hospital—I don't know how they would use it to learn anything about me, but there's always a chance."

"What are you going to do about it?"

I shrug. My bullet wound has begun to throb, and I lean against the wall for support. "I'm sure as hell not meeting him, whoever he is—but I got to admit, I'm curious to see what he has to say. What if he *does* have plague cures?"

Tess stares at me. It's the same expression she wore the very first night I met her—hopeful, curious, and fearful all at once. "Well . . . can't be any more dangerous than your crazy hospital break-in, yeah?"

JUNE

I DON'T KNOW IF IT'S BECAUSE COMMANDER JAMESON has taken pity on me, or if she really does feel the loss of Metias, one of her most valued soldiers, but she helps me arrange his funeral—even though she's never done that for one of her soldiers before. She refuses to say anything about why she chose to do it.

Wealthy families like ours always have elaborate funerals—Metias's takes place inside a building with soaring baroque archways and stained-glass windows. They've covered the bare floors with white carpets; round white banquet tables overflowing with white lilacs fill the room. The only colors come from the Republic flags and circular gold Republic seal hanging behind the room's front altar, the portrait of our glorious Elector looming above them all.

All the mourners wear their best whites. I have on an elaborate white gown, laced and corseted, with a silk overskirt and draped layers in the back. A tiny white-gold brooch of the Republic seal is clipped on its bodice. The hairdresser piled my hair high on my head, with loose ringlets cascading over one shoulder, and a white rose pinned behind my ear. Pearls line the choker wrapped around my throat. My eyelids are coated with glittering white eye shadow, my lashes are bathed in snow, the puffy redness under my eyes erased by shining white powder. Everything about me is stripped of color, just as Metias has been stripped from my life.

Metias once told me that it was not always this way, that only after the first floods and volcanic eruptions, after the Republic built a barrier along the warfront to keep the Colonies' deserters from fleeing illegally into our territory, did people start mourning for the dead by wearing white. "After the first eruptions," he said, "white volcanic ash rained from the sky for months. The dead and dying were covered in it. So now to wear white is to remember the dead."

He told me this because I'd asked him what our parents' funeral was like.

Now I wander among the guests, lost and aimless, responding to the sympathetic words of those around me with appropriate, practiced replies. "I am so sorry for your loss," they say. I recognize some of Metias's professors, fellow soldiers, and superiors. There are even a couple of my classmates from Drake. I'm surprised to see them—I'd never been good at making friends during my three years in college, considering my age and my hefty course load. But they're here, some from afternoon drills and others from my Republic History 421 class. They take my hand and shake their heads. "First your parents, and now your brother. I can't imagine how hard it is for you."

No, you can't. But I smile graciously and bow my head, because I know they mean well. "Thank you for coming," I say. "It means a lot. I know Metias would be proud that he gave his life for his country."

Sometimes I catch an admiring glance from a well-wisher across the room, which I ignore. I have no use for such sentiments. My outfit is not meant for them. Only for Metias do I wear this unnecessarily exquisite gown, to show without words how much I love him.

After a while, I sit at a table near the front of the room, facing the flower-strewn altar that'll soon be occupied with a line of people reading their eulogies to my brother. I bow my head respectfully to the Republic flags. Then my eyes wander to the white coffin next to them. From here I can see just a hint of the person lying inside.

"You look lovely, June."

I glance up to see Thomas bow, then take the seat beside me. He's exchanged his military clothes for an elegant, white-vested suit, and his hair is freshly cut. I can tell the suit is brand-new. It must have cost him a fortune. "Thanks. You too."

"That is—I mean, you look well for the circumstances, given all that's happened."

"I know what you mean." I reach over and pat his hand to reassure him. He gives me a smile. He looks like he wants to say something more, then decides against it and turns his eyes away.

It takes a half hour for everyone to find their seats and another half hour for the waiters to start arriving with plates of food. I don't eat anything. Commander Jameson sits opposite me on the far side of our banquet table, and between her and Thomas are three of my Drake classmates. I exchange a strained smile with them. On my left side is a man named Chian who organizes and oversees all Trials taken in Los Angeles. He administered mine. What I don't understand is why he's here—why he even cares that Metias died. He's a former acquaintance of our parents, so his presence is not unexpected—but why right next to me?

Then I remember that Chian had mentored Metias before he joined Commander Jameson's squad. Metias hated him.

The man now furrows his bushy eyebrows at me and claps a hand on my bare shoulder. It lingers there for a while. "How are you feeling, my dear?" he asks. His words distort the scars on his face—a slice across the bridge of his nose, and another jagged mark that goes from his ear to the bottom of his chin.

I manage a smile. "Better than expected."

"Well, I'll say." He lets out a laugh that makes me cringe. His eyes look me up and down. "That dress polishes you up like a fresh snow blossom."

It takes all my control to keep the smile on my face. *Stay calm,* I tell myself. Chian is not a man to make into an enemy.

"I loved your brother very much, you know," he continues with overdone sympathy. "I remember him as a kid—you should've seen him. He used to run around your parents' living room, holding out his hand like a little gun. He was destined to enter our squads."

"Thank you, sir," I say.

Chian saws off a huge piece of steak and shoves it in his mouth. "Metias was very attentive during the time I mentored him. Natural leader. Did he ever tell you about that?"

A memory flashes through my mind. The rainy night when Metias first started working for Chian. He had taken me and Thomas, who was still in school, out to the Tanagashi sector, where I ate my first bowl of pork edame, with spaghetti and sweet onion rolls. I remember the two of them were in full uniform—Metias with his jacket open and shirt hanging loose; Thomas neatly buttoned up, with his hair carefully slicked back. Thomas teased me over my messy pigtails, but Metias was quiet. Then, a week later, his apprenticeship with Chian ended abruptly. Metias had filed an appeal, and he was reassigned to Commander Jameson's patrol.

"He said it was all classified," I lie.

Chian laughs. "A good boy, that Metias was. A great apprentice. Imagine my disappointment when he was reassigned to the city patrols. He told me he just didn't have the smarts to judge the Trials or organize the kids who finished taking them. Such a modest one. Always smarter than he thought he was—just like you." He grins at me.

I nod. Chian made me take the Trial twice because I got a perfect score in record time (one hour ten minutes). He thought I had cheated. Not only do I have the only perfect score in the nation—I'm probably also the only kid who has ever taken the Trial *twice*. "You're very kind," I reply. "My brother was a better leader than I'll ever be."

Chian shushes me with a wave of his hand. "Nonsense, my dear," he says. Then he leans uncomfortably close. There's something oily and unpleasant about him. "I'm personally devastated by the way he died," he says. "At the hands of that nasty boy. What a shame!" Chian narrows his eyes, making his eyebrows look even bushier. "I was so pleased when Commander Jameson told me that you'd be tracking him. His case needs a pair of fresh eyes, and you're just the doll to do it. What a gem of a test mission, eh?"

I hate him with all my being. Thomas must notice my stiffness, because I feel his hand cover mine under the table. *Just go with it,* he's trying to tell me. When Chian finally turns away from me to answer a question from the man on his other side, Thomas leans toward me.

"Chian has a personal grudge against Day," he whispers.

"Is that so?" I whisper back.

He nods. "Who do you think gave him that scar?"

Day did? I can't keep the surprise from my face. Chian is a rather large man and has worked for the Trial's administration for as long as I can remember. He's a skilled official. Could a teenage boy really wound him like that? And get away with it? I glance over at Chian and study the scar. It's a clean cut made with a smooth-edged blade. Must've happened quickly too, to be such a straight line—I can't imagine Chian holding still while someone sliced him like that. For a moment, just a split second, I'm on Day's side. I glance up at Commander Jameson, who stares at me as if she's reading my thoughts. It makes me uneasy.

Thomas's hand touches mine again. "Hey," he says. "Day can't hide from the government forever—sooner or later we'll dig that street brat out and make an example out of him. He's no match for you, especially when you put your mind to something."

Thomas's kind smile makes me weak, and suddenly I feel like Metias is the one sitting next to me and telling me everything is going to be okay, reassuring me that the Republic won't fail me. My brother had once promised to stay at my side forever. I look away from Thomas and toward the altar, so he doesn't see the tears in my eyes. I can't smile back. I don't think I'll ever smile again.

"Let's get this over with," I whisper.

DAY

IT'S GODDY HOT EVEN THIS LATE IN THE AFTERNOON. I limp through the streets along the rim of Alta and Winter sector, along the lake and out in the open, lost in the crowded shuffle of other people. My wounds are still healing. I wear the army trousers our caretaker gave me with a thin collared shirt Tess found in a garbage bin. My cap is pulled low, and I've added to my disguise with a bandage patch over my left eye. Nothing unusual, really. Not in this sea of workers with factory injuries. Today I'm out on my own—Tess is keeping a low profile several streets down, tucked away on a hidden second-floor ledge. Never any reason to risk both of us if I don't have to.

Familiar noises surround me: street vendors call out to passersby, selling boiled goose eggs and fried dough and hot dogs. Attendants linger at the doors of grocery stores and coffee shops, trying to win customers over. A decades-old car rattles by. The second-shift workers are slowly making their way home. A few girls notice me and blush when I look at them. Boats chug around the lake, careful to avoid the giant water turbines churning along the edge, and the shore's flood sirens are quiet and unlit.

Some areas are blocked off. These I steer clear of—the soldiers have marked them as quarantine zones.

The loudspeakers that line the roofs of the buildings

crackle and pop, and JumboTrons pause in their ads—or, in some cases, warnings about another Patriot rebel attack—to show a video of our flag. Everyone stops in the streets and goes still as the pledge starts.

I pledge allegiance to the flag of the great Republic of America, to our Elector Primo, to our glorious states, to unity against the Colonies, to our impending victory!

When the Elector Primo's name comes on, we salute toward the capital. I mumble the pledge under my breath, but stay silent in the last two passages when the street police aren't looking my way. I wonder what the pledge sounded like before we went to war against the Colonies.

When the pledge ends, life resumes. I go to a Chinese-themed bar covered in graffiti. The attendant at the door gives me a wide smile that's missing several teeth and quickly ushers me in. "We have real Tsingtao beer today," he murmurs. "Leftover cases from an imported gift sent straight to our glorious Elector himself. Goes until six o'clock." His eyes dart around nervously as he says this. I just stare at him. Tsingtao beer? Yeah, right. My father would've laughed. The Republic didn't sign an import deal with China (or, as the Republic likes to claim, "conquer China and take over its businesses") just to send quality imports to the slum sectors. More likely, this guy's pretty far behind in paying his bimonthly government taxes. No other reason to risk slapping fake Tsingtao labels on bottles of his home brew.

I thank the man, though, and step inside. This is as good a place as any to dig up information.

It's dark. The air smells like pipe smoke and fried meat and gas lamps. I bump my way through the mess of tables and chairs—snatching food from a couple of unguarded plates as I go, then stuffing it beneath my shirt—until I reach the bar. Behind me, a large circle of customers are cheering on a Skiz fight. Guess this bar tolerates illegal gambling. If they're smart, they'll be ready at any minute to bribe the street police with their winnings—unless they're willing to admit out loud that they're making tax-free money.

The bartender doesn't bother to check my age. She doesn't even look at me. "What'll it be?" she asks.

I shake my head. "Just some water, please," I say. Behind us I hear a huge roar of cheers as one of the fighters goes down.

She gives me a skeptical glance. Her eyes immediately shift to the bandage on my face. "What happened to your eye, kid?"

"Terrace accident. I tend cows."

She makes a disgusted face, but now she seems interested in me. "What a shame. You sure you don't wanna beer to go with that? Must hurt."

I shake my head again. "Thanks, cousin, but I don't drink. I like to stay alert."

She smiles at me. She's kind of pretty in the flickering lamplight, with glittering green powder over her smooth-lidded eyes and a short, black, bobbed haircut. A vine tattoo snakes down her neck and disappears into her corseted shirt. A dirty pair of goggles—probably protection against bar fights—hangs around her neck. Kind of a shame. If I weren't busy hunting for information, I'd take my time with this girl, chat her up and maybe get a kiss or three out of her.

"Lake boy, yeah?" she asks. "Just decided to waltz in here and break a few girls' hearts? Or are you fighting?" She nods toward the Skiz fight.

I grin. "I'll leave that to you."

"What makes ya think I fight?"

I nod at the scars on her arms and the bruises on her hands. She gives me a slow smile.

I shrug after a moment. "I wouldn't be caught dead in one of those rings. Just taking a break from the sun. You seem like nice company, you know. I mean, as long as you don't have the plague."

A universal joke, but she still laughs. She leans on the counter. "I live on the sector's edge. Pretty safe there so far."

I lean toward her. "You're lucky, then." I grow serious. "A family I know had their door marked recently."

"Sorry t'hear it."

"I want to ask you something, just out of curiosity. You heard anything about a man around here in the last few days, someone who says he has plague meds?"

She raises an eyebrow at me. "Yeah, I heard about that. There's a bunch of people trying to find him."

"Do you know what he's been telling people?"

She hesitates for a moment. I notice that she has a few tiny freckles on her nose. "I hear he's telling people he wants to give a plague cure to someone—one person only. That this person will know who he's talking about."

I try to look amused. "Lucky person, yeah?"

She grins. "No kidding. He said he wants this person to meet him at midnight, *tonight*, at the ten-second place."

"Ten-second place?"

The bartender shrugs. "Hell if I know what that means. Neither does anyone else, for that matter." She leans over the counter toward me and lowers her voice. "Know what I think? I think this guy's just crazy."

I laugh along with her, but my mind is spinning. I have no doubt now that this person is searching for me. Almost a year ago, I broke into an Arcadia bank through the alley that runs behind it. One of the security guards tried to kill me. When he spat at me and told me I'd be cut to pieces by the bank vault's lasers, I taunted him. I told him that it would take me ten seconds to break into that vault room. He didn't believe me . . . but the thing is, no one ever believes what I say until I actually end up doing it. I bought myself a nice pair of boots with that money, and even shopped for an electro-bomb on the black market—a weapon that disables guns in its vicinity. Came in handy when I attacked an air base. And Tess got an entire outfit, brand-new shirts and shoes and pants, and bandages and rubbing alcohol and even a bottle of aspirin. We both got a good amount of food. The rest I gave to my family and other Lake folks.

After several more minutes of flirting, I say good-bye to the bartender girl and leave. The sun's still in the sky, and

I can feel beads of sweat on my face. I know enough now. The government must've found something at the hospital and wants to lure me into a trap. They'll send a guy to the ten-second place at midnight, and then place soldiers along the back alley. I bet they think I'm *real* desperate.

They'll probably also bring along plague meds, though, to tempt me out into the open. I press my lips together in thought. Then I change the direction I'm walking. Off to the financial district.

I have an appointment to keep.

JUNE

2329 HOURS.
BATALLA SECTOR.
72°F INDOORS.

THE LIGHTS IN BATALLA HALL ARE COLD AND FLUORESCENT. I dress in a bathroom on the observation and analysis floor. I'm wearing long black sleeves inside a striped black vest, slender black pants tucked into boots, and a long black robe that wraps around my shoulders and covers me like a blanket. A white stripe runs down the center of it, all the way to the floor. A black mask covers my face and infrared goggles shield my eyes. Other than that, all I have is a tiny microphone and an even tinier earpiece. And a gun. Just in case.

I need to look genderless, generic, unidentifiable. I need to look like a black-market dealer, someone rich enough to afford plague cures.

Metias would've shaken his head at me. *You can't go alone on a classified mission, June,* he would say. *You might get hurt.* How ironic.

I tighten the clasp that holds my cloak in place (steel sprayed with bronze, probably imported from West Texas), then head off toward the stairs that will take me outside Batalla Hall and down toward the Arcadia bank where I'm supposed to meet Day.

My brother has been dead for 120 hours. It already feels like forever. Seventy hours ago, I gained clearance to search the Internet and found out as much about Day as I could. Forty hours ago, I laid out a plan for tracking Day to Commander Jameson. Thirty-two hours ago she approved it. I doubt she even remembers what it is. Thirty hours ago, I sent one scout to every plague-infected sector in Los Angeles—Winter, Blueridge, Lake, and Alta. They spread the word: someone has plague medicine for you, come to the ten-second place. Twenty-nine hours ago, I attended my brother's funeral.

I do not plan on catching Day tonight. I don't even plan on seeing him. He'll know exactly where the ten-second place is, and that I'm either an agent sent by the government or by the black-market dealers that pay taxes to the government. He's not going to show his face. Even Commander Jameson, who's testing me with this first task, knows we won't get a glimpse of him.

But I know he's going to be there. He needs plague meds desperately enough. And him showing up is all I hope for tonight—a clue, a starting point, a narrower direction, something personal about this boy criminal.

I'm careful not to walk under the streetlamps. In fact, I would have traveled by rooftop if I weren't going to the financial sector, where guards line the roofs. All around me the JumboTrons blare their colorful campaigns, the sound of their ads distorted and jolty from the city speakers. One of them shows an updated profile of Day—this time featuring a boy with long, black hair. Next to the JumboTrons are flickering streetlights, and under those walk crowds of night-shift workers, police, and merchants. Every now and then, a tank rolls through, followed by several platoons of troops. (They have blue stripes on their sleeves—soldiers back from the warfront, or soldiers rotating out to the warfront. They keep their guns by their sides, with both hands on the weapon.) They all look like Metias to me, and I have to breathe a little harder, walk a little faster, anything to stay focused.

I take the long way through Batalla, through the sector's side roads and abandoned buildings, not stopping until I'm a good distance outside of military grounds.

The street police won't know I'm on a mission. If they see me dressed like this, equipped with infrared goggles, they'll question me for sure.

The Arcadia bank lies on a quiet street. I go around the bank's back side until I'm standing in front of a parking lot at the end of an alleyway. There, I wait in the shadows. My goggles wash most of the color out of the scene. I look around and see rows of city speakers on the roofs, a stray cat whose tail twitches over the lid of a trash can, an abandoned kiosk with old anti-Colonies bulletins tacked all over it.

The clock on my visor says 2353 HOURS. I pass the time by forcing myself to think through Day's history. Before the robbery at this bank, Day had already appeared on our records three times. Those were only the incidents where we found fingerprints—I can only guess at the number of other crimes he's committed. I take a closer look at the bank's alleyway.

How did he break into this bank in ten seconds, with four armed guards at the back entrance? (The alley is narrow. He could have found enough footholds to jump his way up the walls to the second or third floors—all while using the guards' weapons against them. Probably got them to shoot at each other. Probably smashed through a window. That would've taken just a few seconds. What he did once he got inside, I have no idea.)

I already know how agile Day is. Surviving a two-and-a-half-story fall proves that much. He won't have a chance to do that tonight, though. I don't care how light he is on his feet—you just don't jump out of buildings and then expect to be able to walk properly afterward. Day won't be scampering up walls and stairwells for at least another week.

Suddenly I tense up. It's two minutes past midnight. A clicking sound echoes from somewhere far away, and the cat sitting on the trash can makes a run for it. It could be a cigarette lighter, a gun trigger, the speakers, or a flickering streetlight; it could be anything. I scan the roofs. Nothing yet.

But the hairs on the back of my neck rise. I know he's here. I know he's watching me.

"Come out," I say. The tiny microphone at my mouth makes my voice sound like a man's.

Silence. Not even the kiosk's layers of paper bulletins move. There's no wind tonight.

I remove a vial from a holster at my belt. My other hand doesn't leave the handle of my gun. "I have what you need," I say, and wave around the vial for emphasis.

Still nothing. This time, however, I hear what sounds like the faintest sigh. A breath. My eyes dart to the speakers lining the roofs. (That's what the clicking sound was. He's rewired the speakers so he can talk to me without giving away his location.) I smile behind my mask. It's what I would have done.

"I *know* you need this," I say, gesturing again at the vial. I turn it in my hands and hold it higher. "It has all its official labels, the stamp of approval. I assure you it's the real thing."

Another breath.

"Someone you care about will wish you'd come out to greet me." I look at the time on my goggles. "It's five past midnight. I'll give you two minutes. Then I leave."

The alley falls silent again. Every now and then, I hear another faint breath from the loudspeakers. My eyes shift from the time on my visor to the shadows of the roofs. He's clever. I can't tell where he's broadcasting from. It could be on this street—it could be several blocks down, from a higher floor. But I know he's close enough to see me himself.

The time on my visor shows 0007 HOURS. I turn, tuck the vial back onto my belt, and start to walk away.

"What do you want for the cure, cousin?"

The voice is barely a whisper, but through the speakers it sounds broken and startling, so crackly that I have trouble understanding him. Details race instantly through my mind. (Male. He has a light accent—he's not from Oregon or Nevada or Arizona or New Mexico or West Texas or any other Republic state. Native Southern Californian. He uses the familiar term *cousin,* something Lake sector civilians often use. He's close enough to have seen me put the vial away. He's not so close that the speakers can catch his voice clearly. He must be on an adjacent block with a good vantage point—a high floor.)

Behind the details flashing through my mind emerges a black, rising hatred. This is the voice of my brother's murderer. This may have been the last voice my brother heard.

I wait two seconds before speaking again. When I do, my voice is smooth and calm and shows no sign of my rage. "What do I want?" I ask him. "It depends. Do you have money?"

"Twelve hundred Notes."

(Notes, not Republic gold. He robs the upper class but doesn't have the ability to rob the extremely wealthy. He's probably a one-man operation.) I laugh. "Twelve hundred Notes can't buy you this vial. What else do you have? Valuables? Jewelry?"

Silence.

"Or do you have skills to offer, as I'm sure you do—"

"I don't work for the government."

His weak point. Naturally. "No offense. Just thought I'd ask. And how do you know *I* don't work for someone else? Don't you think you're giving the government too much credit?"

A slight pause. Then the voice comes back. "Your cloak knot. Don't know what it is, but it sure doesn't look civilian."

This surprises me a little. My cloak knot is indeed a Canto knot, a sturdy knot that military officials like to use. Apparently Day has some detailed knowledge of how government uniforms look. Impressive eye. I'm quick to cover up my hesitation. "Good to find another person who knows what a Canto knot is. But I travel a lot, my friend. I see and know a lot of people, people who I might not be affiliated with."

Silence.

I wait, listening for another breath over the speakers. Nothing. Not even a click. I didn't act fast enough, and the brief hesitation in my voice was enough to convince him that he couldn't trust me. I tighten the cloak around me and realize that I've started to sweat in the warmth of the night. My heart hammers against my chest.

Another voice sounds in my head. This time it comes from my tiny earpiece. "Are you there, Iparis?" It's Commander Jameson. I can hear the buzz of other people in her office in the background.

"He left," I whisper. "But he gave me clues."

"Tipped him off about whom you work for, didn't you? Well, it's your first time on your own. I have the recordings at any rate. See you back at Batalla Hall." Her rebuke stings a little. Before I can answer, the static cuts off.

I wait for another minute, just to be sure I hadn't misread Day's exit. Silence. I turn and start back down the alley. I'd wanted to tell Commander Jameson what the easiest solution would be—to simply round up everyone in the Lake sector whose doors are marked. *That* would draw Day out of hiding. But I can already hear Commander Jameson's retort. *Absolutely not, Iparis. It's far too expensive, and headquarters won't approve. You'll have to think of something else.* I glance back once, half expecting to see a black-clad figure following me. But the alley is empty.

I won't be allowed to force Day to come to me—which leaves me only one option. I'll have to go to him.

"EAT SOMETHING, YEAH?"

Tess's voice shakes me out of my vigil. I look away from the lake to see her holding out a piece of bread and cheese, gesturing for me to take it. I should be hungry. I've only eaten half an apple since my encounter with the strange government agent last night. But somehow the bread and cheese—still fresh from the shop where Tess had traded a few precious Notes for it—doesn't seem tempting.

I take it anyway. Far be it from me to waste perfectly good food, especially when we should be saving everything we have for plague meds.

Tess and I are sitting in the sand underneath a pier, at the part of the lake that crosses into our sector. We keep ourselves pressed as closely against the side of the bank as we can so idle soldiers and drunk workers above can't see us past all the grass and rocks. We blend into the shadows. From where we sit, we can taste the salt in the air and see the lights of downtown Los Angeles reflected on the water. Ruins of older buildings dot the lake, buildings abandoned by business owners and residents when the floodwaters rose. Giant waterwheels and turbines churn along the water's edge behind veils of smoke. This is probably my favorite view from our shabby, beautiful little Lake sector.

I take that back. It's my favorite and least-favorite view. Because while the electric lights of downtown make for some nice sightseeing, I can also see the Trial stadium looming off in the east.

"You still have time," Tess says to me. She scoots close enough for me to feel her bare arm against mine. Her hair smells like bread and cinnamon from the shop. "Probably a month or more. We'll find plague medicine before then, I'm sure of it."

For a girl with no family and no home, Tess is surprisingly optimistic. I try to smile for her sake. "Maybe," I say. "Maybe the hospital will let down its guard after a couple weeks." But in my heart I know better.

Earlier in the day, I risked a peek at my mother's house. The strange *X* still marked the door. My mother and John seemed okay, at least strong enough to stand and walk around. But Eden . . . this time Eden was lying in bed with a cloth on his forehead. Even from a distance, I could tell that he'd already lost some weight. His skin looked wan, and his voice sounded weak and hoarse. When I met John later behind our house, he told me that Eden hadn't eaten since the last time I came by. I reminded John to stay out of Eden's room when he could. Who knows how this cracked plague is spreading. John warned me not to pull any more stunts, in case I get myself killed. I had to laugh at that. John won't ever say it to my face, but I know that I am Eden's only chance.

The plague might end Eden's life before he even gets to take the Trial.

Maybe it's a blessing in disguise. Eden would never have to stand outside our door on his tenth birthday, waiting for a bus to take him to the Trial stadium. He'd never have to follow dozens of other children up the stadium stairs and into the inner circle, or run laps while Trial admins study his breathing and posture, or answer pages and pages of stupid multiple-choice questions, or survive an interview in front of a half circle of impatient officials. He'd never have to wait in one of several groups afterward, unsure which groups would return home and which group would be sent off to the so-called "labor camps."

I don't know. If worse came to worst, maybe the plague *would* be a more merciful way to go.

"Eden always gets sick, you know," I say after a while. I take a large bite out of the bread and cheese. "He almost died once when he was a baby. He caught some kind of pox, and had fevers and rashes and cried nonstop for a week. The soldiers came close to marking our door. But it obviously wasn't the plague, and no one else seemed to have it." I shake my head. "John and I never got sick."

Tess doesn't smile this time. "Poor Eden." After a pause, she continues. "I was pretty sick when you first met me. Remember how grimy I looked?"

Suddenly I feel guilty for talking about my problems so much over the last few days. At least I *have* a family to worry about. I put an arm around her shoulder. "Yeah, you looked pretty awful."

Tess laughs, but her eyes stay focused on the downtown lights. She leans her head on my shoulder. It's the way she's leaned against me since the very first week I knew her, when I'd spotted her in an alley in Nima sector.

I still don't know what made me stop and talk to her that afternoon. Maybe the heat had made me soft, or maybe I was just in a good mood because I'd found a restaurant that had thrown out an entire day's worth of old sandwiches.

"Hey," I called out to her.

Two more heads popped up out of the garbage bin. I flinched in surprise. Two of them, an older woman and a teenage boy, immediately scrambled out of the mess and ran down the alley. The third, a girl who couldn't have been more than ten years old, stayed where she was, trembling when she saw me. She was skinny as a rail, with a tattered shirt and trousers. Her hair was short and blunt, cut off abruptly right below her chin, and red in the sunlight.

I waited for a moment, not wanting to scare her like I had the others. "Hey," I said again, "mind if I join you?"

She stared back at me without a word. I could barely make out her face because of all the soot on it.

When she didn't reply, I shrugged and started walking toward her. Maybe I could salvage something useful from the bin.

The instant I got within ten feet of the girl, she let out a strangled cry and darted away. She ran so fast that she tripped, falling onto the asphalt on her hands and knees. I limped over to her. My old knee injury was worse back then—and I can remember stumbling in my rush. "Hey!" I said. "Are you all right?"

She jerked away and held up her scratched hands to shield her face. "Please," she said. "Please, please."

"Please *what*?" Then I sighed, embarrassed by my irritation. Already I could see tears welling up in her eyes. "Stop crying. I'm not going to hurt you." I knelt down beside her. At first she whimpered and started to crawl away, but when I didn't move, she paused to stare at me. Both of her knees had the skin ripped right off them, and the flesh underneath was scarlet and raw.

"You live close by?" I asked her.

She nodded. Then, as if she had remembered something, she shook her head. "No," she said.

"Can I help you get home?"

"I don't have a home."

"You don't? Where are your parents?"

She shook her head again. I sighed and dropped my canvas bag to the ground, then held out a hand to her. "Come on," I said. "You don't want two infected knees. I'll help you clean them up and then you can be on your way again. You can have some of my food too. Pretty good deal, right?"

It took her a long time to put her hand in mine. "Okay," she whispered, so softly that I could barely hear her.

That night, we camped out behind a pawn shop that had a pair of old chairs and a ripped-up couch lying in its alley.

I cleaned the girl's knees with alcohol stolen from a bar, letting her bite down on a rag so she wouldn't shriek and draw attention to us. Other than when I was tending to her scrapes, she never let me get near her. Whenever my hand accidentally brushed her hair or bumped her arm, she would flinch as if burned by steam from a kettle. Finally I just gave up trying to talk to her. I let her have the couch, while I laid out my shirt as a pillow and tried to get comfortable on the pavement.

"If you want to leave in the morning, just go," I said to her. "You don't have to wake me up or say good-bye or anything." My eyelids were growing heavy, but she stayed wide awake, staring unblinkingly at me, even as I fell asleep.

She was still there in the morning. She followed me around as I scavenged in garbage bins, picking out old clothes and edible bits of leftover food. I tried asking her to leave. I even tried shouting at her. An orphan would be a huge inconvenience. But although I made her cry a few times, when I looked over my shoulder she'd still be there, trailing me a short distance away.

Two nights later, as we sat together by a crude fire, she finally spoke to me. "My name is Tess," she whispered. Then she studied my face, like she wanted to guess my reaction.

I only shrugged. "Good to know," I said.

And that was that.

Tess bolts out of her sleep. Her arm whacks my head.

"Ouch," I mutter as I rub my forehead. Pain runs through

my healing arm, and I hear the silver bullets Tess took from my clothes clink together in my pocket. "If you wanted me to wake up, you could've just tapped me."

She holds a finger up to her lips. Now I'm on the alert. We're still sitting underneath the pier, but it's probably a couple hours before dawn, and the skyline has already gone dark. The only light comes from several antique streetlamps lining the edge of the lake. I glance at Tess. Her eyes glint in the darkness.

"Did you hear something?" she whispers.

I frown. Usually I can hear something suspicious before Tess does, but this time I hear nothing at all. We both stay still for a long moment. I hear the occasional lap of waves. The churning sound of metal pushing water. Now and then, a passing car.

I look at Tess again. "What did you hear the first time?"

"It sounded like . . . something gurgling," she whispers.

Before I can think much about it, I hear footsteps and then a voice approaching the pier above us. We both shrink farther into the shadows. It's a man's voice, and his footsteps sound oddly heavy. I realize a second later that the man is walking in step with someone else. A pair of street police.

I push myself farther back against the bank, and some of the loose dirt and rocks give way. They roll silently down into the sand. I keep pushing until my back hits a surface that's hard and smooth. Tess does the same.

"There's something brewing," one of the police says. "Plague's popped up in the Zein sector this time."

Their footsteps clomp overhead and I see their figures walk along the beginning of the pier. Off in the distance, the first signs of light are turning the horizon a murky gray.

"I've never heard of the plague showing up there."

"Must be a stronger strain."

"What are they going to do?"

I try to hear what the other policeman has to say, but by now the two have walked far enough that their voices have turned to murmurs. I take a deep breath. The Zein sector is a good thirty miles away from here—but what if the strange red mark on my mother's door means that they're infected with this new strain? And what will the Elector do about it?

"Day," Tess whispers.

I look at her. She turns against the bank so that her back now faces out toward the lake. She points at the deep indent we've made in the bank. When I turn around, I see what she's pointing to.

The hard surface I'd had my back against is actually a sheet of metal. When I brush away more of the rocks and dirt, I see that the metal is lodged deep in the bank, so that it's probably what's holding the bank up in the first place. I squint at the surface.

Tess looks at me. "It's hollow."

"Hollow?" I put my ear against the ice-cold metal. A wave of noise hits me—the gurgling and hissing sound that Tess heard earlier. This isn't just a metal structure to hold up the lake's shores. When I pull away from it and look closer at the metal, I notice symbols carved on its surface.

One of these is the Republic's flag, imprinted faintly against the metal. Another is a small red number:

318

JUNE

"I SHOULD BE THE ONE GOING OUT THERE. NOT YOU."

I grit my teeth and try not to look at Thomas. His words could have come right out of Metias's mouth. "I'll look less suspicious than you," I reply. "People may find it easier to trust me." We're standing in front of a window in Batalla Hall's north wing, watching Commander Jameson at work on the other side of the glass. Today they caught a spy from the Colonies who was secretly spreading propaganda about "how the Republic is lying to you!" Spies are usually shipped out to Denver, but if they're caught in a big city like Los Angeles, we take them before the capital does. He's dangling upside down in the interrogation room right now. Commander Jameson has a pair of scissors in her hand.

I tilt my head a little as I look at the spy. I already hate him as much as I hate anything about the Colonies—he's not affiliated with the Patriots, that's for sure, but that just makes him more of a coward. (So far, every Patriot we've hunted down has killed himself before getting taken in.) This spy's young, probably in his late twenties. About the same age my brother was. I'm slowly growing used to talking about Metias in past tense.

From the corner of my eye, I can see that Thomas is still looking at me. Commander Jameson officially promoted him to fill my brother's position, but Thomas has little power over what I choose to do on this test mission, and it drives him crazy. He would have balked at letting me go undercover in the Lake sector for days on end, without a pair of strong backups and a team to follow me.

But it's going to happen anyway, starting tomorrow morning.

"Look. Don't worry about me." Through the glass, I see the spy arch his back in agony. "I can take care of myself. Day isn't a fool—if I have a team following me through the city, he'll notice it in no time."

Thomas turns back to the interrogation. "I know you're good at what you do," he replies. I wait for the *but* . . . in his sentence. It doesn't come. "Just keep your microphone on. I'll take care of things back here."

I smile at him. "Thanks." He doesn't look back at me, but I can see his lips tilt up at the edges. Maybe he's remembering when I used to tag along after him and Metias, asking them inane questions about how the military worked.

Behind the glass, the spy suddenly yells something at Commander Jameson and thrashes violently against his chains. She glances over at us and motions us in with a flip of her hand. I don't hesitate. Thomas and I, and another soldier standing close to the interrogation room's door, hurry inside and spread out near the back wall. Instantly I feel how stuffy and hot the room is. I look on as the prisoner continues to scream.

"What'd you say to him?" I ask Commander Jameson.

She looks at me. Her eyes are ice-cold. "I told him that our airships will target his hometown next." She turns back to the prisoner. "He'll start cooperating if he knows what's good for him."

The spy glares at each of us in turn. Blood runs from his mouth to his forehead and hair and drips onto the floor beneath him. Whenever he thrashes, Commander Jameson stomps on the chain around his neck and chokes him until he stops.

Now he snarls and spits blood at our boots, making me wipe mine against the ground in disgust.

Commander Jameson bends down and smiles at him. "Let's start again, shall we? What's your name?"

The spy looks away from her and says nothing.

Commander Jameson sighs and nods to Thomas. "My hands are tired," she says. "You do the honors."

"Yes, ma'am." Thomas salutes and steps forward. He tightens his jaw, then balls up his fist and punches the spy hard in the stomach. The spy's eyes bulge out, and he coughs up more blood onto the floor. I distract myself by studying the details of his outfit. (Brass buttons, military boots, a blue pin on his sleeve. Which means he had disguised himself as a soldier, and we caught him near San Diego, the only city that requires everyone to wear those blue pins. I can tell what gave him away too. One of the brass buttons looks slightly flatter than those made in the Republic. He must have stitched on that button by himself—a button from an old Colonies uniform. Stupid. A mistake only a Colonies spy would make.)

"What's your name?" Commander Jameson asks him again. Thomas flips open a knife and grabs one of the spy's fingers.

The spy swallows hard. "Emerson."

"Emerson *what*? Be specific."

"Emerson Adam Graham."

"Mr. Emerson Adam Graham, of East Texas." Commander Jameson says it in a light, coaxing voice. "A pleasure to meet you, young sir. Tell me, Mr. Graham, why did the Colonies send you over to our fine Republic? To spread their lies?"

The spy lets out a weak laugh. "Fine Republic," he snaps. "Your Republic won't last another decade. And all the better, too—once the Colonies take over your land, they'll make better use of it than you have—"

Thomas hits the spy across the face with the hilt of his knife. A tooth skids across the floor. When I look back at Thomas, his hair has fallen across his face and a cruel pleasure has replaced his usual kindness. I frown. I haven't seen this look on Thomas's face often; it chills me.

Commander Jameson stops him before he can hit the spy again. "It's all right. Let us hear what our friend has to say against the Republic."

The spy's face is scarlet from hanging upside down for too long. "You call this a republic? You kill your own people and torture those who used to be your brothers?" I roll my eyes at that. The Colonies want us to think that letting them take over is a good thing. Like they're annexing us or doing us some kind of favor. That's how they see us, a poor little fringe nation, as if *they're* the more powerful one. That idea *is* in their best interest, after all, since I hear the floods have claimed much more of their land than ours. That's all it's ever been about. Land, land, land. But becoming a union—that has never happened, and that *will* never happen. We'll defeat them first or die trying. "I'll tell you nothing. You can try as hard as you want, but I'll tell you nothing."

Commander Jameson smiles at Thomas, who smiles back. "Well, you heard Mr. Graham," she says. "Try as hard as you want."

Thomas goes to work on him, and after a while, the other soldier in the room has to join him to hold the spy in place. I force myself to look on as they try to pry information out of him. I need to learn this, to familiarize myself with this. My ears ring from the spy's screams. I ignore the fact that the spy's hair is straight and dark like my own, and his skin is pale, and his youth reminds me of Metias over and over again. I tell myself that Metias is not the one whom Thomas is now torturing. That would be impossible.

Metias can't be tortured. He is already dead.

That night, Thomas escorts me back to my apartment and kisses me on the cheek before he leaves. He tells me to be careful, and that he will be monitoring anything that transmits through my microphone. "Everyone will keep an eye on you," he reassures me. "You're not alone out there unless you choose to be."

I manage to smile back. I ask him to take care of Ollie while I'm gone.

When I'm finally inside the apartment, I curl up on the couch and rest my arm on Ollie's back. He's sleeping soundly, but has pressed himself tightly against the side of the couch. He probably feels Metias's absence as much as I do. On the coffee table, stacks of our parents' old photos from Metias's bedroom closet are strewn across the glass. So are Metias's journals, and a booklet where he used to save little mementos of the things we did together—an opera, late-night dinners, early practices at the track. I've been looking through them ever since Thomas left, hoping that the thing Metias had wanted to talk to me about is mentioned somewhere. I flip through Metias's writing and reread the little notes Dad liked to leave at the bottom of their photos. The most recent one shows our parents standing with a young Metias in front of Batalla Hall. All three are making thumbs-up gestures. *Metias's future career is here! March 12th.* I stare at the date. It was taken several weeks before they died.

My recorder sits on the edge of the coffee table. I snap my fingers twice, then listen to Day's voice over and over. What face matches up to this voice? I try to imagine how Day looks. Young and athletic, probably, and lean from years on the streets. The voice sounds so crackled and distorted from the speakers that there are parts I can't understand.

"Hear that, Ollie?" I whisper. Ollie snores a little and rubs his head against my hand. "That's our guy. And I'm going to get him."

I fall asleep with Day's words ringing in my ears.

★ ★ ★

0625 HOURS.

I'm in the Lake sector, watching the strengthening daylight paint the churning waterwheels and turbines gold. A layer of smoke hovers perpetually over the water's edge. Farther across the lake I can see downtown Los Angeles sitting right next to the shore. A street policeman approaches and tells me to stop loitering, to keep moving. I nod wordlessly and continue along the shore.

From a distance, I blend in completely with those walking around me. My half-sleeve collared shirt came from a thrift emporium at the border between Lake and Winter. My trousers are torn and smeared with dirt—my boots' leather is flaking off. I'm very careful about the type of knot I use to tie my shoelaces. It's a simple Rose knot, something any worker would use. I've pulled my hair back into a tight, high ponytail. I wear a newsboy cap over it.

Day's pendant necklace sits snugly in my pocket.

I can't believe how filthy the streets are here. Probably even worse than the dilapidated outskirts of Los Angeles. The ground sits low against the water (not unlike the other poor sectors, which all seem to look the same), so that whenever there's a storm, the lake probably floods all the streets lining the shore with dirty, sewage-contaminated water. Every building is faded, crumbling, and pockmarked—except, of course, the police headquarters. People walk around trash piled against the walls as if it isn't even there. Flies and stray dogs linger near the garbage—as do some people. I crinkle my nose at the smell (smoky lanterns, grease, sewage). Then I stop, realizing that if I'm to pass as a Lake citizen, I should pretend to be used to the stench.

Several men grin at me as I pass by. One even calls out to me. I ignore them and keep going. What a bunch of cons, men who had barely passed their Trials. I wonder if I can catch the plague from these people, even though I'm vaccinated. Who knows where they've been.

Then I stop myself. Metias had told me never to judge the poor like that. *Well, he's a better person than I am,* I think bitterly.

The tiny microphone inside my cheek vibrates a little. Then a faint sound comes from my earpiece. "Ms. Iparis." Thomas's voice comes out as a tiny hum that only I can hear. "Everything working?"

"Yup," I murmur. The little microphone picks up my throat's vibrations. "In central Lake now. I'm going dark for a bit."

"Got it," Thomas says, and his side falls silent.

I make a clicking sound with my tongue to turn off my microphone.

I spend most of this first morning pretending to dig around in the garbage bins. From the other beggars I hear stories about plague victims, which areas the police seem most nervous about, and which have started to recover. They talk about the best places to find food, the best places to find fresh water. The best places to hide during hurricanes. Some of the beggars look too young to have even taken the Trial. The youngest ones talk about their parents or how to pickpocket a soldier.

But no one talks about Day.

The hours drag on into evening, then night. When I find a quiet alley to rest in, with a few other beggars already asleep in the garbage bins, I curl into a dark corner and click my microphone on. Then I take out Day's pendant necklace from my pocket, holding it up slightly so I can study its smooth bumps.

"Calling it a night," I murmur. My throat barely vibrates.

My hearing piece crackles faintly with static. "Ms. Iparis?" Thomas says. "Any luck today?"

"Nope, no luck. I'll try some public places tomorrow."

"Okay. We'll have people over here twenty-four seven."

By "people over here twenty-four seven," I know Thomas means he's the only one there, listening for me. "Thanks," I whisper. "Going dark." I click my microphone off. My stomach rumbles. I pull out a slice of chicken I found in the back of a café's kitchen and force myself to munch on it, ignoring the slime of cold grease. If I need to live like a Lake citizen, I'll have to eat like one. *Maybe I should get a job,* I think. The idea makes me snort a little.

When I finally fall asleep, I have a bad dream, and Metias is in it.

I find nothing substantial the next day, or the day after that. My hair grows tangled and dull in the heat and smoke, and dirt has started to coat my face. When I look at my reflection in the lake, I realize that I look exactly like a street beggar now.

Everything feels dirty. On the fourth day, I make my way to the rim of Lake and Blueridge and decide to spend my time wandering through the bars.

That's when something happens. I stumble into a Skiz fight.

DAY

THE RULES FOR WATCHING—AND BETTING ON—a Skiz fight are simple enough.

1. You pick who you think will win.
2. You bet on that person.

That's about it. The only problem that comes up is when you're too infamous to risk placing a public bet and possibly getting picked up by the police.

This afternoon I'm crouched behind the chimney of a crumbling, one-story warehouse. From here I can see the crowd of people gathered in the abandoned building next door. I'm even close enough to make out some of their conversations.

And Tess. Tess is down there with them, her delicate frame nearly lost in the shuffle, with a pouch of our money and a smile on her face. I watch as she listens to other gamblers discuss the fighters. She asks them a few questions of her own. I don't dare take my eyes off her. Street police who are unhappy with their bribes sometimes break up Skiz fights, arresting people as they go, and as a result, I never stand with the crowd when Tess and I watch the fights. If they catch me and fingerprint me, it's over for both of us. Tess, though, is slender and wily. She can escape a raid much more easily than I can. But that doesn't mean I'll leave her on her own.

"Keep moving, cousin," I mutter under my breath as Tess

stops to laugh at some young gambler's joke. *Don't get too close to her, you trot.*

A noise comes from one end of the crowd. My eyes flick there for a second. One of the fighters is stirring up the onlookers by waving her arms and yelling. I smile. That girl is named Kaede, or so the crowd's chants tell me. Kaede is the very same bartender I met days ago while passing through the Alta sector. She flexes her wrists, then bounces on her feet and shakes out her arms.

Kaede has already won a match. Going by the unspoken rules of Skiz, she must now fight until she loses a round—until her opponent throws her to the ground. Each time she wins, she gets a cut of the overall bet on her opponent. My eyes wander to the girl she just picked out to be her next challenger. The girl is olive-skinned, with furrowed brows and an uncertain expression. I roll my eyes. Surely the crowd must know that this fight's going to be a no-brainer. This challenger will be lucky if Kaede lets her live.

Tess waits for a moment when no one is paying attention to her, then glances up quickly in my direction. I hold up one finger. She grins, then winks at me and looks back to the crowd. She hands money to the person organizing bets—a big, burly guy. We've cast one thousand Notes, almost all our money, in favor of Kaede.

The fight lasts for less than a minute. Kaede strikes early and hard, lunging out and striking the other girl viciously across the face. The other girl wavers. Kaede toys with her like a cat playing with her food before lashing out again with her fist. The challenger crashes to the ground, hitting her head on the cement floor, where she lies in a daze. Knockout. The crowd cheers, and several people help the girl stumble out of the ring. I exchange a brief smile with Tess, who gathers up our winnings and stuffs it into the pouch.

Fifteen hundred Notes. I swallow hard, warning myself not to get too excited. One step closer to a vial of cure.

My attention is back on the cheering crowd. Kaede flips her hair at the audience and strikes a mock pose for them, which makes them go wild. "Who's next?"

The crowd chants back. "Choose! Choose!"

Kaede looks slowly around the circle, shaking her head or sometimes tilting it to one side. I keep my eyes on Tess. She stands on her tiptoes behind several taller people, straining for a good look. Then she taps them hesitantly on their shoulders, says something, and pushes her way forward. I tighten my jaw at the sight. Next time I'll join her. Then she can sit on my shoulders and finally get to see the fights, instead of calling unwanted attention to herself.

A second later, I bolt upright. Tess has pushed her way past one of the larger gamblers. He shouts something at her, something angry, and before Tess can apologize, I see him shove her roughly into the ring's center. She stumbles, and the crowd roars with laughter.

Anger boils up in my chest. Kaede seems amused by the whole thing. "Is that a challenge, kid?" she shouts. A grin breaks out on her face. "Ya look like fun." Tess looks around, bewildered. She tries to take a step back into the crowd, but they block her path. When I see Kaede nod her head in Tess's direction, I rise up from my crouch. This trot's going to choose Tess.

Oh, *hell* no. Not while I'm watching. Not if Kaede wants to live.

Suddenly, a voice rings out from below. I pause. Some girl has made her way to the front of the ring, where she stares at Kaede. She rolls her eyes. "Doesn't seem like a fair fight," she calls out.

Kaede laughs. There's a brief silence.

Then Kaede shouts back, "Who the hell you think ya are, talking t'me like that? Think you're better?" She points at the girl, and the crowd lets out a cheer. I see Tess scurry into the safety of the crowd. This new girl has taken Tess's place, whether she meant to or not.

I let out a long breath. When I've managed to calm down, I take a closer look at Kaede's new opponent.

She's not much taller than Tess and definitely lighter than Kaede. For a second it seems like the crowd's attention has made her uncomfortable and I'm ready to dismiss her as a real contender until I study her again. No, this girl is nothing like the last one. She's hesitating not because she's afraid to fight, or because she fears losing, but because she's thinking. Calculating. She has dark hair tied back in a high ponytail and a lean, athletic build. She stands *deliberately*, with a hand resting on her hip, as if nothing in the world can catch her off guard. I find myself pausing to admire her face.

For a brief moment, I'm lost to my surroundings.

The girl shakes her head at Kaede. This surprises me too—I've never seen anyone refuse to fight. Everyone knows the rules: if you're chosen, you fight. This girl doesn't seem to fear the crowd's wrath. Kaede laughs at her and says something I can't quite make out. Tess hears it, though, and casts me a quick, concerned glance.

This time the girl nods. The crowd lets out another cheer, and Kaede smiles. I lean a little bit out from behind the chimney. Something about this girl . . . I don't know what it is. But her eyes burn in the light, and although it's hot and might be my imagination, I think I see a small smile on the girl's face.

Tess shoots a questioning look at me. I hesitate for a split second, then hold up one finger again. I'm grateful to this mystery girl for helping Tess out, but with my money on the line, I decide to play it safe. Tess nods, then casts our bet in favor of Kaede.

But the instant the new girl steps into the circle and I see her stance . . . I know I've made a big mistake. Kaede strikes like a bull, a battering ram.

This girl strikes like a viper.

JUNE

I'M NOT WORRIED ABOUT LOSING THIS FIGHT.

I'm more worried that I'll accidentally kill my opponent.

If I run right now, though, I'm a dead girl.

I silently scold myself—what a game to involve myself in. When I first saw this crowd of gamblers, I'd wanted to leave it alone. I'd wanted nothing to do with brawls. Not a good place to get caught by street police and taken downtown for questioning. But then I'd thought that maybe I could pick up some valuable information from a group like this—so many locals, some who might even know Day personally. Surely Day isn't a complete stranger to *everyone* in Lake, and if anyone knows who he is, it's the crowd that watches illegal Skiz fights.

But I should not have said anything about the skinny girl they shoved into the ring. I should have let her fend for herself.

It's too late now.

The girl named Kaede tilts her head at me and grins as we face each other in the ring. I take a deep breath. Already she has started to circle me, stalking me like prey. I study her stance. She steps forward with her right foot. She's left-handed. Usually this would work to her advantage and throw off her opponents, but I've trained for this. I shift the way I walk. My ears are drowning in the noise.

I let her strike first. She bares her teeth at me and lunges forward at full speed, her fist raised. But I can see her preparing to kick. I sidestep. Her kick whooshes past me. I use her momentum against her and strike her hard when her back's turned. She loses her balance and nearly falls. The crowd cheers.

Kaede whirls around to face me again. This time her smile is gone—I've succeeded in angering her. She lunges at me again. I block her first two punches, but her third punch catches me across the jaw and makes my head spin.

Every muscle in my body wants to end this now. But I force my temper down. If I fight too well, people might get suspicious. My style is too precise for a simple street beggar.

I let Kaede hit me one last time. The crowd roars. She starts smiling again, her confidence returning. I wait until she's ready to charge. Then I dart forward, duck down, and trip her. She doesn't see it coming—she falls heavily on her back. The crowd screams in approval.

Kaede forces herself onto her feet, even though most Skiz fights would've called her fall the end of the round. She wipes a bit of blood from her mouth. Before she can even catch her breath properly, she lets out an angry shout and lunges for me again. I should've seen the tiny flash of light near her wrist. Kaede's fist punches hard into my side, and I feel a terrible, sharp pain. I shove her away. She winks at me and starts circling again. I hold my side—and that's when I feel something warm and wet at my waist. I look down.

A stab wound. Only a serrated knife could have torn my skin that way. I narrow my eyes at Kaede. Weapons are not supposed to be part of a Skiz fight . . . but this is hardly a fight where the crowd follows all the rules.

The pain makes me light-headed and angry. No rules? So be it.

When Kaede comes at me again, I dart away and twist her arm in a tight hold. In one move, I shatter it. She screams in pain. When she tries to pull away, I continue to hold on, twisting the broken arm behind her back until I see the blood drain from her face. A knife slips out from the bottom of her tank top and clatters to the ground. (A serrated knife, just as I thought. Kaede is not a normal street beggar. She has the skills to get her hands on a nice weapon like that—which means she might be in the same line of business as Day. If I weren't undercover, I'd arrest her right now and take her in for questioning.) My wound burns, but I grit my teeth and maintain my grip on her arm.

Finally Kaede taps me frantically with her other hand. I release her. She collapses to the ground on her knees and her good arm. The crowd goes nuts. I clutch my bleeding side as tightly as I can, and when I look around, I see money exchanging hands. Two people help Kaede out of the ring (she shoots me a look of hatred before she turns away), and the rest of the onlookers start up their chant.

"Choose! Choose! Choose!"

Maybe it's the dizzying pain from my wound that makes me reckless. I can't contain my anger anymore. I turn without a word, roll my shirtsleeves back up to my elbows, and flip my collar up. Then I step out of the ring and start shoving my way out of the circle.

The crowd's chant changes. I hear the boos start. I'm tempted to click my microphone on and tell Thomas to send soldiers, but I keep silent. I'd promised myself not to call for backup unless I had no choice, and I'm certainly not going to ruin my cover over a street brawl.

When I've managed to walk outside the building, I risk a look behind me. Half a dozen of the onlookers are following me, and most of them look enraged. *They're the gamblers,* I think, *the ones who care the most.* I ignore them and continue to walk.

"Get back here!" one of them yells. "You can't just leave like that!"

I break into a run. *Curse* this knife wound. I reach a large trash bin and swing myself up onto it, then get ready to jump to a second-floor windowsill. If I can climb high enough, they won't be able to catch me. I leap as far as I can and manage to grab the edge of the windowsill with one hand.

But my wound has slowed me down. Someone grabs my leg and yanks hard. I lose my grip, scrape myself against the wall, and crash to the ground. I hit my head hard enough to send the world spinning. Then they're on me, dragging me to my feet and back to the screaming crowd. I fight to clear my head. Spots explode across my vision. I try to click my microphone on, but my tongue feels slow and covered with sand. *Thomas*, I whisper, but it comes out as *Metias*. I blindly reach out a hand for my brother, and then I remember that he's no longer there to take it.

Suddenly I hear a pop and a few shrieks, and in the next instant they release me. I fall back to the ground. I try scrambling to my feet, but stumble and fall again. Where did all this dust come from? I squint, trying to see through it. I can still hear the noise and chaos from the onlookers. Someone must've set off a dust bomb.

Then there's a voice telling me to get up. When I look to my side, I see a boy holding out his hand to me. He has bright blue eyes, dirt on his face, and a beat-up old cap on, and at this moment, I think he might be the most beautiful boy I've ever seen.

"Come on," he urges. I take his hand.

In the dust and chaos, we hurry down the street and disappear into the afternoon's lengthening shadows.

DAY

SHE WON'T TELL ME HER NAME.

I can understand that well enough. Lots of kids on the streets of Lake try to keep their identities a secret, especially after participating in something illegal like a Skiz fight. Besides, I don't want to know her name. I'm still upset about losing the bet. Kaede's defeat cost me a thousand Notes. That was money toward a vial of cure. Time is running out, and it's all this girl's fault. Stupid me. If she hadn't been responsible for getting Tess out of the ring, I would've left her to fend for herself.

But I know Tess would've given me sad puppy eyes for the rest of the day. So I didn't.

Tess continues to ask questions as she helps the Girl—that's what I'll call her, I guess—clean the wound in her side as best as she can. I stay quiet for the most part. I'm on guard. After the Skiz fight and my dust bomb, the three of us ended up camping out on the balcony of an old library. (Does it still count as a balcony if the whole wall has collapsed and left this floor open to the air?) In fact, almost all the floors have collapsed walls. The library is part of an ancient high-rise that now lies almost entirely in the water several hundred feet from the lake's eastern edge, completely overgrown with wild grasses. It's a good place for people like us to find some shelter. I watch the streets along the banks for angry gamblers who might still be searching for the Girl. I look over my shoulder from where I sit on the balcony's edge. The Girl says something to Tess, and Tess smiles cautiously in return.

"My name's Tess," I hear her say. She knows better than to say mine, but she keeps on talking. "What part of Lake are you from? Are you from another sector?" She studies the Girl's wound. "That's a nasty one, but nothing that can't heal. I'll try to find some goat milk for you in the morning. It's good for you. Until then you'll just have to spit on it. It'll help with infections."

I can tell from the Girl's face that she knows this already. "Thank you," she murmurs to Tess. She glances in my direction. "I'm grateful for your help."

Tess smiles again, but I can tell even *she* feels a little uncomfortable with this newcomer.

"I'm grateful for yours."

I tighten my jaw. Night will fall in about an hour or so, and I have a wounded stranger added to my duties.

After a while, I rise and join Tess and the Girl. Somewhere in the distance the Republic's pledge has started blaring from the city's speakers. "We'll stay here for the night." I look at the Girl. "How are you feeling?"

"Okay," she replies. But it's obvious she's in pain. She doesn't know what to do with her hands, so she keeps reaching for her wound, then stopping herself. I have a sudden urge to comfort her. "Why did you save me?" she asks.

I snort. "No goddy clue. You cost me a thousand Notes."

The Girl smiles for the first time, but there's something eternally cautious about her eyes. She seems to take in and analyze my every word. She doesn't trust me. "You bet big, don't you? Sorry about that. She made me angry." She shifts. "I'm guessing Kaede was no friend of yours."

"She's a bartender from the rim of Alta and Winter. Just a recent acquaintance."

Tess laughs and gives me a look that I can't quite read. "He likes to be acquainted with cute girls."

I scowl at her. "Bite your tongue, cousin. Haven't you had enough brushes with death for one day?"

Tess nods, a small smile on her face. "I'll go get us some water." She jumps up and heads down the open stairwell to the water's edge.

When she's gone, I sit down next to the Girl, and my hand accidentally brushes past her waist. She takes a small breath—I move away, afraid that I've hurt her.

"That should heal soon, if it doesn't get infected. But you might want to rest a couple of days. You can stay with us."

The Girl shrugs. "Thanks. When I feel better, I'm tracking Kaede down."

I lean back and study the Girl's face. She's a little paler than other girls I see in the sector, and has large dark eyes that shine with flecks of gold in the waning light. I can't tell *what* she is, which isn't unusual around here—Native, maybe, or Caucasian. Or something. She's pretty in a way that distracts me just like she did in the Skiz ring. No, pretty's not the right word. Beautiful. And not only that, but she reminds me of someone. Maybe it's the expression in her eyes, something at once coolly logical and fiercely defiant. . . . I feel my cheeks growing warm and suddenly look away, glad for the coming darkness. Maybe I shouldn't have helped her. Way too distracting. At this moment all I'm thinking about is what I'd give up for the chance to kiss her or to run my fingers through her dark hair.

"So, Girl," I say after a while, "thanks for your help today. For Tess, I mean. Where'd you learn to fight like that? You broke Kaede's arm without even trying."

The Girl hesitates. From the corner of my eye, I can see her watching me. I turn to face her, and she pretends to study the water instead, as if embarrassed to be caught looking. She absently touches her side and then makes a clicking sound with her tongue as if out of habit. "I hang around the edge of Batalla a lot. I like to watch the cadets practice."

"Wow, you're a risk-taker. But your fighting is pretty impressive. I bet you don't have much trouble on your own."

The Girl laughs. "You can see how well I did on my own today." She shakes her head. Her long ponytail swings behind. "I shouldn't have watched the Skiz fight at all, but what can I say? Your friend looked like she could use some help." Then she shifts her gaze to me. That cautious expression still blankets her eyes. "What about you? Were you in the crowd?"

"No. Tess was down there because she likes seeing the action and she's a little nearsighted. I like watching from a distance."

"Tess. Is she your younger sister?"

I hesitate. "Yeah, close enough. It was really Tess I wanted to keep safe with my dust bomb, you know."

The Girl raises an eyebrow at me. I watch her lips as they curl into a smile. "You're so kind," she says. "And does everyone around here know how to make a dust bomb?"

I wave my hand dismissively. "Oh, sure, even kids. It's easy." I look at her. "You're not from the Lake sector, are you?"

The Girl shakes her head. "Tanagashi sector. I mean, I used to live there."

"Tanagashi is pretty far away. You came all this way to see a Skiz fight?"

"Of course not." The Girl leans back and carefully lies down. I can see the center of her bandage turning a dark red. "I scavenge on the streets. I end up traveling a lot."

"Lake isn't safe right now," I say. A splash of turquoise in the corner of the balcony catches my eye. There's a small patch of sea daisies growing from a crack in the floor. *Mom's favorite.* "You might catch the plague down here."

The Girl smiles at me, as if she knows something I don't. I wish I could figure out who she reminds me of. "Don't worry," she says. "I'm a careful girl, when I'm not angry."

When evening finally comes and the Girl has dozed off into a fitful sleep, I ask Tess to stay with her so I can sneak away to check on my family. Tess is happy to do it. Going to the plague-infected areas of Lake makes her nervous, and she always comes back scratching at her arms—as if she can feel an infection spreading on her skin.

I tuck a handful of sea daisies into the sleeve of my shirt and a couple of Notes into my pocket for good measure. Tess helps me wrap both of my hands in cloth before I go to avoid leaving fingerprints anywhere.

The night feels surprisingly cool. No plague patrols wander the streets, and the only sounds come from occasional cars and the distant blare of JumboTron ads. The strange *X* on our door is still there, as prominent as ever. In fact, I'm almost certain that the soldiers have been back at least once, because the *X* is bright and the paint's fresh. They must have run a second check through the area. Whatever made them mark our door in the first place has apparently stuck around. I wait in the shadows near my mother's house, close enough so I can actually peek through the gaps of our backyard's rickety fence.

When I'm sure that no one is patrolling the street, I dart through the shadows toward the house and crawl to a broken board that leads under the porch. I slide the board aside. Then I crawl into the dark, stale-smelling crevice, and pull the board back into place behind me.

Small slivers of light come from between the floorboards in the rooms above me. I can hear my mother's voice toward the back, where our one bedroom is. I make my way over there, then crouch beside the bedroom's vent and look in.

John is sitting on the edge of the bed with his arms

crossed. His posture tells me that he's exhausted. His shoes are caked with dirt—I know Mom must've scolded him about that. John is looking toward the other side of the bedroom, where Mom must be standing.

I hear her voice again, this time loud enough to understand. "Neither of us is sick yet," she says. John looks away and back toward the bed. "It doesn't seem to be contagious. And Eden's skin still looks good. No bleeding."

"Not *yet,*" John replies. "We have to brace ourselves for the worst, Mom. In case Eden . . ."

Mom's voice is firm. "I won't have you saying that in my house, John."

"He needs more than suppressants. Whoever gave them to us is very kind, but it's not enough." John shakes his head and gets up. Even now, *especially* now, he has to protect my mother from the truth of my whereabouts. When he moves away from the bed, I can see that Eden is lying there with a blanket pulled up to his chin, despite the heat. His skin looks oily with sweat. The color of it is strange too, a pale, sickly green. I don't remember other plagues with symptoms like that. A lump rises in my throat.

The bedroom looks exactly the same, the few things in it old and worn but still comfortable. There's the tattered mattress Eden's on, and next to it is the scratched-up chest of drawers that I used to doodle on. There's our obligatory portrait of the Elector hanging on the wall, surrounded by a handful of our own photos, as if he were a member of our family. That's all our bedroom has. When Eden was a toddler, John and I used to hold his hands and help him walk from one end of this room to the other. John would give him high fives whenever he did it on his own.

Now I see Mom's shadow stop in the middle of the room. She doesn't say anything. I imagine her hunched shoulders, her head in her hands, her brave face finally gone.

John sighs. Footsteps echo above me, and I know he must've crossed the room to hug her. "Eden will be okay. Maybe this virus is less dangerous and he'll recover on his own." There's a pause. "I'm going to see what we have for soup." I hear him leave the bedroom.

I'm sure John hated working at the steam plant, but at least he got to leave the house and take his mind off things for a while. Now he's trapped here, with no way to help Eden. It must be killing him. I clench the loose dirt under me and make as tight a fist as I can.

If only the hospital had cures.

Moments later I see Mom walk across the room and sit at the edge of Eden's bed. Her hands are all bandaged up again. She murmurs something comforting to him and leans over to brush his hair from his face. I close my eyes. In my mind I conjure up a memory of her face, soft and beautiful and concerned, her eyes bright blue and her mouth rosy and smiling. My mother used to tuck me in, smoothing down my blankets and whispering a promise of good dreams. I wonder what she's whispering to Eden now.

Suddenly I'm overwhelmed with missing her. I want to rush out from under here and knock on our door.

I push my fists harder into the dirt. No. The risk is too great. *I'll find a way to save you, Eden. I promise.* I curse myself for risking so much money in a Skiz bet instead of finding a more reliable way to get cash.

I pull out the sea daisies that I had tucked into my shirt's sleeve. Some of the blossoms are crumpled now, but I prop them up as carefully as I can and gently pat down dirt around them. Mom will probably never see them here. But *I* know they're here. The flowers are proof to myself that I'm still alive. Still watching over them.

Something red in the dirt beside the daisies catches my eye. I frown, then brush aside more of the dirt to get a better look. There's a symbol here, something inscribed underneath all the dirt and pebbles.

It's a number, just like Tess and I had seen by the bank of the lake, except this time it says: 2544

I used to hide down here sometimes when I was younger, back when my brothers and I would play hide-and-seek. But I don't remember seeing this before. I lean down and put my ear against the ground.

At first there's nothing. Then I hear a faint sound, a whoosh—then a hissing and gurgling. Like some sort of liquid, or steam. There's probably a whole system of pipes down there, something that leads all the way out to the lake. Maybe all around the sector. I brush aside more dirt, but no other symbols or words appear. The number looks faded with age, the paint chipped away in little flakes.

I stay there for a while, quietly studying it. I glance one last time through the vent at the bedroom, then make my way out from under the porch, into the shadows, and away into the city.

JUNE

I WAKE UP AT DAWN. THE LIGHT MAKES ME SQUINT (where is it coming from—behind me?), and for an instant I'm disoriented, unsure of why I'm sleeping in an abandoned building facing the ocean with sea daisies growing at my feet. A sharp pain in my stomach forces a gasp out of me. *I've been stabbed,* I realize in a panic. And then I remember the Skiz fight and the knife and the boy who saved me.

Tess hurries over when she sees me stir. "How are you feeling?"

She still looks wary of me. "Sore," I mutter. I don't want her to think that she wrapped my wound badly, so I add, "Much better than yesterday, though."

It takes me a minute to realize that the boy who had saved me is sitting in the corner of the room, dangling his legs over the balcony and looking out toward the water. I have to hide my embarrassment. On a normal day, with no knife wound, I never would've let a detail like that go unnoticed. He went somewhere last night. When I was slipping in and out of sleep, I'd made a mental note of the direction he took (south, toward Union Station).

"I hope you don't mind waiting a few hours before eating," he says to me. He's wearing his old newsboy cap, but I can see a few strands of white-blond hair beneath it. "We lost the Skiz bet, so there's no money left for food right now."

He blames me for his loss. I just nod. I recall the sound of Day's crackly voice from the speakers and compare it quietly to this boy's. He looks at me for a while without smiling, as if he knows what I'm doing, then returns to his vigil. No, I can't be sure the voice belongs to him. Thousands of people in Lake could match that voice.

I realize that the mouthpiece in my cheek is still turned off. Thomas must be furious with me. "Tess," I say. "I'm going to head down to the water. I'll be back in a minute."

"You sure you can make it by yourself?" she asks.

"I'll be fine." I smile. "If you see me floating unconscious out to sea, though—by all means, come and get me."

The steps of this building definitely used to be part of a stairwell, but now they sit open to the outside. I get to my feet and limp down the stairs one at a time, careful not to slip off the side and plummet down to the water. Whatever Tess did last night seems to be working. Although my side still burns, the pain is a little duller and I can walk with less effort than yesterday. I make it down to the bottom of the building faster than I thought I would. Tess reminds me of Metias, of how he'd nursed me back to health on the day of his induction.

But I can't handle memories of Metias right now. I clear my throat and concentrate on making my way to the water's edge.

The rising eastern sun is now high enough to bathe the entire lake in a shade of murky gold, and I can see the tiny strip of land that separates the lake from the Pacific Ocean. I head all the way down to the floor of the building that sits right at the water's surface. Every wall on this floor is collapsed, so I can walk straight out to the building's edge and ease my legs into the water. When I look into the depths, I can see that this old library continues for many floors. (Perhaps fifteen stories tall, judging from how the buildings on the shore sit and how the land slopes from the shoreline. Approximately six stories should be underwater.)

Tess and the boy sit at the top of the building, several stories above me, safely out of hearing range. I look back at the horizon, click my tongue, and turn on my microphone.

Static buzzes from my earpiece. A second later, I hear a familiar voice. "Ms. Iparis?" Thomas says. "Is that you?"

"I'm here," I murmur. "I'm well."

"I'd like to know what you've been up to, Ms. Iparis. I've been trying to contact you for the past twenty-four hours. I was ready to send some soldiers to collect you—and you and I both know how happy Commander Jameson would be about *that*."

"I'm well," I say again. My hand digs into my pocket and pulls out Day's pendant. "Got a minor injury in a Skiz fight. Nothing serious."

I hear a sigh from the other end. "Well, you're not going to go that long again with your mike off, you hear me?" he says.

"Fine."

"Did you find anything yet?"

I glance up to where the boy is swinging his legs. "Not sure. A boy and girl helped me get out of the Skiz chaos. The girl bandaged up my wound. I'm staying with them temporarily until I can walk better."

"*Walk* better?" Thomas's voice rises. "What kind of minor injury is this?"

"Just a knife wound. No big deal." Thomas makes a choking sound, but I ignore it and keep going. "Anyway, that's not the point. The boy made a fancy little dust bomb to get us out of the Skiz mob. He has some skills. I don't know who he is, but I'll get more information."

"Think he's Day?" Thomas asks. "Day doesn't seem like the kind of boy who goes around saving people."

Most of Day's past crimes involve saving people. All except Metias. I take a deep breath. "No. I don't think so." I lower my voice until it's barely a whisper. Best not to throw wild guesses at Thomas right now, lest he decide to jump the gun and send troops after me. Commander Jameson will boot me right off her patrol if we do something expensive like that, with nothing to show for it. *Besides. These two got me out of serious trouble.* "But they might know something about Day."

Thomas is silent for a moment. I hear some commotion in the background, some static, and then his faint voice along with Commander Jameson's. He must be telling her about my injury, asking her if it's safe to keep me out here alone. I give an annoyed sigh. *As if I've never been wounded before.* After a few minutes, he comes back on again. "Well, be careful." Thomas pauses for a moment. "Commander Jameson says to keep you on your mission if your injury isn't bothering you too much. She's preoccupied with the patrol right now. But I'm warning you. If your mike goes dark again for more than a few hours, I'm going to send soldiers after you—whether or not it blows your cover. Understand?"

I fight to contain my irritation. Commander Jameson doesn't believe I can accomplish anything on this mission—her lack of interest is imprinted in every word of Thomas's response. As for Thomas . . . he rarely sounds so firm with me. I can only imagine how stressed-out he must've been over the last few hours. "Yes, sir," I say. When Thomas doesn't respond, I look up toward the boy again. I remind myself to watch him more closely when I get upstairs and not let this injury distract me.

I stuff the pendant back into my pocket and rise.

I observe my rescuer all day as I follow him around the Alta sector of Los Angeles. I take note of everything, no matter how small the detail.

He favors his left leg, for instance. The limp is so slight that I can't tell when he's walking beside Tess and me. I see it when he sits down or gets up—the slightest hesitation when he bends his knee. It's either a serious injury that never quite healed, or a minor but recent one. A bad fall, maybe.

That's not his only injury. Now and then he winces when he moves his arm. After he does this a couple times, I realize that he must have some sort of wound on his upper arm that stretches painfully whenever he reaches too far up or down.

His face is perfectly symmetrical, a mix of Anglo and Asian, beautiful behind the dirt and smudges. His right eye is slightly paler than his left. At first I think it might be a trick of the light, but I notice it again when we pass by a bakery and admire the loaves of bread. I wonder how it happened or whether it's something he was born with.

I notice other things too: how familiar he is with streets far from the Lake sector, as if he could walk them blindfolded; how nimble his fingers are when they smooth down the wrinkles at his shirt's waist; how he looks at buildings as if memorizing them. Tess never refers to him by name. Just like how they call me "Girl," they use nothing to identify who *he* is. When I grow tired and light-headed from walking, he stops all of us and finds water for me while I rest. He can sense my exhaustion without my uttering a word.

Afternoon approaches. We escape the worst of the sun by hanging out near the market vendors in the poorest part of Lake. Tess squints at the stands from under our awning. We're a good fifty feet away from them. She's nearsighted, but somehow she's able to pick out the differences between the fruit vendors and the vegetable vendors, the faces of the various merchants, who has money and who doesn't. I know this because I can see the subtle movements in her face, her satisfaction at making something out or her frustration at not being able to.

"How do you do that?" I ask her.

Tess glances at me—her eyes refocus. "Hmm? Do what?"

"You're nearsighted. How can you see so much of what's around you?"

Tess seems surprised for a moment, then impressed. Beside her, I notice the boy glance at me. "I can tell subtle differences between colors, even though they may look a little blurry," Tess replies. "I can see silver Notes peeking out of that man's purse, for example." She flicks her eyes toward one of the customers at a vendor.

I nod at her. "Very clever of you."

Tess blushes and glances down at her shoes. For a moment she looks so sweet that I can't help but laugh. Instantly I feel guilty. *How can I laugh so soon after my brother's death?* These two have a strange way of making me lose my composure.

"You're a perceptive one, Girl," the boy says quietly. His eyes are locked on mine. "I can see why you've survived on the streets."

I just shrug. "It's the *only* way to survive, isn't it?"

The boy shifts his eyes away. I release a breath. I realize that I'd been holding it in while his eyes kept me frozen in place. "Maybe you should be the one to help us steal some food, not me," he continues. "Vendors always trust a girl more, especially one like you."

"What do you mean by that?"

"You get right to the point."

I can't help smiling. "As do you." As we settle down to watch the stands, I make some notes to myself. I can afford to linger with these two for one more night, until I heal enough to return to tracking down information about Day. Who knows—maybe they'll even give me a clue.

When evening finally comes and the sun's heat begins to fade, we make our way back to the water's edge and search for a place to camp. All around us I see candlelight flickering to life from window to glassless window, and here and there the locals light small fires along the edges of alleys. New shifts of street police begin making their rounds. Five nights out in the field now. I still can't get used to the crumbling walls, the lines of worn clothing hanging from balconies, the clusters of young beggars hoping for a bite to eat from passersby . . . but at the very least, my disdain has faded. I think back with some shame on the night of Metias's funeral, when I'd left a giant steak untouched on my plate, without a second thought. Tess walks ahead of us, completely unperturbed by her surroundings, her stride cheerful and carefree. I can hear her humming some faint tune.

"Elector's Waltz," I murmur, recognizing the song.

The boy glances at me from where he's walking by my side. He grins. "Sounds like you're a fan of Lincoln, yeah?"

I can't tell him that I own copies of all of Lincoln's songs as well as some signed memorabilia, that I've seen her perform political anthems live at a city banquet or that she once wrote a song honoring each of the Republic's warfront generals. Instead, I smile. "Yeah, guess so."

He returns my smile. His teeth are beautiful, the loveliest I've seen so far on these streets. "Tess loves music," he replies.

"She always drags me past the bars around here and makes us wait nearby while she listens to whatever anthems they're playing inside. I don't know. Must be a girl thing."

Half an hour later, the boy starts to notice my fatigue again. He calls Tess back and guides us over to one of the alleys, where a series of large metal trash bins sit wedged between two walls. He pushes one of them forward to give us some room. Then he crouches down behind it, motions for Tess and me to sit down, and begins unbuttoning his vest.

I blush scarlet and thank every god in the world for the darkness surrounding us. "I'm not cold and I'm not bleeding," I say to him. "Keep your clothes on."

The boy looks at me. I would've expected his bright eyes to look dimmer in the night, but instead they seem to reflect the light coming from the windows above us. He's amused. "Who said anything about *you*, sweetheart?" He takes off his vest, folds it neatly, and places it on the ground next to one of the trash bin's wheels. Tess sits down and unceremoniously rests her head on it, as if it's an old habit.

I clear my throat. "Of course," I mutter. I ignore the boy's low laugh.

Tess stays up and talks with us, but soon her eyelids grow heavy, and she falls asleep with her head on the boy's vest. The boy and I lapse into silence. I let my eyes linger on Tess.

"She seems very fragile," I whisper.

"Yeah . . . but she's tougher than she looks."

I glance up at him. "You're lucky to have her with you." My eyes go to his leg. He sees my gesture and quickly adjusts his posture. "She must've come in handy when she fixed up your leg."

He realizes that I've noticed his limp. "Nah. I got this a long time ago." He hesitates, then decides against saying anything more about it. "How's your wound healing, by the way?"

I wave him off. "No big deal." But I grit my teeth even as I say it. Walking around all day hasn't helped things, and the pain is returning like wildfire.

The boy sees the strain on my face. "We should change those bandages." He gets up and, without disturbing Tess, deftly pulls a roll of white wraps from her pocket. "I'm not as good as she is," he whispers. "But I'd rather not wake her."

He sits beside me and loosens the bottom two buttons of my shirt, then pushes it up until he exposes my bandaged waist. His skin brushes against mine. I try to keep my focus on his hands. He reaches behind one of his boots and pulls out what looks like a compact kitchen knife (patternless silver handle, worn edge—he's used it plenty of times before, and to saw through things much tougher than cloth). One of his hands rests against my stomach. Even though his fingers are callused from years on the streets, they're so careful and gentle that I feel heat rising on my cheeks.

"Hold still," he mutters. Then he places the knife flat between my skin and the bandages and rips the cloth. I wince. He lifts the bandage away from my wound.

Tiny trickles of blood still seep from where Kaede's knife stabbed me, but thankfully, there are no signs of infection. Tess knows her stuff. The boy pulls the rest of the old bandages away from my waist, tosses them aside, and starts wrapping the new bandages around me. "We'll stay here until late morning," he says as he works. "We shouldn't have traveled so much today—but y'know, putting some distance between you and the Skiz folks wasn't such a bad idea."

Now I can't help looking at his face. This is a boy who must've barely passed his Trial. But that doesn't make sense. He doesn't act like a desperate street kid. He has so many more *sides* to him that I wonder if he has always lived in these poor sectors. He glances at me now, notices me studying him, and pauses for a second. Some secret emotion darts across his eyes. *A beautiful mystery.* He must have similar questions about me, how I'm able to pick out so many details of his life. Perhaps he's even wondering what I'll figure out about him next. He's so close to my face now that I can feel his breath against my cheek. I swallow. He draws a little nearer.

For an instant, I think he might kiss me.

Then he quickly looks back down at my wound. His hands brush against my waist as he works. I realize that his cheeks are rosy too. He's as flushed as I am.

Finally he tightens the bandage, tugs my shirt back into place, and pulls away. He leans against the wall beside me and rests his arms against his knees. "Tired?"

I shake my head. My eyes wander to the clothes hanging overhead, several stories up. If we run out of bandages, that's where I can get some fresh ones. "I think I can leave you guys alone after another day," I say after a while. "I know I'm slow-ing you down." But I feel a surge of regret even as the words come out of my mouth. Strange. I don't *want* to leave them so soon. There's something comforting about hanging around with Tess and this boy, as if the absence of Metias hasn't entirely stripped me of everyone who cares about me.

What am I thinking? This is a boy from the slums. I've been trained to deal with guys like this, to watch them from the other side of the glass.

"Where will you go?" the boy asks.

I refocus. My voice comes out cool and collected. "East, maybe. I'm more used to the inner sectors."

The boy keeps his eyes forward. "You can stay longer, if all you're going to do is wander the streets somewhere else. I could use a good fighter like you. We can make quick cash in Skiz fights and split our food supplies. We'll both do better."

He offers this idea with such sincerity that I have to smile. I decide not to ask why he doesn't fight in Skiz himself. "Thanks, but I prefer to work alone."

He doesn't miss a beat. "Fair enough." And with that, he leans his head back against the wall, sighs, and closes his eyes. I watch him for a moment, waiting for him to expose those brilliant eyes to the world again. But he doesn't. After a while, I hear his breathing grow steady and see his head droop, and I know he's fallen asleep.

I think about contacting Thomas. But I'm not in the mood to hear his voice right now. I'm not even sure why. *Tomorrow morning, then, first thing.* I lean my head back too and stare up at the clothes hanging above us. Other than the distant sounds of night-shift crowds and occasional JumboTron broadcasts, it's a peaceful evening, just like at home. The silence makes me think of Metias.

I make sure that the sound of my crying doesn't wake Tess and the boy.

DAY

I ALMOST KISSED THE GIRL LAST NIGHT.

But nothing good can come out of falling for someone on the streets. That's the worst weakness you can have, right up there with having a family stuck in a quarantined zone or a street orphan needing you.

And yet . . . a part of me still wants to kiss her, no matter how cracked a move it might be. This girl can point out a detail on the streets a mile away. ("The shutters on that building's third-floor windows must've been scavenged from a rich sector. Solid cherrywood.") With a knife, and in one throw, she can skewer a hot dog from an unattended stand. I can see her intelligence in every question she asks me and every observation she makes. But at the same time, there's an innocence that makes her completely different from most of the people I've met. She's not cynical or jaded. The streets haven't broken her. They've made her stronger instead.

Like me.

Throughout the morning, we hunt for more opportunities to make money—naive police to pickpocket, stuff in trash bins to resell, unguarded pier crates to pry open—and when that's done, we find a new spot to camp for the night. I try to keep my thoughts on Eden, on the money I need to collect before it's too late, but I start thinking up new ways to mess with the Republic's war campaign instead. I could hitch a ride on an airship, siphon off its precious fuel, then sell it on the market or divvy it up to people who need it. I could destroy the airship altogether before it heads off to the warfront. Or target the electric grids of Batalla or the airfield bases, cut their power and shut them down. These thoughts keep me occupied.

But every now and then, when I steal a glance at the Girl, or feel her eyes on me, I helplessly drift back to thinking about her.

JUNE

NEARLY 2000 HOURS.
AT LEAST 80°F.

THE BOY AND I SIT TOGETHER IN THE BACK OF ANOTHER alley while Tess sleeps a short distance away. The boy has given her his vest again. I watch as he files his nails down by scraping them with the edge of his knife. He's taken the cap off his head, for once, and combed through the tangles in his hair.

He's in a good mood. "You want a sip?" he asks me.

A bottle of nectar wine sits between us. It's cheap stuff, probably made from those bland sea grapes that grow in ocean water. But the boy acts like this wine is the best thing in the world. He'd stolen a case of bottles from a shop at Winter sector's edge earlier in the evening and sold all but this one for a grand total of 650 Notes. It never ceases to amaze me how quickly he gets around the sectors. His agility is on par with the top students at Drake.

"I'll have some if you do," I say. "Can't let your stolen goods go to waste, can I?"

He grins at that. I watch as he stabs his knife into the bottle's cork, then pops it out and throws his head back for a long swig. He wipes a thumb across his mouth and smiles at me. "Delicious," he says. "Have some."

I accept the bottle and take a small sip before handing it back to him. Salty aftertaste, just as I thought. At least it might ease the pain in my side.

We continue taking turns—large swigs for him, small sips for me—until he recorks the bottle, seeming to put it away the instant he feels it dulling his awareness. Even so, his eyes look glossier, and the blue irises take on a lovely, reflective sheen.

He may not let himself lose his ability to focus, but I can tell that the wine has relaxed him. "So tell me," I decide to ask. "Why do you need so much money?"

The boy laughs. "Is that a serious question? Don't we all want more money? Can you ever have enough?"

"You like answering all my questions with your own questions?"

He laughs again. But when he speaks, his voice has a sad tinge to it. "Money is the most important thing in the world, you know. Money can buy you happiness, and I don't care what anyone else thinks. It'll buy you relief, status, friends, safety . . . all sorts of things."

I watch as his eyes take on a faraway look. "It seems like you're in an awful hurry to stock up."

This time he shoots me an amused look. "Why wouldn't I be? You've probably lived on the streets as long as I have. You should know the answer to that, yeah?"

I look down. I don't want him to see the truth. "I guess so."

We sit in silence for a moment.

The boy speaks up. When he does, there's such a tender

quality to his voice that I can't help looking up at him. "I don't know if anyone's ever told you this," he begins. He doesn't blush, and his eyes don't dart away. Instead I find myself staring into a pair of oceans—one perfect, the other blemished by that tiny ripple. "You're very attractive."

I've been complimented on my appearance before. But never in his tone of voice. Of all the things he's said, I don't know why *this* catches me off guard. But it startles me so much that without thinking I blurt out, "I could say the same about you." I pause. "In case you didn't know."

A slow grin spreads across his face. "Oh, trust me. I know."

I laugh. "Nice to hear something honest." I can't break away from his stare. Finally, I manage to add, "Well, I think you've had too much wine, my friend." I keep my voice as light as I can. "A little sleep will do you good."

The words have barely left my mouth when the boy leans closer and places his hand on my cheek. All my training would have me block his hand and pin it to the ground. But now I do nothing but sit perfectly still. He pulls me to him. I take a breath before he touches his lips to mine.

I taste the wine on his lips. He kisses me gently at first and then, as if he's reaching for something more, he pushes me against the wall and kisses me harder. His lips are warm and so soft—his hair brushes against my face. I try to focus. (Not his first time. He's definitely kissed other girls before, and quite a few at that. He's—he seems like he's short of breath. . . .) The details flit away. I grab at them in vain. It takes me a moment to realize I'm kissing him just as hungrily. I feel the knife at his waist against my own skin, and I tremble. It's too warm here, there's too much heat on my face.

He pulls away first. We stare at each other in bewildered silence, like neither of us can quite grasp what just happened.

Then he regains his composure, and as I struggle to regain mine, he leans back against the wall beside me and sighs. "Sorry," he murmurs. He gives me a look laced with mischief. "I couldn't help it. But at least now it's over with."

I stare at him awhile longer, still unable to speak. My mind screams at me to collect my thoughts. The boy returns my look. Then he smiles, as if he knows what sort of effect he has, and turns away. I begin breathing again.

That's when I see a gesture which jolts my mind completely back into place: before he lies down to sleep, he grabs at something around his neck. It's such an unconscious movement that I doubt he even realizes he did it. I stare at his neck but see nothing hanging around it. He had grabbed at the ghost of a necklace, the ghost of some trinket or thread.

And that's when I remember, with a nauseating feeling, the pendant in my pocket. Day's pendant.

WHEN THE GIRL HAS FINALLY FALLEN ASLEEP, I LEAVE her with Tess and head off to visit my family again. The cooler air clears my head. Once I'm a fair distance from the alley, I take a deep breath and quicken my pace. *I shouldn't have done it,* I tell myself. *I shouldn't have kissed her.* I especially shouldn't be glad that I did it. But I am. I can still feel her lips against mine, the smooth, soft skin of her face and arms, the slight trembling of her hands. I've kissed plenty of beautiful girls before, but not like this one. I'd wanted more. I can't believe I managed to pull away.

So much for warning myself against falling for people on the streets.

Now I force myself to concentrate on meeting up with John. I try to ignore the strange *X* on my family's door and make my way directly to the floorboards lining the side of the porch. Candles flicker by the shuttered bedroom window. My mother must be up late watching Eden. I crouch in the darkness for a while, look over my shoulder at the empty streets, then push aside the board and fall to my knees.

Something stirs in the shadows across the street. I pause for a second and squint into the night. Nothing. When I don't see anything else, I lower my head and crawl under the porch.

John's warming some sort of soup in the kitchen. I utter a trio of low whistles that sounds like a cricket; it takes a few tries before John hears it and turns around. Then I leave the porch and head around to the house's back door, where I meet my brother in the darkness.

"I've got sixteen hundred Notes," I whisper. I show him the pouch. "Almost enough for cures. How's Eden?"

John shakes his head. The anxiety on his face unnerves me, because I always expect him to be the strongest of us. "Not good," he says. "He's lost more weight. But he's still alert, and he recognizes us. I think he has a few more weeks."

I nod quietly. I don't want to think about the possibility of losing Eden. "I promise I'll have the money soon. All I need is one more lucky break, and I'll be there, and we'll have it for him."

"You're being careful, right?" he asks. In the dark, we can pass for twins. Same hair, same eyes. Same expression. "I don't want you putting yourself in unnecessary danger. If there's any way for me to help you, I'll do it. Maybe I can sneak out with you sometimes and—"

I scowl. "Don't be stupid. If the soldiers catch you, you'll all die. You know that." John's frustrated expression makes me feel guilty for dismissing his help so quickly. "I'm faster this way. Seriously. Better that only one of us is out there hunting for the money. You won't do Mom any good if you're dead."

John nods, although I can tell he wants to say more. I avoid it by turning away. "I've got to go," I say. "I'll see you soon."

JUNE

DAY MUST HAVE THOUGHT I'D FALLEN ASLEEP. BUT I SEE him get up and leave in the middle of the night, so I follow him. He breaks into a quarantine zone, enters a house marked with a three-lined *X,* and reappears several minutes later.

It's all I need to know.

I climb to the roof of a nearby building. Once there, I crouch in the shadows of a chimney and turn my mike on. I'm so angry with myself that I can't stop my voice from shaking. I'd let myself get carried away with the last person I ever wanted to like. That I ever wanted to ache for.

Maybe Day didn't kill Metias, I tell myself. *Maybe it was someone else.* God—am I making *excuses* to protect this boy now?

I've acted like an idiot in front of Metias's murderer. Have the streets of Lake turned me into some simpleminded girl? Have I just shamed the memory of my brother?

"Thomas," I whisper, "I found him."

A full minute of static passes before I hear Thomas answer me. When he does, he sounds oddly detached. "Can you repeat that, Ms. Iparis?"

My temper rises. "I said I found him. Day. He just visited a house in one of Lake's quarantine zones, a house with a three-lined *X* on its door. Corner of Figueroa and Watson."

"Are you sure?" Thomas sounds more alert now. "You're *absolutely* sure."

I take the pendant out of my pocket. "Yes. No doubt about it."

Some commotion on the other side. His voice grows excited. "Corner of Figueroa and Watson. That's the special plague case we're meant to investigate tomorrow morning. You're sure it's Day?" he asks again.

"Yes."

"Medic trucks will be at the house tomorrow. We're to take the inhabitants to the Central Hospital."

"Then send for extra troops. I want backup when Day shows up to protect his family." I remember the way Day had crawled under the floorboards. "He'll have no time to get them out, so he'll probably hide them somewhere in the house. We should take them to Batalla Hall's hospital wing. No one's to be hurt. I want them there for questioning."

Thomas seems taken aback by my tone. "You'll have your troops," he manages to say. "And I hope to hell you're right."

The feel of Day's lips, our heated kiss, and his hands running across my skin—it should all mean nothing to me now. Worse than nothing. "I am right."

I return to the alley before Day can find me missing.

DURING THE FEW HOURS OF SLEEP I MANAGE TO GET before dawn, I dream of home.

At least, it seems like the home I remember. John sits with our mother at one end of the dining table, reading to her from a book of old Republic tales. Mom nods encouragingly to him when he gets through an entire page without flipping words or letters around. I smile at them from where I stand by the door. John is the strongest of us, but he has a patient, gentle streak that I didn't inherit. A trait from our father. Eden is doodling something on paper at the other end of the table. Eden always seems to be drawing in my dreams. He never looks up, but I can tell he's listening to John's story as well, laughing at the appropriate places.

Then I realize that the Girl is standing next to me. I hold her hand. She gives me a smile, one that fills the room with light, and I smile back.

"I'd like you to meet my mother," I say to her.

She shakes her head. When I look back to the dining table, John and Mom are still there, but Eden's gone.

The Girl's smile fades. She looks at me with tragic eyes. "Eden is dead," she says.

A distant siren shakes me out of my sleep.

I lie quietly for a while, eyes open, trying to catch my breath. My dream is still seared into my mind. I focus on the sound of the siren to distract myself. Then I realize I'm not hearing the normal wail of a police siren. Nor is it an ambulance's siren. This is a siren from a military medic truck, the ones used for transporting injured soldiers to the hospital. It's louder and higher-pitched than the others because military trucks get first priority.

Except we have no injured soldiers coming back to Los Angeles. They get treated at the warfront's border. The other thing these trucks are used for around here is to transport special plague cases to the labs, due to their better emergency equipment.

Even Tess recognizes the sound. "Where are they going?" she asks.

"I don't know," I murmur back. I sit up and look around. The Girl looks like she's been awake for a while already. She sits several feet away with her back against the wall, her eyes pointed out toward the street, her face grave with concentration. She seems tense.

"Morning," I say to her. My eyes dart to her lips. Did I really kiss her last night?

She doesn't look at me. Her expression doesn't change. "Your family had their door marked, didn't they?"

Tess looks at her in surprise. I stare at the Girl in silence, not sure how to respond. It's the first time anyone other than Tess has brought up my family to me.

"You followed me last night." I tell myself that I should be angry—but I don't feel anything except confusion. She must have followed me out of curiosity. I'm amazed—shocked, really—at how silently she can travel.

But something seems different about the Girl this morning. Last night she was as into me as I was into her—but today she's distant, withdrawn. Have I done something to piss her off? The Girl looks directly at me. "Is that what you're saving up all that money for? A plague cure?"

She's testing me, but I don't know why. "Yes," I say. "Why do you care?"

"You're too late," she says. "Because today the plague patrol is coming for your family. They're taking them away."

JUNE

I DON'T HAVE TO SAY MUCH MORE TO CONVINCE DAY TO move. And the medic truck sirens, almost certainly headed for Figueroa and Watson, have come by just as Thomas promised they would.

"What do you mean?" Day says. The shock hasn't even hit him yet. "What do you mean, they're coming for my family? How do you know this?"

"Don't question it. You don't have time for that." I hesitate. Day's eyes look so terrified—so vulnerable—that suddenly it takes all my strength to lie to him. I try to draw on the anger I felt last night. "I did see you visit your family's quarantine zone last night, and I overheard some guards talking about today's sweep. They mentioned the house with the three-lined *X*. Hurry. I'm trying to help you—and I'm telling you that you have to go to them right *now*."

I've taken advantage of Day's greatest weakness. He doesn't hesitate, doesn't stop to question what I say, doesn't even wonder why I didn't tell him right away. Instead he leaps to his feet, pinpoints the direction that the sirens are coming from, and darts out of the alley. I feel a surprising pang of guilt. He trusts me—truly, stupidly, wholeheartedly trusts me. In fact, I don't know if anyone has ever taken my word so readily before. Maybe not even Metias.

Tess watches him go with a look of increasing fright. "Come on, let's follow him!" Tess exclaims. She jumps to her feet and takes my hands. "He might need our help."

"No," I snap. "You wait here. I'll follow him. Keep low and stay quiet—someone will come back for you."

I don't bother to wait for Tess's reply before I take off down the street. When I look over my shoulder, I see Tess standing in the alley with her wide eyes locked on my vanishing figure. I turn back around. Best to keep her out of this. *If we arrest Day today, what will happen to her?* I click my tongue and turn on my mike.

Static blares for a second in my tiny earpiece. Then I hear Thomas's voice. "Talk to me," he says. "What's going on? Where are you?"

"Day's heading toward Figueroa and Watson right now. I'm on his tail."

Thomas sucks in his breath. "Right. We've already deployed. See you in a few."

"Wait for my word—no one's to be harmed—" I start to say, but the static cuts off.

I sprint down the street, my wound throbbing in protest. Day couldn't have gone far—he has less than a half-minute lead on me. I point myself in the direction that I remember Day going the previous night, south toward Union Station.

Sure enough, before long I see glimpses of Day's old cap peeking out far ahead of me in the crowd.

All my anger and fear and anxiety now zero in on the back

of his head. I have to force myself to keep enough distance between us so that he doesn't know I'm following him. A part of me recalls the way he saved me from the Skiz fight, that he had helped me heal this burning wound in my side, that his hands had been so gentle. I want to scream at him. I want to hate him for confusing me so much. Stupid boy! It's a wonder you've evaded the government for so long—but you can't hide now, not when your own family or friends are at risk. *I have no sympathy for a criminal,* I remind myself harshly. *Just a score to settle.*

DAY

USUALLY I'M GRATEFUL FOR THE CROWDS ON THE streets of Lake. They're easy to slip in and out of, throwing off those who might be on your trail or hoping to pick a fight. I've lost count of the number of times I've used the busy streets to my advantage. But today they only slow me down. Even with a shortcut along the lakeside, I'm running just barely in front of the sirens and won't have a chance to widen the gap before I reach my family's house.

I won't have time to get them out. But I have to try. I have to reach them before the soldiers do.

Occasionally I pause to make sure the trucks are still going in the direction I think they are. Sure enough, they continue on a path straight for our neighborhood. I run faster. I don't even stop when I accidentally collide with an old man. He stumbles and falls against the pavement. "Sorry!" I shout. I can hear him yelling at me, but I don't dare waste time looking back.

I'm sweating by the time I near our house, still quiet and taped off as part of the quarantine. I sneak through the back alleys until I'm standing by our crumbling backyard fence. Then I ease my way through a crack in the fence, push aside the loose board, and crawl underneath the porch. The sea daisies that I laid under the vents are still there, untouched, but they've already withered and died. Through the floor's gaps, I see my mother sitting at Eden's bedside. John is rinsing a washcloth in a nearby basin. My eyes dart to Eden. He looks worse now—as if all the color has been stripped from his skin. His breath is shallow and raspy, so loud that I can hear it from down here.

My mind screams for a solution. I could help John, Eden, and my mother escape right now, and risk running into the plague patrols or street police. Maybe we could find refuge in the usual spots Tess and I hide. John and my mother are certainly strong enough to run. But how would Eden keep up? John could only carry him for so long. Maybe I can find a way to sneak them onto a cargo train, and help them escape inland to . . . somewhere, I don't know. If the patrols are already after Eden, then it won't make things any worse if John and Mom just leave their jobs and run. They've already been quarantined, anyway. I could help them get to Arizona, or maybe West Texas, and after a while maybe the patrols won't bother searching for them anymore. Besides, maybe I'm fooling myself to begin with—maybe the Girl is wrong and the patrols aren't even coming for my family. I can keep saving up for Eden's plague medicine. All my anxiety might be for nothing.

But off in the distance, I hear the medic truck's siren growing louder.

They're coming for Eden.

I make up my mind. I scramble from under the porch and hurry to the back door. Out here I can hear the medic trucks much more clearly. They're getting closer. I open the back door and dash up the few steps leading to our living room.

I take a deep breath.

Then I kick open the door and rush into the light.

My mother lets out a startled cry. John whirls around in my direction. We stand there for an instant, staring at each other, unsure of what to do.

"What's wrong?" His face turns pale at my expression. "What are you doing here? Tell me what happened." He tries to steady his voice, but he knows something's terribly wrong—something so serious that it forced me to reveal myself to my entire family.

I pull the worn cap off my head. My hair tumbles down in a tangled mess. Mom holds a bandaged hand over her mouth. Her eyes grow suspicious, then they widen.

"It's me, Mom," I say. "It's Daniel."

I watch the different emotions flash across her face—disbelief, joy, confusion—before she takes a step forward. Her eyes dart between John and me. I can't tell which shocks her more . . . that I'm alive or that John seems to know all about it.

"Daniel?" she whispers.

It's strange to hear her say my old name again. I rush to take Mom's injured hands in my own. They're shaking. "There's no time to explain." I try to ignore the expression in her eyes. They were a strong, bright blue once, just like mine, but sorrow has faded them. How do I face a mother who's thought I was dead for so many years? "They're coming for Eden. You have to hide him."

"Daniel?" Her fingers brush the hair from my eyes. I'm suddenly her little boy again. "My Daniel. You're alive. This must be a dream."

I take her by the shoulders. "Mom, listen. The plague patrol is coming, and they have a medic truck with them. Whatever virus Eden has . . . They're coming to get him. We have to hide you all."

She studies me a moment, then nods. She leads me to Eden's bed. From up close I can see that Eden's dark eyes have somehow turned black. There's absolutely no reflection in them, and I realize with horror that they're black because his irises are bleeding. Mom and I carefully help Eden sit up. His skin is burning hot. John gently lifts him onto his shoulder, whispering soothing words as he does.

Eden lets out a pained yelp, and his head lolls to one side, resting against John's neck. "Connect the two circuits," he murmurs.

The sirens continue to wail outside—they must be less than a couple of blocks away by now. I exchange a desperate look with my mother.

"Under the porch," she whispers. "There's no time to run."

Neither John nor I argue. Mom takes my hand tightly in hers. We make our way out the back entrance. I stop for a second just outside, checking the direction and distance of the patrols. They're almost here. I hurry over to the porch and slide the board to one side. "Eden first," Mom whispers. John adjusts Eden on his shoulder, then kneels down and crawls into the space. I help Mom in next. Then I scoot after them, wiping away any marks we made in the dirt, and carefully lifting the board back into place. I hope it's good enough.

We huddle in the darkest corner, where we can barely even see each other. I stare at the shafts of light coming through the vents. They slice the dirt floor into pieces, and I can just make out the crumpled sea daisies. The medic truck's sirens sound distant for a moment—they're making a turn somewhere—and then all of a sudden, they're deafening. Heavy boots follow in their wake.

Damn trots. They've stopped outside our home and are getting ready to force their way in.

"Stay here," I whisper. I twist my hair up over my head and then stuff it back inside my cap. "I'm going to throw them off."

"No." It's John's voice. "Don't go back out there. It's too dangerous."

I shake my head. "It's too dangerous for you if I stay. Trust me." My eyes flick to Mom, who's working hard to keep her own fear in check while telling Eden a story. I remember how calm she had always seemed when I was little, with her soothing voice and gentle smile. I nod at John. "I'll be right back."

Overhead I hear someone bang on our door. "Plague patrol," a voice calls out. "Open up!"

I dart over to the loose board, carefully pull it aside a couple of feet, and then squeeze my way out. I slide it carefully back into place. Our house's fence shields me from view, but through the cracks I can see the soldiers waiting outside the door. I have to act quickly. They won't be expecting someone to fight back right now, especially someone they can't see. I hurry silently to the back of our house, get a good foothold on a loose brick, and fling myself upward. I grab the edge of our roof, then swing up onto it.

The soldiers can't see me up here, with our wide chimney and the shadows cast by the taller buildings around us. But I have a good view of them. In fact, the view makes me pause. Something's wrong here. We have at least a slim chance against one plague patrol. But there are far more than a dozen soldiers in front of our house. I count at least twenty, maybe more, all with white masks tied tightly around their mouths. Some have full gas masks on. Two military jeeps are parked next to the medic truck. In front of one, a high-ranking official with red tassels and a commander's hat stands waiting. Next to her is a dark-haired young man in a captain's uniform.

And standing in front of him, unmoving and unprotected, is the Girl.

I frown, confused. They must have arrested her—and now they're using her for something. That means they must've caught Tess too. I search the crowd, but Tess is nowhere to be seen. I turn back to the Girl. She seems calm, unfazed by the sea of soldiers surrounding her. She tightens her own mask around her mouth.

And then, in an instant, I realize why the Girl had looked so familiar. Her eyes. Those dark, gold-flecked eyes. The young captain named Metias. The one I'd escaped from on the night I raided the Los Angeles Central Hospital. He had the exact same eyes.

Metias must be her relative. Just like him, she works for the military. I can't believe my stupidity. I should have seen this earlier. I quickly scan the faces of the other soldiers, wondering if Metias himself is here as well. But I just see the Girl.

They've sent her to hunt me down.

And now, because of my idiocy, she has tracked me right to my family. She may have even killed Tess. I close my eyes—I'd trusted this girl, had been duped into kissing her. Even falling for her. The thought makes me blind with rage.

A loud crash rings out from our house. I hear shouts, then screams. The soldiers have found them—they've broken through the floorboards and dug them out. *Go down there! Why are you hiding on this roof? Help them!* But that would only reveal their relation to me, and their fates would be sealed. My arms and legs freeze up.

Then two soldiers with gas masks emerge from behind the house, dragging my mother between them. Following close behind are soldiers restraining John, who shouts at them to leave our mother alone. A pair of medics come out last. They've strapped Eden to a gurney and are wheeling him toward the medic truck.

I have to do something. From my pocket, I pull the three silver bullets Tess had given me, the three bullets from my hospital break-in. I fit one of them into my makeshift sling-shot. A memory of my seven-year-old self launching the flaming snowball into the police headquarters flickers through my mind. Then I point the slingshot at one of the soldiers holding John, pull back as far as I can, and fire.

It scrapes his neck so hard that I see blood spray from the impact. The soldier crumples, clutching frantically at his mask. Instantly other soldiers point their guns up toward the roof. I'm crouched, motionless, behind the chimney.

The Girl steps forward. "Day." Her voice echoes down the street. I must be delirious because I think I hear sympathy in her voice. "I know you're here, and I know why." She points toward John and my mother. Eden has already disappeared inside the medic truck.

Now my mother knows I'm the criminal she sees on all the JumboTron warnings. But I say nothing. I fit another bullet to my slingshot and point it in the Girl's direction.

"You want your family to be safe. I understand that," she continues. "I wanted my family to be safe too."

I pull back my arm.

The Girl's voice becomes more pleading, even urgent. "Now I'm giving you a chance to save yours. Turn yourself in. Please. No one will get hurt."

One of the soldiers standing near her lifts his gun higher. On instinct, I swing the slingshot toward him and fire. It hits him right in the knee and sends him tumbling forward.

The soldiers fire a volley of bullets at me. I huddle behind the chimney. Sparks fly. I grit my teeth and close my eyes—I can do nothing in this situation. I'm helpless.

Once the gunfire stops, I look out from the chimney and see the Girl still standing there. Her commander crosses her arms. The Girl doesn't flinch.

Then I see the commander step forward. When the Girl starts to protest, she pushes her aside. "You can't stay there forever," the commander shouts up at me. Her voice is much colder than the Girl's. "And I know you won't leave your family to die."

I fit the last bullet into my slingshot and point it straight at her.

The commander shakes her head at my silence. "Okay, Iparis," she says to the Girl. "We've tried your tactic. Now let's try mine." She turns to the dark-haired captain and nods once. "Cop her."

I have no time to stop what happens next.

The captain lifts his gun and points it at my mother. Then he shoots her in the head.

JUNE

THE WOMAN THOMAS SHOOTS HASN'T EVEN CRUMPLED TO the ground yet when I see the boy launch himself from the rooftop. I freeze. This is all wrong. *No one's supposed to get hurt.* Commander Jameson did not tell me that she intended to kill anyone from the house—we were supposed to take them all back to Batalla Hall for arrest and questioning. My eyes dart to Thomas, wondering if he feels the same horror I do. But he remains expressionless, his gun still drawn.

"Get him!" Commander Jameson yells out. The boy lands on one of the soldiers and knocks him to the ground in a shower of dirt. "We're taking him alive!"

The boy who I now know is Day lets out a wrenching scream and charges at the nearest soldier even as they close in around him. Somehow he manages to get a hold of the soldier's gun, although another soldier instantly knocks it from his hands.

Commander Jameson looks at me and pulls the pistol from her belt.

"Commander, don't!" I blurt out, but she ignores me. Metias flashes through my mind.

"I'm not going to wait for him to kill off my soldiers," she snaps back at me. Then she aims at Day's left leg and fires. I wince. The bullet misses its mark (she was aiming for his kneecap)—but it hits the flesh of his outer thigh. Day lets out a scream of agony, then goes down amid a circle of soldiers. The cap flips off his head. His blond hair spills out from beneath it. One soldier kicks him hard enough to knock him out. Then they cuff him, blindfold and gag him, and drag him into one of the waiting jeeps. It takes me a moment to turn my attention to the other prisoner we pulled from the house, a young man who's probably Day's brother or cousin. He's screaming something unintelligible at us. The soldiers shove him into the second jeep.

Thomas gives me an approving look over his mask, but Commander Jameson just frowns at me. "I can see why Drake labeled you a troublemaker," she says. "This isn't college. You don't question my actions."

A part of me wants to apologize, but I'm too overwhelmed by what just happened, too angry or anxious or relieved. "What about our plan? Commander, with all due respect, we didn't discuss killing civilians."

Commander Jameson lets out a sharp laugh. "Oh, Iparis," she replies. "We'd be here all night if we kept negotiating. See how much faster that was? Much more persuasive to our target." She looks away. "No matter. Time for you to get in a jeep. Back to headquarters." She makes a quick motion with her hand, and Thomas barks out an order. The other soldiers hurry back into their formations. She climbs into the first jeep.

Thomas approaches, then tips his hat at me. "Congratulations, June." He smiles. "I think you really did it. What a run! Did you see the look on Day's face?"

You just murdered someone. I can't bring myself to look at

Thomas. Can't bring myself to ask him how he can bear to follow orders so blindly. My eyes wander to where the woman's body lies on the pavement. Medics have already surrounded the three wounded soldiers, and I know they'll be placed carefully in the medic truck and taken back to headquarters. But the woman's body lies unattended and abandoned. A few heads peek out at us from the other houses along the street. Some of them see the body and quickly turn away, while others keep a timid gaze on Thomas and me. Some small part of me wants to smile at the sight, to feel the joy of avenging my brother's death. I pause, but the feeling doesn't come. My hands clench and unclench. The pool of blood underneath the woman is starting to make me feel sick.

Remember, I tell myself, *Day killed Metias.* Day killed Metias, Day killed Metias.

The words echo empty and uncertain in my mind.

"Yeah," I say to Thomas. My voice sounds like a stranger's. "I think I really did it."

PART TWO

★★★

THE GIRL WHO SHATTERS THE SHINING GLASS

DAY

THE WORLD'S A BLUR. I REMEMBER GUNS AND LOUD voices, and the splash of ice water over my head. Sometimes I recognize the sound of a key turning in a lock and the metallic smell of blood. Gas masks look down at me. Somebody won't stop screaming. There's a medic truck siren wailing all the time. I want to turn it off, and I keep trying to find its switch, but my arms feel weird. I can't move them. A horrible pain in my left leg keeps my eyes and cheeks moist with tears. Maybe my entire leg's wasted.

The moment the captain shot my mother plays over and over in my head, like a movie stuck on the same scene. I don't understand why she doesn't move out of the way. I yell at her to move, to duck, to do *anything*. But she just stays there until the bullet hits her and she crumples to the ground. Her face is pointed right at me—but it's not my fault. *It's not.*

The blurring comes into focus after an eternity. What's it been, four or five days? A month, maybe? I have no idea. When I finally open my eyes, I see that I'm now in a small, windowless cell with four steel walls. Soldiers stand on either side of a small, vaultlike door. I grimace. My tongue is cracked and bone-dry. Tears have dried against my skin. Something that feels like metal cuffs binds my hands tightly to the back of a chair, and it takes me a second to realize that I'm sitting. My hair hangs over my face in stringy ribbons. Blood stains my vest. A sudden fear seizes me: *my cap*. I'm exposed.

Then I feel the pain in my left leg. It's worse than anything I've ever experienced, worse even than the first time I got cut in that knee. I break out in a cold sweat and see stars flicker in the corners of my vision. At that moment, I would give anything for a painkiller, or ice to put out the fire in my injured thigh, or even another bullet to put me out of my misery. *Tess, I need you. Where are you?*

When I dare to look down at my leg, though, I see that it's wrapped in a tight, blood-soaked bandage.

One of the soldiers notices me stirring. He presses his hand against his ear. "He's awake, ma'am."

Minutes later—maybe it's hours—the metal door swings open and the commander who ordered my mother's death strides in. She has her full uniform on, cloak and all, and her triple-arrow insignia shines silver under the fluorescent lights. *Electricity. I'm in a government building.* She says something to the soldiers on the other side of the door. Then it swings shut again, and she saunters over to me with a smile.

I'm not sure if the red haze clouding my vision is because of the pain from my leg or my rage at her presence.

The commander stops in front of my chair, then leans down close to my face. "My dear boy," she says. I can hear the amusement in her voice. "I was so excited when they told me you were awake. I just had to come and see you myself. You should feel pretty lucky—the medics say you're plague-free, even after spending time with that infected lot you call a family."

I jerk back and spit at her. Even this movement is enough to make my leg tremble from white-hot pain.

"What a beautiful boy you are." She gives me a smile laced with poison. "A pity you chose the life of a criminal. You could have become a celebrity in your own right, you know, with a face like that. Free plague vaccinations every year. Wouldn't that have been nice?"

I could tear the skin off her face right now if I weren't tied up. "Where are my brothers?" My voice comes out as a hoarse croak. "What have you done with Eden?"

The commander just smiles again and snaps her fingers at the soldiers behind her. "Believe me when I say I would love to stay and chat with you, but I have a training session to lead. There's also a person much more eager to see you than I am. I'll let her take it from here." The commander exits without another word.

Then I see someone else—someone smaller, with a more delicate frame—enter the cell with the swoosh of a black cape. It takes me a minute to recognize her. No more torn trousers or muddy boots; no dirt on her face. The Girl is clean and polished, her dark hair pulled back into a high, glossy ponytail. She wears a fancy uniform: gold epaulettes shine from the top of her cloaked military robe, white ropes loop around her shoulders, and a double-arrow insignia is printed on both sleeves. Her cape hangs all the way to her feet, swathing her in gold-trimmed black. An elaborate Canto knot holds the top of her robe firmly in place. I'm surprised at how young she looks, even younger than when I first met her. Surely the Republic wouldn't give a girl my age such a high rank. I look at her mouth—the same lips I kissed are now coated in a light sheen of gloss. A cracked thought hits me and I want to laugh. If she had not led to the death of my mother and my capture, if I did not wish she were *dead*, I would find her absolutely breathtaking.

She must've seen the recognition on my face. "You must be as thrilled as I am to meet again. Call it an act of extreme kindness that I requested your leg be bandaged up," she snaps. "I want to see you stand for your execution, and I won't have you dying from infection before I'm through with you."

"Thanks. You're very kind."

She ignores my sarcasm. "So. You're Day, then."

I stay silent.

The Girl crosses her arms and regards me with a penetrating glare. "I suppose I should call you Daniel, though. Daniel Altan Wing. I managed to get that much out of your brother John."

At the mention of John's name, I lean forward and instantly regret it as my leg explodes in pain. "Tell me where my brothers are."

Her expression doesn't change. She doesn't even blink. "They are no longer your concern." She takes several steps forward. Here she has a precise, deliberate step, unmistakably that of the Republic's elite. She disguised it surprisingly well on the streets. It only makes me angrier.

"Here's how it works, Mr. Wing. I'm going to ask you a question, and you're going to give me an answer. Let's start with an easy one. How old are you?"

I meet her gaze. "I should've never saved you from that Skiz fight. I should've left you to die."

The Girl looks down, then takes a gun from her belt and strikes me hard across the face. For a second I can see only blinding white light—the taste of blood fills my mouth. I hear something click, then feel cold metal against my temple. "Wrong answer. Let me be clear. You give me another wrong answer, and I'll make sure you can hear your brother John's screams all the way from here. You give me a third wrong answer, and your little brother, Eden, can share the same fate."

John and Eden. At least they're both still alive. Then I realize from the hollow sound of her gun's click that her gun isn't loaded. *Apparently she just wants to slap me around with it.*

The Girl doesn't move her gun away. "How old are you?"

"Fifteen."

"That's better." The Girl lowers her gun a little. "Time for a few confessions. Were you responsible for the break-in at the Arcadia bank?"

The ten-second place. "Yes."

"Then you must be responsible for stealing sixteen thousand five hundred Notes from there as well."

"You got that right."

"Were you responsible for vandalizing the Department of Intra-Defense two years ago, and destroying the engines of two warfront airships?"

"Yes."

"Did you set fire to a series of ten F-472 fighter jets parked at the Burbank air force base right before they were to head out to the warfront?"

"I'm kinda proud of that one."

"Did you assault a cadet standing guard at the edge of the Alta sector's quarantine zone?"

"I tied him up and delivered food to some quarantined families. Bite me."

The Girl rattles off a few more past offenses, some of which I can barely remember. Then she names one more crime, my latest.

"Were you responsible for the death of a city patrol captain during a raid on the Los Angeles Central Hospital? Did you steal medical supplies and break into floor three?"

I lift my chin. "The captain named Metias."

She gives me a cold look. "That's right. My brother."

So. This is why she hunted me down. I take a deep breath. "Your brother. I didn't kill him—I couldn't have. Unlike you trigger-happy trots, I don't kill people."

The Girl doesn't reply. We stare at each other for a moment. I feel a weird tinge of sympathy and quickly push it away. I can't feel sorry for a Republic agent.

She motions to one of the soldiers standing by the door. "The prisoner in 6822. Cut off his fingers."

I lunge forward, but my cuffs and the chair stop me. My leg explodes with pain. I'm not used to someone having this much power over me. "Yes, I was responsible for breaking in!" I shout. "But I'm serious when I tell you that I didn't kill him. I admit I hurt him—yes—I had to escape, and he tried to stop me. But there's no way my knife throw could've caused anything more than a wounded shoulder. Please—I'll answer your questions. I've given you answers to everything so far."

The Girl looks at me again. "Nothing more than a wounded shoulder? Maybe you should've double-checked." There's a deep fury in her eyes, something that takes me aback. I try to remember the night I faced Metias—the moment when he had his gun pointed at me and I had my knife pointed at him. I'd thrown it at him . . . it had hit his shoulder. I'm sure of it.

Am I?

After a moment, she tells the soldier to hold off. "According to the Republic's databases," she goes on, "Daniel Altan Wing died five years ago from smallpox, in one of our labor camps."

I snort at that. *Labor camps.* Yeah, right, and the Elector is fairly elected every term, too. This girl either actually believes all that made-up crap or she's taunting me. An old memory struggles to resurface—a needle injected into one of my eyes, a cold metal gurney and an overhead light—but it vanishes as soon as it comes.

"Daniel *is* dead," I reply. "I left him behind a long time ago."

"That was when you began your little crime spree on the streets, I guess. Five years. Seems like you grew used to getting away with things. Started letting your guard down, didn't you? Did you ever work for anybody? Did anybody ever work for you? Were you ever affiliated with the Patriots?"

I shake my head. A terrifying question emerges in my mind, a question I'm too afraid to bring up. *What has she done with Tess?*

"No. They've tried recruiting me before, but I prefer to work alone."

"How did you escape the labor camps? How did you end up terrorizing Los Angeles when you should've been working for the Republic?"

So this is what the Republic thinks of children who fail the Trial. "What does it matter? I'm here now."

This time I strike some sort of nerve with the Girl. She kicks my chair back until it can go no further, then slams my head against the wall. Stars burst across my vision. "I'll tell you why it matters," she hisses. "It matters because if you hadn't escaped, my brother would be alive right now. And I want to make sure no other filthy street con assigned to the labor camps escapes the system—so that this scenario won't play out *ever* again."

I laugh in her face. The pain in my leg only fuels my anger. "Oh, is *that* all you're worried about? A bunch of renegade

Trial takers who managed to escape their *deaths*? Those ten-year-olds are a dangerous bunch, yeah? I'm telling you that you got your facts wrong. I didn't kill your brother. But you killed my mother. *You might as well have held the gun to her head!*"

The Girl's face hardens—but behind that I can see something waver, if only for a moment, and she looks like the girl I'd met on the streets. She leans over me, so close that her lips touch my ear and I can feel her breath against my skin. A shiver runs down my spine. She lowers her voice to a whisper that only I can hear. "I'm sorry about your mother. My commander had promised me she wouldn't hurt any civilians, and she went back on her word. I . . ." Her voice quivers. She actually sounds a little apologetic, like that will help. "I wish I could have stopped Thomas. You and I are enemies, make no mistake about that . . . but I did not wish for such a thing to happen." Then she straightens and begins to turn away. "That'll do for now."

"Wait." With great effort, I swallow my temper and clear my throat. The question I'd been afraid to think about escapes before I can stop it. "Is she alive? What'd you do with her?"

The Girl glances back at me. The expression on her face tells me she knows exactly who I'm talking about. *Tess. Is she alive?* I brace myself for the worst.

But instead the Girl just shakes her head. "I don't know. I have no interest in her." She nods at one of the soldiers. "Withhold water from him for the rest of the day and move him to a cell at the end of the hall. Maybe he'll be less temperamental in the morning." It's weird to see the soldier salute someone so young.

She's keeping Tess a secret, I realize. *For my sake? For Tess's sake?*

Then the Girl's gone, and I'm left alone in the cell with the soldiers. They haul me off the chair, across the floor, and out the door. My bad leg drags along the tiles. I can't hold back the tears that spring to my eyes. The pain makes me light-headed, like I'm drowning in a bottomless lake. The soldiers are taking me down a wide hallway that seems to be a mile long. Troops are everywhere, along with doctors wearing goggles and white gloves. I must be in the medical ward. Probably because of my leg.

My head slumps forward. I can't hold it up anymore. In my mind, I see the image of my mother's face as she lies crumpled on the ground. *I didn't do it,* I want to scream, but no sound comes out. The pain of my wounded leg reclaims me.

At least Tess is safe. I try to send a mental warning to her, to tell her to get out of California and run as far as she can.

That's when, halfway down the hall, something catches my attention. A small red number—a *zero*—printed in the same style as the ones I'd seen underneath the porch of our house and under the banks of our sector's lake. It's here. I turn my head to get a better look as we pass the double doors it's sprayed on. The doors have no windows, but a gas-masked figure clad in white enters and I get a brief glimpse inside. I don't see much more than blurs as we walk by—but I do manage to catch one thing. Something in a bag on a gurney. A body. On the bag is a red *X*.

Then the doors slide shut again, and we continue on.

A series of images begin to run through my mind. The red numbers. The three-lined *X* mark on my family's door. The medic trucks that took Eden away. Eden's eyes—black and bleeding.

They want something from my little brother. Something to do with his illness. I picture the three-lined *X* again.

What if it was no accident that Eden got the plague? What if it's no accident when *anyone* gets it?

JUNE

That evening, I force myself into a dress to attend an impromptu ball with Thomas on my arm. The gala is being held to celebrate the capture of a dangerous criminal, and to reward us all for bringing him to justice. Soldiers go out of their way to hold open doors for me when we arrive. Others throw me salutes. Clusters of chatting officials smile at me when I pass, and my name is scattered through almost every conversation I overhear. *That's the Iparis girl. . . . She looks awfully young. . . . Only fifteen years old, my friend. . . . The Elector himself is impressed. . . .* Some words are more heavily laced with envy than others. *Not as big a deal as you might think. . . . Truly it's Commander Jameson that deserves the recognition. . . . Just a child . . .*

No matter their tone, though, the topic is me.

I try to take pride in all this. I even tell Thomas, as we wander the lavish ballroom with its endless banquet tables and chandeliers, that arresting Day has filled the gaping hole Metias's death left in my life. But even as I say it, I don't believe it. Everything here feels wrong somehow, everything about this room—as if it's all an illusion that will shatter if I reach out and touch it.

I feel wrong . . . like I did a terrible thing by betraying a boy who trusted me.

"I'm glad you're relieved," Thomas says. "At least Day's

good for something." His hair is carefully combed back, and he looks taller than usual in a flawless, tasseled captain's uniform. He touches my arm with one gloved hand. Before the murder of Day's mother, I would've smiled at him. Now I feel a chill at his touch and pull away.

Day is good for forcing me into this dress, I want to say, but instead I just smooth down the already smooth fabric of my gown. Both Thomas and Commander Jameson had insisted I wear something nice. Neither would tell me why. Commander Jameson had simply waved a dismissive hand when I asked her. "For once, Iparis," she'd said, "do what you're told and don't question it." Then she added something about a surprise, the unexpected appearance of someone I care very much about.

For an illogical moment, I'd thought she might mean my brother. That somehow he had been brought back to life and I would see him on this night of celebration.

For now I just let Thomas navigate me around the crowds of generals and aristocrats.

I ended up choosing a corseted sapphire dress lined with tiny diamonds. One of my shoulders is covered in lace, and the other is hidden behind a long curtain of silk. My hair stays straight and loose—a discomfort for someone who spends most training days with her hair pulled securely away from her face. Thomas occasionally glances down at me, and his cheeks turn rosy. I don't see what the big deal is, though. I've worn nicer dresses before, and this one feels too modern and lopsided. This dress could've bought a kid in the slum sectors several months' worth of food.

"The commander informed me that they'll sentence Day tomorrow morning," Thomas says a moment later, after we finish greeting a captain from the Emerald sector.

At the mention of Commander Jameson, I turn my face away, unsure that I want Thomas to register my reaction. It seems that she's already forgotten about what happened to Day's mother, as if twenty years has passed. But I decide to be polite and look up at Thomas. "So soon?"

"The sooner the better, right?" The sudden edge in his voice startles me. "And to think you were forced to spend so much time in his company. I'm amazed he didn't kill you in your sleep. I'm—" Thomas pauses, then decides against finishing his sentence.

I think back to the warmth of Day's kiss, the way he'd bandaged my wound. Since his capture, I've puzzled over this a hundred times. The Day that killed my brother is a cruel, ruthless criminal. But who is the Day I met on the streets? Who is this boy that would risk his own safety for a girl he didn't know? Who is the Day that grieves so deeply for his mother? His look-alike brother, John, did not seem like a bad person when I questioned him in his cell—bargaining his life for Day's, bargaining hidden money for Eden's freedom. How could such a coldhearted criminal be a part of this family? The memory of Day bound to his chair, agonizing over his wounded leg, makes me both angry and confused. I could have killed him yesterday. I could've just loaded some bullets into my gun and shot him dead and been done with it. But I'd left my gun empty.

"Those street cons are all the same," Thomas goes on, echoing what I said to Day in his cell. "Did you hear that Day's sick brother, the little one, tried to spit on Commander Jameson yesterday? Tried to infect her with whatever mutated plague he's carrying?"

The subject of Day's younger brother isn't something I've investigated. "Tell me," I say, pausing to look at Thomas. "What exactly does the Republic want with that boy? Why take him to the hospital lab?"

Thomas lowers his voice. "I can't say. Much of it is confidential. But I do know that several generals from the warfront have come to see him."

I frown. "They came just for him?"

"Well, many of them are here for a meeting of some sort. But they did make a point of stopping by the lab."

"Why would the warfront be interested in Day's little brother?"

Thomas shrugs. "If there's something we need to hear about, the generals will tell us."

Moments later, we're intercepted by a large man with a scar from his chin to his ear. Chian. He grins broadly at the sight of us and puts a hand on my shoulder. "Agent Iparis! Tonight is your night. You're a star! I tell you, my dear, everyone in the higher circles is talking about your prodigious performance. Especially your commander—she's gushing about you like you're her daughter. Congratulations on your agent promotion and that nice little reward. Two hundred thousand Notes should buy you a dozen elegant dresses."

I manage a polite nod. "You are very kind, sir."

Chian smiles, distorting his scar, and claps his gloved hands together. His uniform has enough badges and medals to sink him to the ocean's bottom. Surprisingly, one of the badges is purple and gold, which means Chian was a war hero once—although I have a hard time believing that he ever risked his life to save his comrades. It also means he's suffered the loss of a limb. His hands seem intact, so he must have a prosthetic leg. The subtle angle he's leaning toward tells me that he favors his left.

"Follow me, Agent Iparis. And you too, Captain," Chian instructs. "There's someone who wants to meet you."

This must be the person Commander Jameson mentioned. Thomas shoots me a secretive smile.

Chian leads us through the banquet hall and across the dance floor, toward a thick navy curtain walling off a large part of the room. Republic flag stands are positioned at both ends of the curtain, and as we approach, I see that the curtain has a faint pattern of the flag on it as well.

Chian holds open the curtain for us, then closes it behind him as we step inside.

There are twelve velvet chairs arranged in a circle, and in each sits an official in full black uniform, his or her shoulders adorned with shining gold epaulettes, sipping from delicate glasses. I recognize a few. Some are generals from the war-front, the same ones Thomas mentioned earlier. One of them spots us and approaches, a younger official following close behind him. But as they leave the circle, the rest of the group rises and bows in their direction.

The older official is tall, with graying hair at his temples and a chiseled jaw. His skin looks wan and sickly. He wears a gold-rimmed monocle over his right eye. Chian is standing at attention, and when Thomas releases my arm, I look over to see him doing the same. The man waves a hand, and everyone relaxes their stance. Only now do I finally recognize him. He looks different in person than he does in his portraits or on the city's JumboTrons, where his skin has a much warmer color and no wrinkles. I also pick out the bodyguards scattered among the officials.

This is our Elector Primo.

"You must be Agent Iparis." His lips tug upward at my stunned expression, but there is little warmth in his smile. He grasps my hand in one quick, firm shake. "These gentlemen tell me great things about you. That you're a prodigy. And more important, you've put one of our most irritating criminals behind bars. So I thought it fitting that I congratulate you in person. If we had more patriotic young people like you, with minds as sharp as yours, we'd have won the war against the Colonies long ago. Wouldn't you agree?" He pauses to look around at the others, and everyone murmurs in agreement. "I congratulate you, my dear."

I bow my head. "Such an honor to meet you, sir. It is my pleasure, Elector, to do what I can for our country." I'm amazed by how calm my voice is.

The Elector motions to the young official beside him. "This is my son, Anden. Today is his twentieth birthday, so I thought I would bring him with me to this lovely celebration."

I turn to Anden. He's very much like his father, tall (six feet two inches) and quite regal looking, with dark curly hair. Like Day, he has some Asian blood. But unlike Day, his eyes are green and his expression uncertain. He wears white condor flight gloves with elaborate gold lining, which means he's already completed fighter pilot training. Left-handed. Gold cuff links on the sleeves of his black military tuxedo coat have the Colorado coat of arms engraved on them. Which means he was born there. Scarlet waistcoat, double row of buttons. He wears his air force rank first, unlike the Elector.

Anden smiles at my lingering gaze, gives me a perfect bow, then takes my hand in his. Instead of shaking my hand like the Elector did, he holds it up to his lips and kisses the back of it. I'm embarrassed by how much my heart leaps. "Agent Iparis," he says. His eyes stay on me for a moment.

"A pleasure," I reply, unsure of what else to say.

"My son will run for the Elector's position in late spring." The Elector smiles at Anden, who bows. "Exciting, don't you think?"

"I wish him great luck in the election, then, although I'm sure he will not need it."

The Elector chuckles. "Thank you, my dear. That will be all. Please, Agent Iparis, enjoy yourself tonight. I hope we have a chance to meet again." Then he turns away. Anden follows in his wake. "Dismissed," the Elector calls as he goes.

Chian ushers us out of the curtained area and back to the main ballroom. I can breathe again.

0100 HOURS. RUBY SECTOR.
73°F INDOORS.

After the celebration ends, Thomas escorts me back to my apartment without saying a word. He lingers for a moment outside my door.

I'm the first to break the silence. "Thanks," I say. "That was fun."

Thomas nods. "Yeah. I've never seen Commander Jameson look so proud of any of her soldiers before. You're the Republic's golden girl." But then he falls right back into silence. He's unhappy, and I somehow feel responsible.

"Are you all right?" I ask.

"Hmm? Oh, I'm fine." Thomas runs a hand through his slicked hair. A bit of gel comes off on his glove. "I didn't know the Elector's son would be there." I see a mysterious emotion in his eyes—anger? Jealousy? It clouds his face and gives him an ugly look.

I shrug it off. "We met the Elector himself. Can you believe it? I call that a successful night. I'm glad you and Commander Jameson convinced me to wear something nice."

Thomas studies me. He doesn't seem amused. "June, I've been meaning to ask you . . ." He hesitates. "When you were out with Day in Lake sector, did he kiss you?"

I pause. My mike. That's how he knows—my mike

must've turned on when we kissed, or perhaps I hadn't shut it off properly. I meet Thomas's gaze. "Yes," I reply steadily, "he did."

That same emotion returns to his eyes. "Why'd he do it?"

"Perhaps he found me attractive. But most likely it was because he drank some cheap wine. I went with it. Didn't want to compromise the mission after coming so far."

We stand in silence for a moment. Then, before I can protest, one of Thomas's gloved hands brushes my chin as he leans in to kiss me on the lips.

I pull away before his mouth can touch mine—but now his hand is around the back of my neck. I'm surprised at how repulsed I feel. All I can see standing in front of me is a man with blood on his hands.

Thomas gives me a long look. Then, finally, he releases me and moves away. I can read the displeasure in his eyes. "Good night, Ms. Iparis." He hurries away down the hall before I can respond. I swallow. I certainly can't get in trouble for staying in character while out on the streets, but it doesn't take a genius to see how upset Thomas is. I wonder if he'll act on this information and, if so, what he'll do.

I watch him disappear, then open my door and slowly step inside.

Ollie greets me enthusiastically. I pet him, let him out onto our patio, and then throw off the lopsided dress and hop in the shower. When I'm done, I climb into a black vest and shorts.

I try in vain to sleep. But too much has happened today . . . Day's interrogation, meeting the Elector Primo and his son, and then Thomas. Metias's crime scene returns to my thoughts—but as I replay it in my mind, I see his face turn into that of Day's mother. I rub my eyes, heavy with exhaustion. My mind whirls with information, attempting to process all of it and getting jumbled in the middle each time. I try to imagine my thoughts as blocks of data organized into neat little boxes, each clearly labeled. The pattern makes no sense tonight, though, and I'm too tired to make sense of it. The apartment feels empty and foreign. I almost miss the streets of Lake. My eyes wander over to a small chest sitting under my desk, full of the 200,000 Notes I received for capturing Day. I know I should put it in a safer place, but I can't bring myself to touch it. After a while, I get out of bed, fill a glass with water, and wander over to my computer. If I'm not going to sleep, I might as well continue sifting through Day's background and evidence.

I run a finger across my monitor, take a sip of water, and then enter my clearance code for accessing the Internet. I open the files Commander Jameson has forwarded to me. They're full of scanned documents, photos, and newspaper articles. Every time I look through things like this, I hear Metias's voice in my mind. "Some of our tech used to be better," he'd tell me. "Before floods, before thousands of data centers were wiped out." He would let out a mock sigh, then wink at me. "Something to be said for writing my journals by hand, eh?"

I skim through the information I've already read before, starting on the new documents. My mind sorts through the details.

BIRTH NAME: DANIEL ALTAN WING
AGE/GENDER: 15/M; PREV. LABELED DECEASED AT AGE 10
HEIGHT: 5'10"
WEIGHT: 147 LBS
BLOOD TYPE: O
HAIR: BLOND, LONG. FFFAD1.
EYES: BLUE. 3A8EDB.
SKIN: E2B279
DOMINANT ETHNICITY: MONGOLIAN

Interesting. High ratio for what grade school taught us was an extinct country.

SECONDARY ETHNICITY: CAUCASIAN
SECTOR: LAKE
FATHER: TAYLOR ARSLAN WING. DECEASED.
MOTHER: GRACE WING. DECEASED.

My mind pauses on this for a moment. Again I picture the woman crumpled on the street in her own blood, then quickly shake the image away.

SIBLINGS: JOHN SUREN WING, 19/M
EDEN BATAAR WING, 9/M

And then come the pages and pages of documents detailing Day's past crimes. I try to skim these as fast as I can, but in the end I can't help pausing on the last one.

FATALITIES: CAPTAIN METIAS IPARIS

I close my eyes. Ollie whimpers at my feet as if he knows what I'm reading, then shoves his nose against my leg. I keep a hand absently on his head.

I didn't kill your brother. That's what he told me. *But you might as well have put a gun to my mother's head.*

I force myself to scroll to a different document. I've already memorized that crime report from back to front, anyway.

Then something catches my eye. I sit up straighter. The document in front of me shows Day's Trial score. It's a scanned paper with a giant red stamp on it, very different from the bright blue stamp I'd seen on mine.

DANIEL ALTAN WING

SCORE: 674 / 1500

FAILED

Something about that number bothers me . . . 674? I've never heard of anyone scoring so low. One person I knew in grade school did fail, inevitably, but his score was close to 1000. Most failing scores are something like 890. Or 825. Always 800-plus. And those are the kids that are expected to fail, the ones who don't pay attention or don't have the capacity to.

But *674*?

"He's too smart for that," I say under my breath. I read it over again in case I missed something. But the number's still there. Impossible. Day is well-spoken and logical, and he can read and write. He should have passed his Trial's interview portion. He's the most agile person I've ever met—he should have aced his Trial's physical. With high scores on those sections, it should have been impossible for him to score lower than 850—still failing, but higher than 674. And he would've gotten 850 only if he left his entire written portion blank.

Commander Jameson will not be happy with me, I think. I open up a search engine and point to a classified URL.

Final Trial scores are common knowledge, but the actual Trial documents are never revealed—not even to criminal investigators. But my brother was Metias, and we never had trouble finding our way into the Trial databases with his hacks. I close my eyes, recounting what he'd taught me.

Determine the OS and get root privs. See if you can reach the remote system. Know your target, and secure your machine.

I find an open port in the system after an hour of scanning and then take over admin privileges. The site beeps once before displaying a single search bar. I soundlessly tap out Day's name on my desk.

DANIEL ALTAN WING.

The front page of his Trial document comes up. The score still says 674 / 1500. I scroll to the next page. Day's answers. Some of the questions are multiple-choice, while others require several sentences to answer. I skim through all thirty-two pages before I confirm something very odd.

There are no red marks. In fact, every single one of his answers is untouched. His Trial looks as pristine as mine.

I scroll all the way back to the first page. Then I read each question carefully and answer it in my head. It takes me an hour to go through all of them.

Every answer matches.

When I reach the end of his Trial document, I see the separate scores for his interview and physical sections. Both are perfect. The only thing that's weird is a brief note written next to his interview score: *Attention.*

Day didn't fail his Trial. Not even close. In fact, he got the same score I did: 1500 / 1500. I am no longer the Republic's only prodigy with a perfect score.

DAY

"GET ON YOUR FEET. IT'S TIME."

The butt of a rifle hits me in the ribs. I'm yanked out of a dream-filled sleep—first of my mother walking me to grade school, then of Eden's bleeding irises and the red number under our porch. Two pairs of hands drag me up before I can see properly, and I scream as my wounded leg tries to take some of my weight. I didn't think it was possible for it to hurt more than it did yesterday, but it does. Tears spring to my eyes. When my vision sharpens, I can tell that my leg is swollen under the bandages. I want to scream again, but my mouth is too dry.

The soldiers drag me out of my cell. The commander who had visited me the day before is waiting in the hall for us, and when she sees me, she breaks into a smile. "Good morning, Day," she says. "How are you?"

I don't reply. One of the soldiers pauses to give the commander a quick salute. "Commander Jameson," he says, "are you ready for him to proceed to sentencing?"

The commander nods. "Follow me. And please gag him, if you don't mind. We wouldn't want him yelling obscenities the whole time, would we?" The soldier salutes again, then stuffs a cloth into my mouth.

We make our way through the long halls. Again we pass the

double doors with the red number—then several doors under heavy guard and still others with large glass panels. My mind whirls. I need a way to confirm my guess, a way to talk to someone. I'm weak from dehydration, and the pain has made me sick to my stomach.

Now and then, I see a person inside one of the glass-paneled rooms, cuffed to a wall and screaming. I can tell from their tattered uniforms that they are POWs from the Colonies. *What if John's inside one of these rooms? What will they do with him?*

After what seems like an eternity, we step into an enormous main hall with a high ceiling. Outside, a crowd is chanting something, but I can't make out the words. Soldiers line the row of doors that lead to the front of the building.

And then the soldiers part—we're outside. The daylight blinds me, and I hear the shouts of hundreds of people. Commander Jameson holds up a hand, then turns to her right while the soldiers drag me up to a platform. Now I can finally see where I am. I'm in front of a building at the heart of Batalla, the military sector of Los Angeles. An enormous crowd has turned out to watch me, held back and patrolled by an almost equally large platoon of gun-wielding soldiers. I had no idea this many people cared enough to see me in person today. I raise my head as high as I can and see the JumboTrons embedded in the surrounding buildings. Every single one has a close-up of my face accompanied by frantic news headlines.

NOTORIOUS CRIMINAL KNOWN AS DAY
ARRESTED,
TO BE SENTENCED TODAY OUTSIDE
BATALLA HALL

DANGEROUS MENACE TO SOCIETY
FINALLY CAUGHT

TEEN RENEGADE KNOWN AS DAY CLAIMS
TO WORK ALONE,
NO AFFILIATION WITH THE PATRIOTS

I stare at my face on the JumboTrons. I'm bruised, bloody, and listless. A bright streak of blood stains one thick strand of my hair, painting a dark red streak into it. I must have a cut on my scalp.

For a moment I'm glad that my mother isn't alive to see me like this.

The soldiers shove me toward a raised block of cement in the center of the platform. To my right, a judge cloaked in scarlet robes and gold buttons waits behind a podium. Commander Jameson stands beside him, and to her right is the Girl. She's decked out in her full uniform again, stoic and alert. Her expressionless face is turned toward the crowd—but once, just once, she turns to look at me before quickly looking away.

"Order! Please, order in the crowd." The judge's voice

crackles over the JumboTrons' loudspeakers, but the people continue to shout, and soldiers push back against them. The entire front row is clogged with reporters, their cameras and microphones shoved in my direction.

Finally, one of the soldiers barks out a command. I look over at him. It's the young captain who shot my mother. His soldiers fire several shots into the air. This settles the crowd. The judge waits a few seconds to make sure the silence holds, then adjusts his glasses.

"Thank you for your cooperation," he begins. "I know this is a rather warm morning, so we'll keep the sentencing brief. As you can see, our soldiers are present and serve to remind you all to keep calm during these proceedings. Let me begin with an official announcement that on December twenty-first, at eight thirty-six A.M., Ocean Standard Time, the fifteen-year-old criminal known as Day was arrested and taken into military custody."

A huge cheer erupts. But as much as I expected this, I also hear something else that surprises me. Boos. Some—many—of the people in the crowd don't have their fists in the air. A few of the louder protesters are approached by street police, cuffed, and dragged away.

One of the soldiers restraining me strikes me in the back with his rifle. I fall to my knees. The instant my wounded leg hits the cement, I scream as loud as I can. The sound's muffled by my gag. The pain blinds me—my swollen leg trembles from the impact, and I can feel a gush of fresh blood on my bandages. I almost keel over before the soldiers prop me up. When I look toward the Girl, I see her wince at the sight of me and turn her eyes to the ground.

The judge ignores the commotion. He begins by listing off my crimes, then concludes, "In light of the defendant's past felonies and, in particular, his offenses against the glorious nation of the Republic, the high court of California recommends the following verdict. Day is hereby sentenced to death—"

The crowd erupts again. The soldiers hold them back.

"—by firing squad, to be carried out four days from today, on December twenty-seventh at six P.M., Ocean Standard Time, in an undisclosed location—"

Four days. How will I save my brothers before then? I lift my head and fix my eyes on the crowd.

"—to be broadcast live across the city. Civilians are encouraged to stay vigilant for any possible criminal activity that may occur before and after the event—"

They will make an example of me.

"—and to report any suspicious activity immediately to the street police or to the police headquarters closest to you. This officially concludes our sentencing."

The judge straightens and steps away from the podium. The crowd continues to push against the soldiers. They're shouting, cheering, booing. I feel myself being dragged back onto my feet. Before they can start ushering me inside Batalla Hall, I catch a last glimpse of the Girl staring at me. Her expression looks blank . . . but behind it, something flickers. The same emotion I'd seen on her face before she knew my real identity. It's only there for a moment and then it's gone. *I'm supposed to hate you for what you did,* I think. But her eyes linger on me in a way that refuses to let me.

After the sentencing, Commander Jameson doesn't let her soldiers take me back to my cell. Instead we step into an elevator held up by enormous cogs and chains and go up a level, then another, and another. The elevator takes us to the roof of Batalla Hall, twelve stories high, where the shadows from surrounding buildings don't protect us from the sun.

Commander Jameson leads the soldiers to a flat circular stand in the middle of the roof, a stand with the Republic's seal embedded in it and strings of heavy chains hooked around its rim. The Girl brings up the rear. I can still feel her eyes on my back. When we reach the center of the circle, the soldiers force me to stand while they bind my shackled hands and feet to the chains.

"Keep him up here for two days," Commander Jameson says. Already the sun has blurred my vision and the world looks bathed in a haze of sparkling diamonds. The soldiers let go of me. I sink to the ground on my hands and my good knee, chains clacking as I go. "Agent Iparis, head this up. Check on him now and then and make sure he doesn't die before his execution date."

The Girl's voice pipes up. "Yes, ma'am."

"He's allowed one cup of water a day. One food ration." The commander smiles, then tightens her gloves. "Be creative when you're giving it to him, if you wish. I'll bet you can make him beg for it."

"Yes, ma'am."

"Good." Commander Jameson addresses me one final time. "Looks like you're finally behaving. Better late than never." Then she walks away and disappears into the elevator with the Girl, leaving the rest of the soldiers to stand guard.

The afternoon is quiet.

I slip in and out of consciousness. My injured leg throbs to the beat of my heart, sometimes fast and sometimes slow, sometimes so hard that I think I'm going to pass out. My mouth cracks each time I move it. I try to think about where Eden might be—the Central Hospital lab, or a medical division of Batalla Hall, or even a train headed to the warfront. They'll keep him alive, that I'm sure of. The Republic won't kill him until the plague does.

But John. What they've done with him I can only guess. They may keep him alive, in case they want to squeeze more information out of me. Maybe both of us will be executed at the same time. Or he could already be dead. A new pain stabs at my chest. I think back to the day I took my Trial, when John came to pick me up and saw me being taken away in a train with others who had failed. After I'd escaped from the lab and developed the habit of watching my family from a distance, I occasionally saw John sitting at our dining room table with his head in his hands, sobbing. He's never said it aloud, but I think he blames himself for what happened to me. He thinks he should have protected me more. Helped me study more. Something, *anything.*

If I can escape, I still have time to save them. I can still use my arms. And I have one good leg. I could still do it . . . if I only knew where they were. . . .

The world fades in and out. My head slumps against the cement stand, and my arms lie motionless against the chains. Memories of my Trial day flash before me.

The stadium. The other children. The soldiers guarding every entrance and exit. The velvet ropes that kept us separated from the kids of rich families.

The physical trial. The written exam. The interview.

The interview, more than anything. I remember the panel that questioned me—a group of six psychiatrists—and the official who'd led them, the man named Chian, who had a uniform adorned with medals. He asked the most questions. *What is the Republic's national pledge? Good, very good. It says here on your school report that you like history. What year did the Republic officially form? What do you enjoy doing in school? Reading . . . yes, very nice. A teacher once reported you for sneaking into a restricted area of the library, looking for old military texts. Can you tell me why you did that? What do you think of our illustrious Elector Primo? Yes, he is indeed a good man, and a great leader. But you are mistaken to call him those things, my boy. He's not a man like you and me. The correct way to address him is our* glorious father. *Yes, your apology is accepted.*

His questions went on forever, dozens and dozens of them, each more mind-bending than the last, until I couldn't even be sure why I answered as I did. Chian wrote notes on my interview report the whole time, while one of his assistants recorded the session with a tiny microphone.

I thought I'd answered well enough. At least, I was careful to say things that I thought would please him.

But then they led me onto a train, and the train took us to the lab.

The memory makes me shiver even as the sun continues to beat down, baking my skin until it hurts. *I have to save Eden,* I say to myself over and over again. *Eden turns ten . . . in one month. When he recovers from the plague, he'll have to take the Trial. . . .*

My injured leg feels like it could burst right out of my bandages and swell to the size of the roof.

Hours pass. I lose track of time. Soldiers rotate in and out of their shifts. The sun changes position.

Then, just as the sun mercifully starts to set, I see someone emerge from the elevator and make her way toward me.

JUNE

I HARDLY RECOGNIZE DAY, EVEN THOUGH IT'S ONLY BEEN seven hours since the sentencing. He lies crumpled in the center of the Republic seal. His skin looks darker, and his hair is completely matted down with sweat. Dried blood still clings to one long strand of hair, as if he chose to dye it. It looks almost black now. He turns his head in my direction as I approach. I'm not sure if he can see me, though, because the sun hasn't completely set and is probably blinding him.

Another prodigy—and not just an average one. I've met other prodigies before but certainly never one that the Republic decided to keep hidden. Especially one with a perfect score.

One of the soldiers lining the circular stand salutes me. He's sweaty, and his pith helmet doesn't protect his skin from the sun. "Agent Iparis," he says. (His accent's from Ruby sector, and his uniform's row of buttons are freshly polished. Pays attention to details.)

I glance at the other soldiers before looking back at him. "You're all dismissed for now. Tell your men to get some water and shade. And send an order up for your replacements to come early."

"Yes, ma'am." The soldier clicks his heels together before shouting a dismissal to the others.

When they leave the roof and I'm alone with Day, I remove my cape and kneel down to see his face better. He squints at me, but stays quiet. His lips are so cracked that a little blood has trickled down to his chin. He's too weak to talk. I look down toward his wounded leg. It's much worse than it was this morning, not surprisingly, and is swollen to twice its normal size. An infection must've set in. Blood oozes from the edges of the bandage.

I absently touch the knife wound at my own side. It doesn't hurt as much anymore.

We'll need to get that leg checked. I sigh, then remove the canteen hanging at my belt. "Here. Have some water. I'm not allowed to let you die yet." I dribble water on his lips. He flinches at first, but then opens his mouth and lets me pour a thin stream in. I wait while he swallows (he takes forever) and then let him take another long drink.

"Thanks," he whispers. He lets out a dry laugh. "Guess you can go now."

I study him for a moment. His skin is burned and his face drenched with sweat, but his eyes are still bright, if a bit unfocused. I suddenly remember the first moment I saw him. Dust everywhere . . . and out of that emerged this beautiful boy with the bluest eyes I'd ever seen, holding his hand out to help me to my feet.

"Where are my brothers?" he whispers. "Are they both alive?"

I nod. "Yes."

"And Tess is safe? No one's arrested her?"

"Not to my knowledge."

"What are they doing with Eden?"

I think back to what Thomas told me, that the generals from the warfront have come to see him. "I don't know."

Day turns his head away and closes his eyes. He concentrates on breathing. "Well, don't kill them," he murmurs. "They didn't do anything . . . and Eden . . . he's not a lab rat, you know." He's silent for a minute. "I never got your name. Guess it's no big deal now, is it? You already know mine."

I stare at him. "My name is June Iparis."

"June," Day murmurs. I feel a strange warmth at the sound of my name on his lips. He turns to face me. "June, I'm sorry about your brother. I didn't know anything would happen to him."

I'm trained not to take the word of a prisoner—I know that they'll lie, that they'll say anything they can to make you vulnerable. But this feels different. Somehow . . . he sounds so genuine, so serious. What if he *is* telling me the truth? What if something else happened to Metias that night? I take a deep breath and force myself to look down. Logic above all else, I tell myself. Logic will save you when nothing else will.

"Hey." I remember something else now. "Open your eyes again and look at me."

He does as I say. I lean over to study him. Yes, it's still there. That strange little blemish in one of his eyes, a ripple in an otherwise ocean-blue iris. "How did you get that thing in your eye?" I gesture at my own. "That imperfection?"

Something must've sounded funny, because Day laughs once before bursting into a coughing fit. "That *imperfection* was a gift from the Republic."

"What do you mean?"

He hesitates. I can tell he's having trouble forming his thoughts. "I've been in the lab of the Central Hospital before, you know. On the night I took my Trial." He tries to lift a hand to point at his eye, but the chains clank together and drag his arm back down. "They injected something."

I frown. "The night of your tenth birthday? What were you doing in the lab? You were supposed to be on your way to the labor camps."

Day smiles as if he's about to fall asleep. "I thought you were a smart one. . . ."

Apparently the sun hasn't baked all the attitude out of him yet. "And what about your old knee injury?"

"Your Republic gave me that, too. On the same night I got my eye *imperfection.*"

"Why would the Republic give you those wounds, Day? Why would they want to damage someone who got a perfect fifteen hundred on his Trial score?"

This catches Day's attention. "What are you talking about? I failed my Trial."

He doesn't know either. Of course he wouldn't. I lower my voice to a whisper. "No, you didn't. You got a perfect score."

"Is this some kind of trick?" Day moves his injured leg a little and tenses up in pain. "A perfect score . . . hah. I don't know anyone who's ever gotten a fifteen hundred."

I cross my arms. "I did."

He raises an eyebrow at me. "You did? You're the prodigy with the perfect score?"

"Yes." I nod at him. "And apparently, so were you."

Day rolls his eyes and looks away again. "That's ridiculous."

I shrug. "Believe what you want."

"Doesn't make sense. Shouldn't I be in your position? Isn't that the point of your precious Trial?" Day looks like he wants to stop, hesitates, and then continues. "They injected something into one of my eyes that stung like wasp poison. They also cut up my knee. With a scalpel. Then they force-fed me some kind of medicine, and the next thing I knew . . . I was lying in a hospital basement with a bunch of other corpses. But I wasn't dead." He laughs again. It sounds so weak. "Great birthday."

They experimented on him. Probably for the military. This I'm sure of now, and the thought makes me ill. They were taking tiny tissue samples from his knee, as well as from his heart and his eye. His knee: they must have wanted to study his unusual physical abilities, his speed and agility. His eye: maybe it wasn't an injection but an extraction, something to test why his vision was so sharp. His heart: they fed him medicine to see how low his heart rate could go, and they were probably disappointed when his heart temporarily stopped. That's when they thought he died. The reasoning for all this becomes clear—they wanted to develop those tissue samples into something, I don't know what—pills, contact lenses, whatever could improve our soldiers, to make them run faster, see better, think smarter, or endure harsher conditions.

All this flies through my head in a second before I can stop it. No way. This isn't in line with Republic values. Why waste a prodigy in this way?

Unless they saw something dangerous in him. Some defiant spark, the same rebellious spirit he has now. Something that made them think it'd be riskier to educate him than to sacrifice his possible contributions to society. Last year thirty-eight kids scored higher than 1400.

Maybe the Republic would want to make this one disappear.

But Day is not just any prodigy. He has a perfect score. What was it that made them nervous?

"Can I ask *you* a question now?" Day asks. "Is it my turn?"

"Yes." I look over to the elevator, where a new rotation of guards has just arrived. I hold up a hand and tell them to stay where they are. "You can ask."

"I want to know why they took Eden away. The plague. I know you rich folks have it easy—new plague vaccinations every year and whatever meds you need. But haven't you wondered . . . haven't you wondered why it never goes away? Or why it comes back so regularly?"

My eyes dart back to him. "What are you trying to say?"

Day manages to focus his eyes on me. "What I'm *trying* to say . . . yesterday, when they dragged me out of my cell, I saw that red *zero* stamped on some double doors in Batalla Hall. I've seen numbers like it in Lake too. Why would they show up in the poor sectors? What are they doing out there—what are they pumping into the sectors?"

I narrow my eyes. "You think the Republic is *intentionally* poisoning people? Day, you're on dangerous ground."

But Day doesn't stop. Instead his voice takes on a more urgent tone. "That's why they wanted Eden, right?" he whispers. "To see the results of their mutated plague virus? Why else?"

"They want to prevent whatever new disease he's spreading."

Day laughs, but again it makes him cough. "No. They're using him. They're using him." His voice grows quiet. "They're using him. . . ." His eyes grow heavy. The strain of talking has worn him out.

"You're delirious," I reply. But while Thomas's touch now repulses me, I feel no revulsion toward Day. I *should*. But the feeling just doesn't come. "A lie like that is treason against the Republic. Besides, why would Congress authorize such a thing?"

Day doesn't take his eyes off me. And just when I think he's lost the strength to respond, his voice comes out sounding even more insistent. "Think about it this way. How do they know what vaccines to give you every year? They *always* work. Don't you find it strange that they can make vaccines that match the new plague that's popped up? How can they predict which vaccine they'll need?"

I sit back on my heels. I've never questioned the annual vaccinations we're required to have—never had any reason to doubt them. And why should I? *My father used to work behind those double doors, working hard to find new ways to combat the plague.* No. I can't listen to this anymore. I pluck my cape from the ground and tuck it under my arm.

"One more thing," Day whispers as I stand. I glance down

at him. His eyes burn right into me. "You think we go to labor camps if we fail? June, the only labor camps are the morgues in hospital basements."

I don't dare linger. Instead I walk away from the platform, away from Day. But my heart pounds against my chest. The soldiers waiting by the elevator stand even straighter as I approach. I arrange my face in an expression of pure irritation. "Unchain him," I order one of the soldiers. "Take him down to the hospital wing and get that leg of his fixed. Give him some food and water. He won't last the night otherwise."

The soldier salutes me, but I don't bother to look at him before shutting the elevator door.

DAY

I HAVE NIGHTMARES AGAIN. THIS TIME THEY'RE OF TESS.

I'm running in the streets of Lake. Somewhere ahead of me, Tess is running too, but she doesn't know where I am. She turns left and right, desperate to see my face, but all she finds are strangers and street police and soldiers. I call out for her. But my legs can barely move, as if I'm wading through a thick sludge.

Tess! I shout. *I'm here, I'm right behind you!*

She can't hear me. I look on helplessly as she runs right into a soldier, and when she tries to turn away from him, he grabs her and throws her to the ground. I scream something. The soldier lifts his gun and points it at Tess. Then I see that it's not Tess, but my mother, who lies in a puddle of blood. I try to run to her. But instead I stay hidden behind a chimney on a roof, crouched like a coward. It's my fault she's dead.

Then suddenly I'm back in the hospital lab again, and the doctors and nurses are standing over me. I squint in the blinding light. Pain shoots through my leg. They're cutting open my knee again, pulling back my flesh to reveal the bones underneath, scraping at it with their scalpels. I arch my back and scream. One of the nurses tries to hold me down. My flailing arm knocks over a tray somewhere.

"Hold still! Damn it, boy, I'm not going to hurt you."

It takes me a minute to wake up. The blurry hospital scene shifts, and I realize I'm staring up at a similar fluorescent light and that a doctor is hovering over me. He wears goggles and a face mask. I give a shout and try to bolt upright. But I'm tied to an operating table by a pair of belts.

The doctor sighs and slides his face mask down. "Look at me. Bandaging up a criminal like you when I could be helping soldiers from the warfront."

I look around, confused. Guards line the walls of this hospital room. A nurse is cleaning bloody equipment at the sink. "Where am I?"

The doctor gives me an impatient look. "You're in Batalla Hall's hospital wing. Agent Iparis ordered me to fix up your leg. Apparently we're not allowed to let you die before your formal execution."

I lift my head as far as I can and look down at my leg. Clean bandages cover up the wound. When I try to move the leg a little, I notice with surprise that the pain is far less than before. I glance at the doctor. "What did you do?"

He only shrugs, then peels off his gloves and starts washing his hands at one of the sinks. "Patched things up a bit. You'll be able to stand for your execution." He pauses. "Don't know if that's what you wanted to hear."

I slump back down onto the gurney and close my eyes. The diminished pain in my leg is such a relief that I try to savor it, but pieces of my nightmare still linger in my mind, too fresh to put away. Where is Tess now? Can she make it without someone there to watch her back? She's nearsighted. Who will help her when she can't make out the shadows at night?

As for my mother . . . I'm not strong enough to think about her right now.

Someone raps loudly on the door. "Open up," a man calls out. "Commander Jameson's here to see the prisoner." The prisoner. I smile at that. The soldiers don't even like calling me by my name.

The guards in the room barely have time to unlock the door and move out of the way before Commander Jameson bursts in, clearly annoyed. She snaps her fingers. "Get this boy off the gurney and put him in some chains," she barks. Then she shoves one finger into my chest. "*You.* You're just a kid—you never even went to college, you failed your Trial! How were you ever able to outsmart soldiers on the streets? How do you cause so much *trouble*?" She bares her teeth at me. "I knew you'd be a bigger nuisance than you're worth. You have a knack for wasting my soldiers' time. Not to mention the soldiers of several other commanders."

I have to grit my teeth to keep from shouting back at her. Soldiers hurry over to me and start undoing the gurney's belts.

Beside me, the doctor bows his head. "If you don't mind, Commander," he says, "has something happened? What's going on?"

Commander Jameson fixes her furious gaze on him. He shrinks away. "Protesters in front of Batalla Hall," she snaps. "They're attacking the street police."

The soldiers pull me off the gurney and onto my feet. I wince as my weight transfers onto my bad leg. "Protesters?"

"Yes. Rioters." Commander Jameson grabs my face. "My own soldiers had to be called in to help, which means my schedule is entirely disrupted. I've already had one of my best men sent in here with lacerations on his face. Filthy cons like you don't know how to treat our military boys." She shoves my face away in disgust and turns her back on me. "Take him away," she calls out to the soldiers holding me. "Be quick about it."

We exit the hospital room. Soldiers rush back and forth in the hallway. Commander Jameson keeps pressing a hand against her ear, listening intently, then shouting orders. As I'm dragged toward the elevators, I see several large monitors—something I pause to admire for a second, as I've never seen them in the Lake sector—broadcasting exactly what Commander Jameson just told us. I can't hear the voice-over, but the text headlines are unmistakable: *Disturbance outside Batalla Hall. Units responding. Await further orders.* This isn't a public broadcast, I realize. The video shows the square in front of Batalla Hall packed with several hundred people. I pick out the line of black-clad soldiers struggling to contain the crowd near the front. Other soldiers run along rooftops and ledges, hurrying into position with their rifles. I get a good look at some of the protesters as we pass the last monitor, the ones clustered together under the street lights.

Some of them have painted a bloodred streak into their hair.

Then we arrive at the elevators and the soldiers shove me inside. *They're protesting because of me.* The thought fills me with excitement and dread. No way will the military let this slide. They'll seal off the poor sectors entirely and arrest every last rioter in the square.

Or they'll kill them.

JUNE

When I was young, Metias was sometimes called away to deal with minor rebellions, and afterward he'd tell me about them. The story was always the same: a dozen or so poor folk (usually teens, sometimes older) causing trouble in one of the sectors, angry about the plague quarantines or taxes. Several dust bombs later, they were all arrested and taken to court.

But I've never seen a riot like this one, with hundreds of people risking their lives. Nothing even close to this.

"What's wrong with these people?" I ask Thomas. "They've lost their minds." We're standing on the raised platform outside Batalla Hall with his entire patrol facing the crowd in front of us, while another of Commander Jameson's patrols is pushing people back with shields and batons.

Earlier, I'd peeked in on Day as the doctor operated on his leg. I wonder if he's awake and seeing this chaos on the hall monitors. I hope not. No need for him to see what he's started. The thought of him—and his accusation against the Republic, that the Republic creates the plagues, kills kids who fail the Trial—fills me with rage. I pull my gun out of its holster. Might as well have it ready. "Ever seen something like this?" I ask, trying to keep my voice even.

Thomas shakes his head. "Only once. A long time ago." Some of his dark hair falls across his face. It's not combed back as nicely as usual—he must've been out in the crowds earlier. One hand lingers on the gun strapped to his belt, while the other rests on a rifle slung around his shoulder. He doesn't look at me. He hasn't looked at me straight on since he tried kissing me last night in the hall. "A bunch of fools," he replies. "If they don't back down soon, the commanders will make them regret it."

I glance up to see several commanders standing on one of Batalla Hall's balconies. It's too dark now to be sure, but I don't think Commander Jameson is with them. I know she's giving orders through her mouthpiece, though, because Thomas listens intently with one hand pressed against his ear. But whatever she's saying is only for Thomas, and I have no idea what she's telling him. The crowd below us continues to push. I can tell from their clothes—torn shirts and trousers, mismatched shoes filled with holes—that almost all of them are from the poor sectors near the lake. Secretly, I will them to disperse. *Get out of here before things get worse.*

Thomas leans over to me and nods toward the center of the crowd. "See that pitiful bunch?"

I'd already noticed what he's pointing out, but I still follow his gaze politely. A group of protesters have streaked their hair scarlet, imitating the bloodstained lock Day had when he'd stood out here for his sentencing. "A poor choice for a hero," Thomas goes on. "Day will be dead in less than a week."

I nod once but say nothing.

A few screams echo from the crowd. One patrol has made its way around to the back of the square, and now they have the crowd boxed in, pushing people in toward the square's center. I frown. This isn't protocol for handling an unruly mob. In school, we were taught that dust bombs or tear gas is more than enough to do the job. But there's no sign of that—none of the soldiers wear gas masks. And now yet another patrol has started chasing away the stragglers gathered outside the square, where the streets are too chaotic and narrow to protest properly.

"What's Commander Jameson telling you?" I ask Thomas.

Thomas's dark hair falls across his eyes and covers his expression. "She says to stay put and wait for her command."

We don't do anything for a good half hour. I keep one hand in my pocket, absently rubbing Day's pendant. Somehow, the crowd reminds me of Skiz. There's probably even some of the same people.

That's when I see soldiers running along the tops of the square's buildings. Some hurry along ledges, while others are gathered in a straight line across the roofs. Odd. Soldiers usually have black tassels and a single row of silver buttons on their jackets. Their arm insignias are navy blue or red or silver or gold. But these soldiers have no buttons on their jackets. Instead, a white stripe runs diagonally across their chests and their armbands are gray. It takes me another second to realize who they are.

"Thomas." I tap him and point up to the roofs. "Executioners."

No surprise on his face, no emotion in his eyes. He clears his throat. "So they are."

"What are they doing?" My voice rises. I glance to the protesters in the square, then back up to the roofs. None of the soldiers have dust bombs or tear gas. Instead, each one has a gun slung around his shoulder. "They're not dispersing them, Thomas. They're trapping them in."

Thomas gives me a stern look. "Hold steady, June. Pay attention to the crowd."

As my eyes stay turned up toward the roofs, I notice Commander Jameson step out onto the top of Batalla Hall flanked by soldiers. She speaks into her mouthpiece.

Several seconds pass. A terrible feeling builds up in my chest—I know where this is going.

Thomas suddenly murmurs something into his mike. A response to a command. I glance at him. He catches my gaze for a second, and then he looks toward the rest of the patrol standing on the platform with us. "Fire at will!" he shouts.

"Thomas!" I want to say more, but at that instant, shots ring out from both the roofs and the platform. I lunge forward. I don't know what I plan to do—wave my arms in front of the soldiers?—but Thomas grabs my shoulder before I can step forward.

"Stay back, June!"

"Tell your men to stand down," I shout, scrambling out of his grasp. "Tell them—"

That's when Thomas throws me to the ground so hard that I feel the wound in my side break open.

"Damn it, June," he says. *"Stay back!"*

The ground's surprisingly cold. I crouch there, for once at a loss, unable to move. I don't really understand what just happened. The skin around my wound burns. Bullets rain down on the square. People in the crowd collapse like levees in a flood. *Thomas, stop. Please stop.* I want to get up and scream in his face, to hurt him somehow. *Metias would kill you for this, Thomas, if he were alive.* But instead I cover my ears. The gunshots are deafening.

The gunfire lasts only a minute, if that—but it seems like forever. Thomas finally shouts an order to cease fire, and those in the crowd who haven't been shot fall to their knees and throw their hands up over their heads. Soldiers rush to them, cuffing their arms behind their backs, forcing them together into clusters. I push myself up onto my knees. My ears still ring from the gunfire. . . . I scan the scene of blood and bodies and prisoners. There are 97, 98 dead. No, at least 120. Hundreds more are in custody. I can't even concentrate enough to count them.

Thomas glances at me before stepping off the platform—his face is grave, even guilty, but I know with a sinking feeling that he feels guilty only for throwing me to the ground. Not for this massacre he's leaving behind. He heads back toward Batalla Hall with several soldiers. I turn my face away so I don't have to watch him.

DAY

WE RIDE UP SEVERAL FLOORS UNTIL I HEAR THE elevator's chains come to a scraping halt. Two soldiers drag me out into a familiar hallway. They're returning me to my cell, I guess, at least for now. For the first time since waking up on the gurney, I realize I'm exhausted and slump my head against my chest. The doctor must've injected me with something to keep me from flailing too much during the operation. Everything around me looks blurred at the edges, as if I'm sprinting.

Then the soldiers come to a sudden stop halfway down the corridor, a good distance away from my cell. I look up in mild surprise. We stand outside one of the rooms I'd noticed earlier, the ones with clear glass windows. Interrogation chambers. So. They want more information before they execute me.

Static, then a voice comes through one of the soldiers' earpieces. The soldier nods. "Let's take him in," he says. "Captain says he'll arrive shortly."

I stand inside, waiting as the minutes tick by. Guards with blank faces stand at the door, while two others hold my shackled arms. I know this room is supposed to be more or less soundproof . . . but I swear I hear the sound of guns and the vibrations of distant screams. My heart pounds. The troops must be firing on the crowd in the square. Are they dying because of me?

More time passes. I wait. My eyelids grow heavy. I want nothing more than to curl into a ball in the corner of my cell and sleep.

Finally I hear footsteps approaching. The door swings open to reveal a young man dressed in black, with dark hair that falls over his eyes. Silver epaulettes sit on each shoulder. The other soldiers click their heels together.

The man waves them off. Now I recognize him. This is the captain who shot my mother. June had mentioned him before. Thomas. Commander Jameson must've sent him.

"Mr. Wing," he says. He approaches me and crosses his arms. "What a pleasure to formally meet you. I was beginning to worry that I'd never get the chance."

I will myself to stay silent. He looks uncomfortable being in the same room as me, and his expression says that he *really* hates me.

"My commander wants me to ask you some standard procedural questions before your execution date. We'll try to keep it cordial, although of course we started off on the wrong foot."

I can't help choking out a laugh. "Really? You think so?"

Thomas doesn't reply, but I see him swallow hard in an effort not to react. He reaches into his cloak and pulls out a small gray remote. He points it at the room's blank wall. A projection comes up. Some police report, with pictures of a person I don't recognize.

"I'm going to show you a series of photos, Mr. Wing," he says. "The people you'll see are suspected of Patriot involvement."

The Patriots had tried in vain to recruit me. Cryptic notes scrawled on alley walls above where I slept. An escort on a street corner who slipped me a note. A small parcel of money with a proposition. After ignoring their offers for a while, I stopped hearing from them. "I've never worked with the Patriots," I snap. "If I ever kill, I'll do it on my own terms."

"You may claim no affiliation with them, but perhaps some have crossed your path. And perhaps you'd like to help us find them."

"Oh, sure. You killed my mother. You can imagine I'm *dying* to help you out."

Thomas manages to ignore me again. He glances at the first photo projected on the wall. "Know this person?"

I shake my head. "Never seen him before."

Thomas clicks the remote. Another photo pops up. "How about this one?"

"Nope."

Another photo. "How about this?"

"Nope."

Yet another stranger pops up on the wall. "Seen this girl before?"

"Never seen her in my life."

More unfamiliar faces. Thomas goes through them without blinking an eye or questioning my responses. What a stupid puppet of the state. I watch him as we continue, wishing I weren't chained so I could beat this man to the ground.

More photos. More strange faces. Thomas doesn't question a single one of my terse responses. In fact, it seems like he can't wait to get out of this room and far away from me.

Then a photo pops up of someone I do recognize. The blurry image shows a girl with long hair—longer than the bobbed cut I remember. No vine tattoo yet. Apparently Kaede is a Patriot.

I don't dare let the recognition show on my face. "Look," I say. "If I knew any of these people, do you really think I'd tell you?"

Thomas is trying so hard to hold his composure. "That will be all, Mr. Wing."

"Oh, come on, that's not all. I can tell you'd give anything to take a swing at me. So do it. I dare you."

His eyes have taken on a furious glow, but he still holds back. "My orders were to ask you a series of questions," he says tightly. "That's it. We're done here."

"Why? You afraid of me or something? Only brave enough to shoot people's mothers?"

Thomas narrows his eyes, then shrugs. "She's just one less slum con to deal with."

I clench my fist and spit right in his face.

This seems to break his resolve. His left fist hits me hard across the jaw, and my head snaps to the side. Spots explode before my eyes.

"Think you're a star, don't you?" he says. "Just because you pulled some pranks and played charity worker to some street scum? Well, let me tell you a secret. *I'm* from a poor sector too. But I followed the rules. I worked my way up,

I *earned* my country's respect. The rest of you people just sit around and complain and blame the state for your bad luck. Bunch of dirty, lazy cons." He punches me again. My head rocks back, and I taste blood in my mouth. My body trembles from the pain. He grabs my collar and pulls me close. My shackles clank. "Ms. Iparis told me about what you did to her on the streets. How *dare* you force yourself onto someone of her rank."

Ah. Here is what's really bothering him—I guess he found out about the kiss. I can't help grinning, even though my face screams in pain. "Awww. Is that what's got you down? I've seen the way you look at her. You want her bad, yeah? Is that something you're also trying to *earn* your way up to, trot? Hate to burst your bubble, but I didn't force her into *anything*."

A deep scarlet rage flashes across his face. "She's looking forward to your execution, Mr. Wing. I can guarantee you *that*."

I laugh. "Sore loser, huh? Here, I'll make you feel better. I'll tell you all about what it was like. Hearing about it is the next best thing, isn't it?"

Thomas grabs my neck. His hands are shaking. "I'd be careful if I were you, boy," he spits. "Maybe you've forgotten that you still have two brothers. Both at the mercy of the Republic. Watch your tongue, unless you want to see their bodies lined up next to your mother's."

He hits me again, then one of his knees slams into my stomach. I gasp for air. I picture Eden and John and force myself to calm down, force away the pain. *Stay strong. Don't let him get to you.*

He hits me two more times. He's breathing hard now. With a great effort, he lowers his arms and exhales. "That will be all, Mr. Wing," he says in a low voice. "I'll see you on your execution day."

I can't speak through the pain, so I just try to keep my eyes focused on him. He has a strange expression, as if he's angry or disappointed that I've forced him from his orderly state.

He turns and leaves the room without a word.

JUNE

THAT NIGHT, THOMAS SPENDS HALF AN HOUR STANDING outside my door, trying out a dozen different kinds of apologies. He is really sorry. He didn't want me to get hurt. He didn't want me to resist Commander Jameson's orders. He didn't want me to get in trouble. He was trying to protect me.

I sit on my couch with Ollie, staring off into space. I can't get the sound of those machine guns out of my head. Thomas has always been disciplined.

Today was not different. He didn't hesitate—not for a second—to obey our commander. He'd carried out the extermination as if he were preparing for a routine plague sweep or for a night guarding an airfield. Is it worse that he followed the orders so faithfully or that he doesn't even know that this is what I want him to apologize for?

"June, are you listening to me?"

I concentrate on scratching Ollie behind his ears. Metias's old journals are still strewn on the coffee table, along with our parents' photo albums. "You're wasting your time," I call back to him.

"Please. Just let me in. I want to see you."

"I'll see you tomorrow."

"I won't be long, I promise. I'm really sorry."

"Thomas, I'll see you tomorrow."

"June—"

I raise my voice. "I said *I'll see you tomorrow.*"

Silence.

I wait another minute, trying to distract myself by petting Ollie. After a while I get up and look through the peephole. The hallway's empty.

When I'm finally convinced he's gone, I lie awake on the couch for another hour. My mind races from the events in the square, to Day's appearance on the rooftop, to Day's outrageous claims about the plague and the Trial, and then back to Thomas. The Thomas that follows Commander Jameson's orders without question is a different Thomas from the one who worried about my safety in the Lake sector. Growing up, Thomas was awkward but always polite, especially to me. Or maybe it's me who's changed. When I tracked Day's family down and watched Thomas shoot his mother, when I looked on today as the crowd in the square was gunned down . . . I stood by both times and did nothing. Does that make me the same as Thomas? Are we doing the right thing by following our orders? Surely the Republic knows best?

And as for what Day told me . . . my temper rises at the thought of it. My father had worked behind those double doors—Metias had mentored under Chian in overseeing the Trials. Why would we poison and kill our own people?

I sigh, sit up, and grab one of Metias's journals off the coffee table.

This one is about an exhausting week of cleanup duty after Hurricane Elijah tore through Los Angeles. Another spells out his first week in Commander Jameson's patrol. A third one is short, only a paragraph long, and complains about working two night shifts in a row. This makes me smile. I can still remember his words. “I can barely stay awake,” Metias had told me after his first night shift. “Does she honestly think we can guard *anything* after pulling an all-nighter? I was so out of it today that the Colonies' Chancellor himself could've walked into Batalla Hall and I wouldn't have known it.”

I feel a tear on my cheek and quickly wipe it away. Ollie whines next to me. I reach out and let my hand sink into the thick white fur around his neck, and he drops his head into my lap with a sigh.

Metias had fretted over such small things.

My eyes grow heavy as I continue to read. The words start to blur together on the page, until I can't quite understand what each entry means anymore. Finally I put the journal aside and drift off into sleep.

Day appears in my dreams. He holds my hands in his own, and my heart pounds at the touch. His hair falls around his shoulders like a silk drape, one streak of it scarlet with blood, and his eyes look pained. “I didn't kill your brother.” He pulls me close. “I promise you, I couldn't have.”

When I wake up, I lie still for a while and let Day's words run through my head. My eyes wander over to the computer desk. How had that fateful night played out? If Day hit Metias's shoulder, then how did the knife end up in my brother's chest? This brief thought makes my heart ache. I look at Ollie.

“Who would want to hurt Metias?” I ask him. Ollie looks back at me with mournful eyes. “And why?”

I push myself off the couch several minutes later, then wander over to my desk and turn on my computer.

I go back to the crime report from the Central Hospital. Four pages of text, one page of photos. It's the photos that I decide to take a closer look at. After all, Commander Jameson had given me only a few minutes to analyze Metias's body, and I'd used the time poorly—but how could I have concentrated? I'd never doubted that the murderer was anyone but Day. I hadn't studied the photos as closely as I should have.

Now I double-click on the first photos and enlarge them to full screen. The sight makes me light-headed. Metias's cold, lifeless face tilts up to the sky, and his hair fans out in a small circle under his head. Blood stains his shirt. I take a deep breath, close my eyes, and tell myself to concentrate this time. I'd always managed to get through reading the text of the report, but I could never bring myself to study the photos. Now I have to. I open my eyes and focus back on my brother's body. I wish I'd studied the wounds more closely in person when I had the chance.

First I make sure the knife in the photo is indeed buried in his chest. Bits of blood stain the hilt. I can't see any of the blade. Then I look at Metias's shoulder.

Although it's covered up by his sleeve, I can see that a sizable circle of blood stains the cloth there. It couldn't all be spillover from the chest—there must be another wound. I enlarge the photo again. Nope, too blurry. Even if there is a knifelike slice in the sleeve over his shoulder, I can't see it at this angle.

I close the photo and click on another one.

That's when I realize something. All the photos on this page are taken at an angle. I can barely make out the details on his shoulder and even on the knife. I frown. Poor crime scene photography. Why weren't there close-up photos of the actual wounds? I scroll through the report again, searching for pages I might have missed. But that was it. I go back to the same page, then try to make sense of it.

Maybe the other photos are classified. What if Commander Jameson took them out to spare me the pain? I shake my head. No, that's stupid. Then she wouldn't have sent any photos with this report at all. I stare at the screen, then dare to imagine the alternative.

What if Commander Jameson took them out to hide something from me?

No, no. I sit back and stare at the first photo again. Why would Commander Jameson want to hide the details of my brother's murder from me? She *loves* her soldiers. She was outraged by Metias's death—she even arranged for his funeral. She *wanted* him on her patrol. She was the one who made him captain.

But I doubt the crime scene photographer was so rushed that he would take such a bad set of photos.

I think about it from several angles, but keep coming to the same conclusion. This report is incomplete. I run a hand through my hair in frustration. I don't understand it.

Suddenly I look closer at the knife in the photo. It's grainy, and details are almost impossible to make out, but something triggers an old memory that makes my stomach churn. The blood on the knife's hilt is dark, but there's another mark there too, something darker than the blood. At first I think it's a part of the faint pattern on the knife, but these marks are on top of the blood. They look black, thick and textured. I try to remember what the knife looked like on the night it happened, when I had a chance to look at it myself.

These black marks look like rifle grease. Almost like the streak of grease that was on Thomas's forehead when I first saw him that night.

DAY

WHEN JUNE VISITS ME AGAIN THE NEXT MORNING, even she looks shocked—if just for a second—at my figure, slumped against one wall of my cell. I tilt my head in her direction. She hesitates at the sight of me but quickly regains her composure.

"I assume you made someone angry," she says, then snaps her fingers at the soldiers. "Everyone out. I want a private word with the prisoner." She nods up at the security cameras positioned in each corner. "And cut those too."

The soldier in charge salutes. "Yes, ma'am." As several of them hurry to click off the cameras, I see her take out two knives sheathed at her belt. *Somehow I must've made her angry too.* A laugh bubbles out of my throat and turns into a coughing fit. Well, I guess we should just get it all out of the way.

When the soldiers leave and the door slams shut behind June, she walks over and crouches beside me. I brace myself for the feeling of a blade against my skin.

"Day."

She hasn't moved. Instead, she puts her knives back by her belt and pulls out a canteen of water. Just a display for the soldiers, I guess. She splashes some of the cool liquid on my face. I flinch, but then I open my mouth to catch some of it. Water never tasted so good.

June squirts some water directly into my mouth, then puts the canteen away. "Your face looks awful." There's concern—and something else—in her expression. "Who did this to you?"

"Nice of you to ask." I'm amazed she even cares. "You can thank your captain friend for this."

"Thomas?"

"That's the guy. I don't think he's very happy that I got a kiss from you and he hasn't. So he interrogated me about the Patriots. Apparently Kaede's a Patriot. Small world, huh?"

Anger flashes across June's face. "He never mentioned this to me. Last night he—well, I'll take it up with Commander Jameson."

"Thanks." I blink water out of my eyes. "I was wondering when you'd come." I hesitate for a second. "Do you know anything about Tess yet? If she's alive?"

June looks down. "Sorry," she replies. "I have no way of knowing where she is. She should be safe, as long as she stays low. I haven't mentioned her to anyone. She hasn't appeared in any of the recent arrests . . . or deaths."

I'm frustrated by the lack of news, but relieved at the same time. "How are my brothers?"

June tightens her lips. "I have no access to Eden, although I'm sure he's still alive. John is doing as well as can be expected." When she looks up again, I see confusion and sadness in her eyes. "I'm sorry you had to deal with Thomas yesterday."

"Thanks, I guess," I whisper. "Is there any particular reason why you're nicer than usual today?"

I don't expect June to take this question seriously, but she does. She stares at me, and then seats herself in front of me with her legs folded underneath her. She seems different today. Subdued, maybe, even sad. Uncertain. An expression I've never seen before, even when I first met her on the streets. "Something bothering you?"

June stays silent for a long while, with her eyes cast down. Finally, she looks at me. *She's searching for something,* I realize. *Is she trying to find a way to trust me?* "I studied my brother's crime scene report again last night." Her voice trickles to a whisper so that I have to lean forward to hear her.

"And?" I say.

June's eyes search mine. She hesitates again. "Day, can you say, honestly and truly . . . that you didn't kill Metias?"

She must have found something. She wants a confession. The night at the hospital flashes through my thoughts—my disguise, Metias watching me as I entered the hospital, the young doctor I'd held hostage, the bullets bouncing off the refrigerators. My long fall to the ground. Then the face-off with Metias, the way I'd thrown my knife at him. I'd *seen* it hit his shoulder, so far from his chest that it couldn't possibly have killed him. I hold June's gaze with my own.

"I did not kill your brother." I reach out to touch her hand and wince at the pain that shoots up my arm. "I don't know who did. I'm sorry for injuring him at all—but I had to save my own life. I wish I'd had more time to think it through."

June nods quietly. The look on her face is so heartbreaking

that I wish for a second that I could hold her. *Someone* needs to hold her. "I really miss him," she whispers. "I thought he would be around for a long time, you know, someone I could always lean on. He was all I had left. And now he's gone, and I wish I knew why." She shakes her head slowly, as if defeated, and then lets her eyes meet mine again. Her sadness makes her impossibly beautiful, like snow blanketing a barren landscape. "And I *don't* know why. That's the worst part, Day. I don't know why he died. Why would someone want him dead?"

Her words are so similar to my thoughts about my mother that I can barely breathe. I didn't know that June had lost her parents—although I should have guessed it from the way she carries herself. June was not the one who shot my mother. She was not the one who brought the plague into my home. She was a girl who'd lost her brother, and someone had led her to believe I did it, and in anguish she had tracked me down. If I'd been in her place, would I have done anything differently?

She's crying now. I give her a small smile, then sit up straighter and stretch my hand out toward her face. The shackles on my wrist clank together. I wipe away the tears from under one of her eyes. Neither of us says anything. There's no need to. She's thinking . . . if I'm right about her brother, then what else am I right about?

After a moment, June takes my hand and holds it against her cheek. Her touch sends warmth coursing through me. She's so lovely. I ache to pull her to me now and press my lips against hers and wash away the sorrow in her eyes. I wish I could go back to that night in the alley for just one second.

I'm the first one to speak. "You and I may have the same enemy," I say. "And they've pitted us against each other."

June takes a deep breath. "I'm not sure yet," she says, even though I can tell by her voice that she agrees with me. "It's dangerous for us to talk like this." She looks away, reaches into her cloak, and pulls out something I thought I had lost at the hospital. "Here. I want to give this back to you. I have no more use for it."

I want to snatch it from her hand, but the chains weigh me down. In her palm is my pendant necklace, the smooth bumps on its surface scraped and dirty but still more or less whole, the necklace part lying in a pile in her palm.

"You had it," I whisper. "You found it at the hospital that night, didn't you? That's how you recognized me when you finally found me—I must've reached for it."

June nods quietly, then takes my hand and drops the pendant into my palm. I look at it in wonder.

My father. I can't keep the memory of him away now that I'm staring at my pendant again. I think back to the day he visited us after six months without a word. When he was safely inside and we'd draped curtains over the windows, he wrapped his arms around Mom and kissed her for such a long time. He kept one hand pressed protectively on her stomach. John waited patiently to greet him, hands in his pockets. I was still young enough to hug his leg. Eden wasn't born yet—he was still inside Mom's growing belly.

"How are my boys?" my father said after he finally let go of Mom. He patted my cheek and smiled at John.

John gave him a big, toothy grin. He had managed to grow his hair long enough to tie it back in a tail. He held up a certificate. "Look!" he said. "I passed my Trial!"

"You did!" My father clapped John on the back and shook his hand as if he were a man. I can still remember the relief in his eyes, the tremor of joy in his words. Back then, we all worried that John would be the one to fail the Trial, considering his trouble with reading. "I'm proud of you, Johnny. Good job."

Then he looked at me. I remember studying his face. Dad's official job in the Republic was to clean up after the warfront's soldiers, of course, but there were always hints that this wasn't the only job he had. Hints like the stories he sometimes told about the Colonies and their glittering cities, their advanced technology and festive holidays. At that moment, I wanted to ask him why he was always gone even after his warfront rotation should've returned him home, why he never came to see us.

But something else distracted me. "There's something in your vest pocket, Dad," I said. Sure enough, a circular bump was pressed against the cloth.

He chuckled, then took out the object. "So there is, Daniel." He glanced up at our mother. "He's very perceptive, isn't he?"

Mom smiled at me.

My father hesitated, then ushered us all into the bedroom. "Grace," he said to Mom, "look what I found."

She studied it closely. "What is it?"

"It's more proof." At first my father tried to show it only

to Mom, but I managed to get a good look as he turned it over in his hands. A bird on one side, a man's profile on the other. UNITED STATES OF AMERICA, IN GOD WE TRUST, QUARTER DOLLAR embossed on one side, and LIBERTY and 1990 on the other. "See? Evidence." He pressed it into her palm.

"Where did you find this?" Mom asked.

"In the southern swamplands between the two warfronts. It's a genuine coin from nineteen-ninety. See the name? United States. It was *real*."

My mother's eyes gleamed with excitement, but she still gave Dad a grave look. "This is a dangerous thing to own," she whispered. "We're not keeping this in our house."

My father nodded. "But we can't destroy it. We have to safeguard it—for all we know, this might be the last coin of its kind in the world." He folded my mother's fingers over the coin. "I'll make a metal casing for it, something that covers both sides. I'll weld it shut so the coin's secure inside."

"What will we do with it?"

"Hide it somewhere." My father paused for a second, then looked at John and me. "Best place might be somewhere obvious to everyone. Give it to one of the boys, maybe as a locket. People will think it's just a child's ornament. But if soldiers find it in the house in a raid, hidden under some floorboard, they'll know for sure that it's important."

I stayed silent. Even at that age, I understood my father's concern. Our house had been searched on routine inspections by troops before, just like every other house on our street. If Dad hid it somewhere, they'd find it.

Our father left early the next morning, before the sun even rose. We would see him only one more time after that. Then he never came home again.

This memory flashes through my mind in an instant. I look up at June. "Thank you for finding this." I wonder if she can hear the sadness in my voice. "Thank you for giving it back to me."

JUNE

I CAN'T STOP THINKING ABOUT DAY.

When I lie down in my apartment for a brief rest later in the afternoon, I dream of him. I dream that Day has his arms wrapped around me and is kissing me again and again, his hands running up my arms and through my hair and around my waist, his chest pressed against mine, his breath against my cheeks and neck and ears. His long hair brushes against me, and his eyes drown me in their depths. When I wake up and find myself alone again, I can hardly breathe.

His words run through my mind until I can't even understand them anymore. That someone else has killed Metias. That the Republic is intentionally spreading the plague in the poor sectors. I think back to how we were on the streets of Lake, when he would risk his safety because I needed to rest. Then today, wiping the tears from my cheek.

I can't find the anger I used to have toward him. And if I discover proof that someone else killed Metias, for whatever reason, then I have no reason to hate him at all. I'd once been fascinated by his legend—all the stories I'd heard before I met him. Now I can feel that same sense of fascination returning. I picture his face, so beautiful even after pain and torture and grief, his blue eyes bright and sincere. I'm ashamed to admit that I enjoyed my brief time with him in his prison cell.

His voice can make me forget about all the details running through my mind, bringing with it emotions of desire or fear instead, sometimes even anger, but always triggering something. Something that wasn't there before.

1912 HOURS. TANAGASHI SECTOR. 78°F.

"I heard you had a private conversation with Day this afternoon," Thomas says to me as we sit together, eating bowls of edame in a café. The café is the same one that we visited when Metias was alive. Thomas's choice of location doesn't ease my thoughts. I can't forget the rifle grease smeared on the hilt of the knife that killed my brother.

Maybe he's testing me. Maybe he knows what I suspect.

I take a bite of pork so I don't have to answer. I'm glad that the two of us are sitting a good distance apart. Thomas had spent a great deal of effort convincing me to "forgive" him, to let him take me out to dinner. *Why* he did this, I can't be sure. To draw me out? To get me to say something by accident? To see if I would refuse, and then take this information to Commander Jameson? It doesn't take much evidence to start an investigation against someone. Maybe this whole evening is just bait.

But then again, maybe he's really trying to make up with me.

I don't know. So I tread carefully.

Thomas watches me eat. "What did you say to him?"

There's jealousy in his voice. My words come out cool and detached. "Don't bother, Thomas." I reach out and touch his arm, to distract him. "If a boy killed someone you loved, wouldn't you keep trying to figure out why he'd done it? I thought he might talk to me if the guards weren't around. But I've given up on him. I'll be happier when he's dead."

Thomas relaxes a little, but he still studies my face. "Maybe you should stop seeing him," he suggests after another long silence. "It doesn't seem to be helping you. I can ask Commander Jameson to send someone else to give Day his water rations. I hate to think of you having to interact so much with your brother's murderer."

I nod in agreement and take another bite of edame. To stay silent now would look bad. What if I'm eating dinner with my brother's murderer? *Logic. Caution and logic.* Out of the corner of my eye, I see Thomas's hands. What if those are the hands that stabbed Metias straight through the heart?

"You're right," I say without missing a beat. I make myself sound grateful, thoughtful. "I haven't gotten anything useful out of him yet. He'll be dead soon, anyway."

Thomas shrugs. "I'm glad you think so." He drops fifty Notes on our table as the waiter comes by. "Day is just a criminal on death row. His words shouldn't matter to a girl of your standing."

I take another bite before answering. "They don't," I reply. "I might as well be talking to a dog." But to myself I think, *Day's words will matter if he's telling the truth.*

★ ★ ★

Long after Thomas has escorted me back to my apartment and left, and long after midnight has passed, I sit awake at my computer and study Metias's crime report. I've looked at the photos enough times now to keep myself from turning away, but it still leaves a queasy feeling in my stomach. Every photo is taken from an angle facing away from his wounds. The longer I stare at the black smears on the knife hilt, the more convinced I am that they're remnants of rifle grease.

When I can't look at the photos any longer, I go back to the couch and sift through Metias's journals again. If my brother had any other enemies, surely there'd be a clue somewhere in his writing. But he was no fool, either. He never would've written down anything that could be used as evidence. I read through pages and pages of his old entries, all of them about irrelevant, mundane things. Sometimes he talks about us. These I have more trouble reading.

One entry talks about the night of his induction ceremony into Commander Jameson's squad, when I'd fallen ill. Another is about the celebration we had together when I scored a 1500 on my Trial. We placed an order for ice cream and two whole chickens, and at one point in the evening, I even experimented with making a chicken and ice cream sandwich, which maybe wasn't the best idea I've ever had. I can still hear us laughing, still smell the warm aromas of baked chicken and fresh bread.

I press my fists against my closed eyes and take a deep breath. "What am I doing?" I whisper to Ollie, who tilts his head at me from where he's lying on the couch. "I'm befriending a criminal, and pushing away people I've known my entire life."

Ollie looks back at me with that universal dog wisdom, then promptly goes back to sleep. I stare at him for a while. Not long ago, Metias would've dozed there with his arm draped around Ollie's back. I wonder if Ollie's imagining that now.

It takes me a moment to realize something. I open my eyes, then look back at the last page I'd read in Metias's journal. I think I saw something . . . there. I narrow my eyes at the bottom of the page.

A misspelled word. I frown. "That's odd," I say out loud. The word is *refrigerator*, spelled with an extra *d. Refridgerator*. Never in my life have I known Metias to misspell anything. I study it for a second longer, shake my head, and decide to move on. I make a mental note of the page.

Ten minutes later, I find another one. This time the word is *elevation,* but Metias spells it *elevatien.*

Two misspelled words. My brother would never have done this by accident. I look around, as if there might be a surveillance camera in the room. Then I lean toward the coffee table and start sifting through all the pages of Metias's journals. I store the misspelled words in my head. No reason to write them down for someone else to find.

I find a third word: *bourgeoisie,* spelled *bowrgeoisie.* Then a fourth one: *emanating,* spelled *emamating.*

My heart starts to pound.

By the time I finish going through all twelve of Metias's journals, I've uncovered twenty-four misspelled words. All of them come from the journals written in the last few months.

I lean back on the couch, then close my eyes so I can picture the words in my mind. That many misspelled words from Metias can be nothing other than a message to me—the one person who was most likely to go through his writing. A secret code. This must be why he'd pulled all the boxes out of the closet that fateful afternoon . . . this might be the important thing he'd wanted to talk about. I shift the words around, trying to form a sentence that makes sense, and when that fails, I move the letters around to see if each one might be an anagram for something else.

No, nothing.

I rub my temples. Then I try something else—what if Metias wanted me to put together the individual letters that are either missing from each word or in the word when they aren't supposed to be there? I quietly make a list of these letters in my head, starting with the *d* in *refridgerator*.

D L W G W U N O W M J W U T C E E L O F O O M B

I frown. It makes no sense. I scramble the letters over and over again in my head, trying to come up with various combinations of words. When I was little, Metias played word games with me—he'd throw a bunch of letter blocks onto the table and ask me what words I could form with them. Now I try playing this game again.

I play it for a while before I stumble across a combination that makes me open my eyes.

JUNE BUG. Metias's nickname for me. I swallow hard and try to stay calm. Slowly, I line up the leftover letters and try to form words with them. Combinations fly through my mind until one of them makes me pause.

FOLLOW ME JUNE BUG.

The only letters left after that are three *W*'s, then *CTOOMD*. Which left one logical option.

WWW FOLLOW ME JUNE BUG DOT COM

A website. I run the letters through my mind several more times, to make sure my assumption is correct. Then I glance at my computer.

First I type in Metias's hack that allows me to access the Internet. I put up the defenses and shells that my brother taught me—there are eyes everywhere online. Then I disable my browser's history, and type in the URL with trembling fingers.

A white page pops up. Only one line of text appears at the top.

Let me take your hand, and I will give you mine.

I know exactly what Metias wants me to do. Without hesitating, I reach a hand out and press it flat against my monitor.

At first, nothing happens. Then I hear a click, see a faint light scan across my skin, and the white page disappears. In its place appears what looks like a blog. My breath catches in my throat. There are six brief entries here. I lean forward in my chair and start reading.

What I see makes me dizzy with horror.

July 12

This is for June's eyes only. June, you can easily delete all traces of this blog at any time by pressing your right palm against the screen and typing: Ctrl+Shift+S+F. I have no other place to write this, so I'll write it here. For you.

Yesterday was your fifteenth birthday. I wish you were older, though, because I can't quite bring myself to tell a fifteen-year-old girl what I found—especially when you should be celebrating.

Today I found a photograph taken by our late father. It was the very last one in the very last photo album they owned, and I'd never noticed it before because Dad had hidden it behind a larger photo. You know I flip through our parents' pictures all the time. I like reading their little notes, it feels like they can still talk to me. But this time I noticed that the last photo in that album felt unusually thick. When I fiddled with it, the secret photo fell out.

Dad had taken a photo of his workplace. The lab in Batalla Hall. Dad never talked to us about his work. Yet he'd taken this photo. It was blurry and oversaturated, but I could make out the shape of a young man on a gurney pleading for his life with a bright red biohazard sign imprinted on his hospital gown.

Do you know what Dad wrote at the bottom of that photo?

Resigning, April 6.

Our father had tried to resign the day before he and Mom were killed in a car wreck.

September 15

I've been trying to find clues for weeks. Still nothing. Who knew the deceased civilians database was so difficult to hack?

But I'm not giving up yet. There's something behind our parents' death, and I'm going to find out what it is.

November 17

You asked me why I seemed so out of it today. June, if you're reading this, you probably remember this day, and now you'll know why.

I've been hunting for clues ever since my last entry here. For the past few months I've tried asking subtle questions of other lab workers, and of Dad's old friends, and searching online. Well, today I found something.

Today I finally managed to hack the Los Angeles deceased civilians database. Most complicated thing I've ever done. I was going about it the wrong way. There's a security hole on their servers that I hadn't noticed before because they'd buried it behind all sorts of—well, anyway, it resulted in me getting in. And much to my surprise, I actually found a report on our parents' car accident.

Except it was not an accident. June, I'll never be able

to say this to you out loud, so I desperately hope that you'll see it here.

Commander Baccarin, another former student of Chian (you remember Chian, right?), submitted the report. The report said that Dr. Michael Iparis had roused the suspicions of the Batalla Hall lab administrators when he first questioned the true purpose of his research. He'd always worked on understanding the plague viruses, of course, but he must have uncovered something that upset him enough to make him quietly file for a change in work assignment. Remember that, June? It was just a few weeks before the car crash.

The rest of the report didn't go into the plagues, but it told me what I needed to know. June, the Batalla Hall lab administrators ordered Commander Baccarin to keep an eye on our father. When Dad tried to get reassigned, Baccarin knew that he'd figured out the reason for his research. As you can imagine, this didn't go over very well. Commander Baccarin was ordered to "find a way to smooth the whole matter over." The report ends by saying that the matter was resolved, without military casualties.

Dated a day after the car accident.

They killed them.

November 18

They fixed the security hole on the server. I'll have to find another way around it.

November 22

It turns out the deceased civilians database has more information about the plagues than I guessed. Of course I should've known that, what with the plagues killing off hundreds of people every year. But I always thought the plagues were spontaneous. They're not.

June bug, you need to know this. I don't know when you'll find these entries, but I know you'll find them eventually. Listen to me carefully: when you are finished reading, don't tell me you know about anything. I don't want you doing something rash. Understand? Think about your safety first. You can find a way to help, I know you can. If anyone can, you can. But for my sake don't do anything that'll draw attention to you. I'll kill myself if the Republic strikes you down for reacting to knowledge that I gave you.

If you want to rebel, rebel from inside the system. That's much more powerful than rebelling outside the system. And if you choose to rebel, bring me with you.

Dad found out that the Republic engineers the annual plagues.

They start off in the most obvious place. Those high-rise terraces full of grazing animals isn't where most of our meat comes from. Did you know that? I should've guessed it. The Republic has thousands of underground factories for the animals. They're hundreds of feet deep. At first Congress didn't know what to do with the crazy viruses that kept developing down there and killing off entire factories of animals. Inconvenient, right? But then they remembered the Colonies war. And so every time an interesting new virus appears in the meat factories, the scientists take samples and craft them into viruses that can infect humans. Then they develop an equivalent vaccine and cure for it. And then they hand out mandatory vaccinations to everyone but a few slum sectors. Rumor has it that there's a new strain developing in Lake and Alta and Winter.

They pump that virus into the slum sectors through a system of underground pipes. Sometimes into the water supply, sometimes just directly into a few specific homes to see how it spreads. That starts off a new round of plague. When they think they've seen enough evidence for what that virus strain can do, they secretly prick everyone (everyone still alive, that is) in those sectors with the cure during a routine sweep, and the plague dies down until the next test strain. They also run individual plague experiments on some of the children who fail the Trial. They don't go to labor camps, June.

None of them do.

They die.

Do you see where I'm going with this? They use the plagues to cull the population of weak genes, the same way the Trials pick out the strongest. But they're also creating viruses to use against the Colonies. They've been using biological weapons against them for years. I don't give a damn what happens to the Colonies or exactly what our Republic wants to inflict on them—but June, our own people are lab rats. Dad worked in those labs, and when he tried to quit, they killed him. And Mom. They thought they would tell everybody. Who wants a mass riot? Certainly not Congress.

We're all going to die like this, June, if someone doesn't step in. One of these days, a virus will get out of hand, and no vaccine or cure will be able to stop it.

November 26

Thomas knows. He knows what I suspect, that I think the government may have killed our parents intentionally.

I keep wondering how he knew that I'd hacked into the deceased civilians database, and all I can think of is that I left a trace, and the tech guys who fixed that security hole found it and mentioned it to him. So he approached me earlier today and asked me about it.

I told him I was still grieving over our parents' deaths and got a little paranoid. Told him I didn't find anything. I said you knew nothing about it, that he shouldn't mention it to you. He said he'd keep it a secret. I think I can trust him. It's just a little nerve-racking to have anyone know even the smallest bit about my suspicions. I mean, you know how he gets sometimes.

I've made up my mind. By the end of the week, I'll tell Commander Jameson that I'm going to withdraw from her patrol. I'll complain about the hours and say that I don't see you enough. Something like that. I'll update here when I'm reassigned.

I follow Metias's instructions and delete every last trace of his blog.

Then I curl up on the couch and sleep until Thomas calls. I press a button on my phone and the voice of my brother's murderer fills my living room. Thomas, the soldier who would happily carry out any order from Commander Jameson, even if it's to kill a childhood friend. The soldier who used Day as a convenient scapegoat.

"June?" he says. "Are you all right? It's almost ten hundred hours, and I haven't seen you. Commander Jameson wants to know where you are."

"I'm not feeling well," I manage. "I'm going to sleep awhile longer."

"Oh." A pause. "What are your symptoms?"

"I'll be fine," I reply. "Just dehydrated and feverish. I think I ate something bad last night at the café. Tell Commander Jameson I should feel a little better by evening."

"Okay, then. Sorry to hear it. Feel better soon." Another pause. "If you're still feeling sick by tonight, I'll file a report and send the plague patrol over to check you. You know, protocol. And if you need me to come over, just call me."

You're the last person I want to see. "I'll let you know. Thanks." I hang up.

My head hurts. Too many memories, too many revelations. No wonder Commander Jameson had Metias's body taken away so fast. I'd been stupid enough to think she did it out of sympathy. No wonder she organized his funeral. Even my test mission to track Day must've been a diversion to distract me while they tossed out any remaining evidence.

I think back to the evening when Metias decided to resign from shadowing Chian and joining the Trial enforcers. He'd been quiet and withdrawn when he picked me up from school. "Are you all right?" I remember asking him.

He didn't answer. He just took my hand in his and headed for the train station. "Come on, June," he said. "Let's just go home."

When I looked at his gloves, I saw tiny specks of blood staining them.

Metias didn't touch his dinner, or ask me how my day went—which annoyed me until I realized just how upset he was. Finally, right before bedtime, I went over to where he was lying on the couch and snuggled under his arm. He kissed my forehead.

"I love you," I whispered, hoping to get something out of him.

He turned to look at me. His eyes were so sad.

"June," he said, "I think I'm going to appeal for a different mentor tomorrow."

"You don't like Chian?"

Metias stayed silent for a while. Then he lowered his eyes as if ashamed. "I shot someone at the Trial stadium today."

This was what bothered him. I kept quiet and let him go on.

Metias ran a hand through his hair. "I shot a girl. She'd failed her Trial and tried to escape the stadium. Chian screamed at me to shoot her . . . and I listened."

"Oh." I didn't know it back then, but now I can tell that Metias felt like he had shot *me* when he killed that little girl. "I'm sorry," I whispered.

Metias stared off into the distance. "Few people ever kill for the right reasons, June," he said after a long silence. "Most do it for the wrong reasons. I just hope you never have to be in either category."

The memory fades, and I'm left hanging on to the ghosts of his words.

I don't move for the next few hours. When the Republic's pledge starts up outside, I can hear the people on the streets below chanting along, but I don't bother to stand. I don't salute when the Elector Primo's name comes up. Ollie sits next to me, staring, whining every now and then. I look back at him. I'm thinking, calculating. I have to do something. I think of Metias, of my parents, then of Day's mother, and his brothers. The plague has gotten its claws around all of us, in one way or another. The plague murdered my parents. The plague infected Day's brother. It killed Metias for uncovering the truth of it all. It took from me the people I love. And behind the plague is the Republic itself. The country I used to be proud of. The country that experiments on and kills children who fail the Trial. Labor camps—we'd all been fooled. Had the Republic murdered relatives of my Drake classmates too, all those people who died in combat or in accidents or of illnesses? What else is secret?

I rise, walk over to my computer, and pick up my glass of water. I stare blankly into it. Somehow, the sight of my fingers' disjointed reflections against the glass startles me—reminds me of Day's bloody hands, of Metias's broken body. This antique glass was a gift, supposedly imported from the Republic's islands of South America. It's worth 2,150 Notes. Someone could've bought a plague cure with the money spent on this glass that I use to drink water out of. Maybe the Republic doesn't even own those islands. Maybe nothing I've been taught is true.

In a sudden fit of anger, I lift the glass and hurl it against the wall. It shatters into a thousand glittering pieces. I stand there unmoving, trembling.

If Metias and Day had met somewhere other than the hospital's back streets, would they have become allies?

The sun changes position. Afternoon comes. I still don't move from where I stand.

Finally, when the sunset bathes my apartment in orange and gold, I break out of my trance. I clean up the shining shards of broken glass. I dress in my full uniform. I make sure my hair is pulled back flawlessly, that my face is clean and calm and devoid of emotion. In the mirror, I look the same. But I am a different person inside. I'm a prodigy who knows the truth, and I know exactly what I'm going to do.

I'm going to help Day escape.

DAY

I TRY TO BREAK OUT OF MY PRISON TONIGHT. THIS is how it happens.

As night falls on the third to last day of my life, I hear more shouting and pandemonium coming from the monitors outside my cell. Plague patrols have completely sealed off the Lake and Alta sectors. The steady rise and fall of gunfire coming from the screens tells me that the people living in those sectors must be facing off against the troops. Only one side has the advantage of guns. Guess who's winning.

My thoughts wander back to June. I shake my head, amazed by how much I've allowed myself to open up to her. I wonder what she's doing right now and what she's thinking about. Maybe she's thinking about me. I wish she were here. Somehow I always feel better with her. It's as if she can completely sympathize with my thoughts and help me channel them away, and I can always take comfort in her lovely face.

Her face might give me courage, too. I've had trouble building up my courage without Tess, or John, or my mother.

I've been thinking about this all day. If I can find a way out of this cell, and arm myself with a soldier's weapons and vest, I have a fighting chance to get out of Batalla Hall. I've seen the outside of this building several times now. The sides are not as slick as the Central Hospital was, and if I manage to break out of a window I could run along one of the ledges wrapping around the side of the building, even with my healing leg. The soldiers won't be able to follow me. They'd have to shoot at me from the ground or the air, but I'm fast when I can find footholds, and I can tolerate the pain in my hands. I'll have to find some way to break John out too. Eden probably isn't in Batalla Hall anymore, but I remember quite clearly what June said to me on the first day of my capture. *The prisoner in 6822.* That must be John . . . and I'm going to find him.

But first I have to figure out how to get out of this cell.

I look over at the soldiers lined up against the wall and near the door. There are four. Each wears a standard uniform: black boots, black shirt with a single row of silver buttons, dark gray trousers, bulletproof vest, and a single silver armband. Each has a close-range rifle and an additional gun in his belt's holsters. My mind races. In a room like this, with four steel walls that bullets could bounce off of, the rifles probably use something other than lead ammo. Rubber, perhaps, to stun me if needed. Even tranquilizers. But nothing that can kill me or kill them. Nothing, that is, unless it's shot from a very close range.

I clear my throat. The soldiers turn to me. I wait a few more seconds, then make a gagging sound and hunch over. I shake my head as if to clear my thoughts, then lean back against the wall and close my eyes.

The soldiers seem alert now. One of them points his rifle at me. They stay silent.

I keep up my act for another few minutes, gagging twice

more as the soldiers continue to watch me. Then, without warning, I pretend to dry heave, then burst into a fit of coughs.

The soldiers look at each other. For the first time, I see an uncertain light come into their eyes.

"What's wrong?" one of them snaps at me. It's the one with the cocked rifle. I don't answer him. I pretend to concentrate too hard on holding back another heave.

Another soldier glances at him. "Maybe it's the plague."

"That's nonsense. The medics checked him already."

The soldier shakes his head. "He *was* exposed to his brothers. That young one's Patient Zero, isn't he? Maybe the medics didn't pick it up back then."

Patient Zero. I knew it. I gag again, trying to turn away from the guards as I do it, so they think I don't want their attention. I heave and spit on the floor.

The guards hesitate. Finally, the one with the cocked rifle nods at the soldier standing next to him. "Well, I don't want to stick around in here if it *is* some weird mutated plague. Call for a bio team. Let's have him brought to the medical ward cells." The other soldier nods, then raps on the door. I hear it unlock from the outside. A soldier from the hallway ushers him outside, then quickly relocks the door.

The first soldier walks toward me. "The rest of you, keep your rifles on him," he says over his shoulder. He holds out a pair of handcuffs. I pretend not to notice his approach, so busy am I with my gagging and coughing. "Get up." He grabs one of my arms and pulls me roughly to my feet. I grunt in pain.

He reaches up and unlocks one of my hands from its chain, then clips it into the handcuffs. I don't fight him. Then he unlocks the second hand. He gets ready to shove it into the handcuffs.

Suddenly I twist, and for a split second I'm free. Before he can react, I whirl, yank the gun out of his holster, and point it straight at him. The other two guards fix their rifles on me, but they don't fire. They can't do it without hitting the first soldier.

"Tell your boys outside to open the door," I say to the soldier I'm holding hostage.

He swallows hard. The other soldiers don't dare to blink. "Open the door!" he shouts. There's commotion in the hall, then a few clicks. The first soldier bares his teeth at me. "There are dozens of them out there," he snaps. "You'll never make it."

I just wink at him.

The instant the door opens a sliver, I grab the soldier's shirt and shove him against a wall. One of the others attempts to fire at me—I duck to the floor and roll. Shots are fired all around me. They sound like rubber pellets. I break out of my roll in time to trip a soldier flat on his back. Even this makes me grit my teeth in pain. *Damn this sore leg.* I dart right through the opening before they can close it.

I take in the hallway scene in the blink of an eye. Soldiers litter the walkway. Ceiling tiles. Right-angle turn at the end of the hall. The walls say *4th Floor*. The soldier who opened the door has started reacting—his hand goes to his gun as if in slow motion. I leap up, push off against one wall, and grip the top ledge of the door. My injured leg throws me off completely—I nearly fall back to the ground. More shots ring out. I swing up toward the ceiling and grab the crisscrossing metal between the tiles. *Room 6822—sixth floor.* I swing back down, kicking one soldier in the head with my good leg. He goes down, and I roll with him. I feel two rubber bullets hit him in the shoulder. He cries out. I crouch down and dart through the hall, dodging soldiers and guns, slipping out of the hands that reach for me.

I have to get to John. If I can get him out, we can help each other escape. If I can—

Then something heavy hits me across the face. My vision goes dark. I fight to concentrate, but I feel myself fall to the floor. I try to spring back to my feet, but someone knocks me down again, and a sharp pain makes my back twitch. A soldier must've hit me with the butt of a rifle. I feel hands pin my arms and legs down. My breath escapes me in a gasp.

Everything happens so fast that I can barely register all of it. My head swims. I think I'm going to pass out.

A familiar voice sounds out above me. It's Commander Jameson. "What the hell is this!" She continues to shout at her soldiers. My vision gradually comes back. I realize I'm still trying to fight my way out of the soldiers' grasp.

A hand grabs my chin. Suddenly I'm looking directly into Commander Jameson's eyes. "A foolish attempt," she says.

She glances at Thomas, who salutes her. "Thomas. Take him back to his cell. And put some qualified guards on his watch, for once." She releases my chin and rubs her gloved hands together. "I want the current guards dismissed and thrown off my patrol."

"Yes, ma'am." Thomas salutes again, then starts barking out orders. My free hand is clipped into the handcuffs that are still hanging off the other wrist. From the corner of my eye, I see another black-clad official standing next to Thomas. It's June. My heart leaps into my throat. She narrows her eyes at me. In her hand I see the rifle she used to hit me.

They drag me kicking and shouting back to my cell. June stands by as soldiers chain me to the wall again. Then, when they step back, she leans down near my face. "I would highly suggest you not try that again," she snaps.

There's nothing but cold fury in her eyes. By the door, I see Commander Jameson smile. Thomas looks on with a serious face.

Then, June leans over again and whispers in my ear. "Don't try it again," she says, "because you won't be able to do it alone. You'll need my help."

Of all the things I could've imagined coming out of her mouth, this is certainly not one of them. I try to keep my expression from changing, but my heart stops beating for a second. *Help? June wants to help me?* This is the girl who'd just knocked me to a state of half consciousness in the hallway. Is she trying to throw me into a trap? Or does she really mean it?

June pulls away from me the instant she utters the last word. I pretend to be angry, as if she's just whispered something insulting. Commander Jameson lifts her chin. "Well done, Agent Iparis." June gives her a quick salute. "Follow Thomas down to the lobby, and I'll meet you there."

June and the captain leave. I'm alone with Commander Jameson and a new rotation of soldiers standing near the cell's door.

"Mr. Wing," she says to me after a while. "An impressive effort tonight. You are truly as agile as Agent Iparis claimed. I hate seeing such talents wasted on worthless criminals, but life isn't very fair, is it?" She smiles at me. "Poor boy. You truly believed you could break out of a military stronghold, didn't you?"

Commander Jameson walks over to me, bends down, and rests her elbow on one knee. "Let me tell you a short story," she says. "Some years ago, we caught a young renegade who had a great deal in common with you. Bold and brash, stupidly defiant, just as inconvenient. He tried to escape before his execution date too. Do you know what happened to him, Mr. Wing?" She reaches over, puts her hand on my forehead, and pushes me backward until my head presses against the wall. "That kid made it as far as the stairwell before we got him. When his execution date came, the court granted me permission to kill him personally instead of putting him in front of the firing squad." Her hand tightens on my forehead. "I think he would have preferred the firing squad."

"Someday you'll die in a worse way than he did," I snap back.

Commander Jameson lets out a laugh. "Ill-tempered until the end, aren't you?" She releases my head and tilts my chin up with a finger. "What fun you are, my beautiful boy."

I narrow my eyes. Before she can stop me, I dart out of her grasp and sink my teeth deep into her hand. She shrieks. I bite down as hard as I can, until I taste blood. Commander Jameson slams me into the wall. The hit knocks me loose. She clutches her hand, performing an agonized dance while I blink, fighting to stay awake. A couple of soldiers try to help her, but she shoves them away.

"I'm looking forward to your execution, Day," she snarls at me. Her hand oozes blood. "I'll be counting down the minutes!" Then she storms away and slams the cell door behind her.

I close my eyes and bury my head in my arms so that no one can see my face. Blood lingers on my tongue—I shudder at the metallic taste. I haven't had the nerve to think about my execution date. What does it feel like to stand in front of a firing squad with no way out? My thoughts wander around and then zoom in on what June whispered to me. *You won't be able to do it alone. You'll need my help.*

She must have discovered something—who really killed her brother, or some other truth about the Republic. She has no reason to trick me now. . . . I have nothing to lose and she has nothing to gain. I wait for the realization to sink in.

A Republic agent is going to help me escape. She'll help me save my brothers.

I must be losing my mind.

JUNE

I LEARNED AT DRAKE THAT THE BEST WAY TO TRAVEL UNSEEN at night is by rooftop. I'm practically invisible at that height—the people on the ground keep their attention fixed on the street—and besides, up there I get the best view of where I'm headed.

Tonight I'm on my way back to the border of Lake and Alta, where I'd gotten into the Skiz fight with Kaede. I need to find her now, before I have to return to Batalla Hall in the morning and go over details of Day's botched escape with Commander Jameson. Kaede is going to be my best ally for Day's upcoming execution.

Shortly after midnight, I get dressed in all black. Black hiking boots. A thin black aviator jacket. Knives at my belt. A small black backpack strapped to my shoulders. I don't bring my guns—I don't want anyone to track me to the plague sectors.

I make my way to the top of my high-rise, until I'm standing alone on the roof with the wind whistling all around me. I can smell the moisture in the air. A few terraces still have animals grazing at this hour. The sight of them makes me wonder whether I've been living over an underground meat factory all this time. From here I can see all of downtown Los Angeles, as well as many of its surrounding sectors, and the thin rim of land that separates the enormous lake from the

Pacific Ocean. It's easy to pick out where the wealthy sectors border the poorest ones—where the steady light from electricity gives way to flickering lanterns, bonfires, and steam power plants.

I use an air rope launcher to connect a thin cable between two buildings. Then I glide silently from high-rise to high-rise until I'm well out of the Batalla and Ruby sectors. Here the going gets a little trickier. The buildings aren't as tall, and the roofs are crumbling, some threatening to collapse entirely if too much force hits them. I choose targets carefully. A few times I'm forced to aim the launcher lower than the roof, and then shimmy my way to the top once I get to that side. By the time I reach the outskirts of Lake sector, I can feel sweat dripping down my neck and back.

The lake's edge sits just a few blocks away. When I take a good look across the sector, I see that red tape lines almost every block, and plague patrol soldiers with gas masks and black capes stand at every street corner. *X*s mark rows and rows of doors. I see one patrol going from door to door, pretending to do another routine sweep. I have a hunch that they are doling out cures right now, just as Metias said, and in a few more weeks, this plague will have "magically" trickled away. I make a point not to look anywhere close to where Day's house is—or perhaps, was. As if his mother's body might still be lying there on the street.

It takes me another ten minutes to reach the place outside of Lake where I met Day. Here the rooftops are too fragile for my air rope launcher. I carefully inch my way down to the ground—I'm agile, but I'm not Day—and follow shadowed alleys to the lakefront. Wet sand crunches under my feet.

I make my way through the back alleys, careful to avoid the streetlights, the street police, and the endless street crowd. Day once told me that he'd met Kaede in a bar here, at the edge of Alta and Winter. Now I scan the area as I go. From the rooftops I could already tell that there were about a dozen bars that matched the location and his description—here on the ground, I count out nine of them.

Several times I stop in an alley to gather my thoughts. If I'm caught here and anyone discovers what I'm doing, they'll probably kill me. No questions asked. The thought makes my heart quicken.

But then I remember my brother's words. It's enough to make my eyes sting, to make me clench my teeth. I've gone too far to turn back now.

I wander through several bars without luck. They all look so similar—dim lantern light, smoke and chaos, the occasional Skiz fight happening in a dark corner. I check each fight, although I've learned my lesson about standing far enough away from the circles. I ask each bartender if he knows a girl with a vine tattoo. No Kaede.

About an hour passes.

Then I find her. (Actually, she finds me.) I don't even get a chance to step inside the bar.

I've barely walked out of an adjacent alley and am heading toward this bar's side door when I feel something fly right past my shoulder. A dagger. Instantly I leap out of the way—

my eyes dart up. Someone leaps down from the second floor, lunges for me, and knocks both of us into the shadows. My back slams into the wall. I reach instinctively for the knife at my belt before I see who my attacker is.

"It's you," I say.

The girl facing me looks furious. Street light reflects off her vine tattoo, and heavy black makeup outlines her eyes. "All right," Kaede says. "I know you're looking for me. You want t'see me so badly that you've been wandering through Alta's bars for over an hour. What do you want? A rematch or something?"

I'm about to respond when I see another movement in the shadows behind Kaede. I freeze. Someone else is here with us.

When Kaede sees my eyes dart away, she raises her voice. "Stay back, Tess," she says. "You don't wanna see this."

"Tess?" I squint into the darkness. The figure standing there looks small enough, with a delicate frame and hair that seems to be tied back in a messy braid. Large, luminous eyes peer at me from behind Kaede. I find myself itching to break into a smile—I know this is news that will make Day very happy.

Tess steps forward. She looks healthy enough, although dark circles have appeared under her eyes. The suspicious look on her face sends a wave of shame through me.

"Hello," she says. "How is Day? Is he okay?"

I nod. "For the moment. I'm glad to see you're okay too. What are you doing here?"

She gives me a cautious smile, then glances nervously at Kaede. Kaede shoots her an angry look and presses me harder against the wall. "How about you answer that question first?" she snaps.

Tess must have joined the Patriots. I drop my own knife to the ground. Then I hold my empty hands out to both of them. "I'm here to negotiate with you." I meet her stare with calm eyes. "Kaede, I need your help. I need to talk to the Patriots."

This catches her off guard. "What makes you think I'm a Patriot?"

"I work for the Republic. We know a lot of things, some that might surprise you."

Kaede narrows her eyes at me. "You don't need my help. You're lying," she says. "You're a Republic soldier, and you turned Day in. Why should we trust you?"

I reach around, unzip my backpack, and pull out a thick wad of Notes. Tess lets out a tiny gasp. "I want to give you this," I reply, handing the money to Kaede. "And there's more where that came from. But I need you to listen to me, and I don't have much time."

Kaede flips through the bills with the hand on her good arm and tests one on the tip of her tongue. Her other arm is wrapped in a tight cast. Suddenly I wonder if Tess was the one to bandage up that arm. The Patriots must find her useful.

"I'm sorry about that, by the way," I say, gesturing at her arm. "I'm sure you understand why I did it. I still have the wound you gave me."

Kaede lets out a dry laugh. "Whatever," she says. "At least we got ourselves another medic in the Patriots now." She pats her cast and winks at Tess.

"Glad to hear it," I say, looking sideways at Tess. "Take good care of her. She's worth it."

Kaede studies my face a little longer. Then, she finally releases me and nods at my belt. "Drop your weapons."

I don't argue. I pull four knives from my belt, hold them out slowly so she can see, then toss them to the alley floor. Kaede kicks them out of my range.

"You have any tracking gear?" she says. "Any listening devices?"

I let Kaede check both my ears and my mouth. "Nothing," I reply.

"If I hear so much as one pair of footsteps heading our way," Kaede says, "I'll kill you right here. Understand?"

I nod.

Kaede hesitates, then lowers her arm and guides us deeper into the shadows of the alley. "No way I'm taking you to see any other Patriots," she says. "I don't trust you enough for that. You can talk to us two, and I'll see if it's worth passing along."

I wonder how large an operation the Patriots are. "Fair enough."

I start telling Kaede and Tess about everything I've discovered. I begin with Metias, and then his death. I tell her about my hunt for Day and what had happened when I turned him in. What Thomas had done to Metias. But I don't mention to her why my parents died or what Metias had revealed about the plagues in his blog entries. I'm too ashamed to say it straight to the face of two people living in the poor sectors.

"So your brother's friend murdered him, huh?" Kaede lets out a low whistle. "For figuring out that the Republic killed your parents? And Day's been framed?"

Kaede's nonchalant tone annoys me, but I brush it aside. "Yes."

"Yeah, that's a sad story. Tell me what the hell this has t'do with the Patriots."

"I want to help Day escape before his execution. And I've heard that the Patriots have wanted to recruit him for a long time. You probably don't want to see him dead, either. Maybe the Patriots and I can come to some sort of arrangement."

The anger in Kaede's eyes has turned into skepticism. "So you want revenge for your brother's death or something? Gonna turn your back on the Republic for Day's sake?"

"I want justice. And I want to free the boy who didn't kill my brother."

Kaede grunts in disbelief. "You're living a sweet life, you know. Tucked in a cozy apartment in some rich sector. You know if the Republic finds out you've been talking to me, they'll put you in front of a firing squad. Same as Day."

The mention of Day standing before a firing squad sends chills down my spine. From the corner of my eye, I see Tess wince as well. "I know," I reply. "Are you going to help me?"

"You're fond of Day, aren't you?" Kaede says.

I hope the darkness hides the rising color in my cheeks. "That's irrelevant."

She lets out a laugh. "What a joke! Poor little rich girl's fallen in love with the Republic's most famous criminal. And it's even worse since you're the reason he's there in the first place. Right?"

Stay calm. "Are you going to help me?" I ask again.

Kaede shrugs. "We've always wanted Day. He'd make a perfect Runner for us, y'know? But we're not in the business of doing good deeds. We're professionals, we have a long agenda, and it doesn't involve charity projects." Tess opens her mouth to protest, but Kaede motions for her to stay quiet. "Day may be a popular figure out here on the streets, but he's still one guy. What's in it for us? Just the joy of getting him on board? The Patriots aren't going to risk a dozen lives just to free a single criminal. It's inefficient."

Tess lets out a sigh. I exchange a look with her, and I can tell that this is something she's been trying in vain to convince Kaede to do ever since Day was arrested. This might even be the reason why Tess joined the Patriots in the first place—to beg them to save Day.

"I know." I take off my backpack and toss it to Kaede. She doesn't open it. "That's why I brought this. There are two hundred thousand Notes in there, minus what I handed you earlier. A decent fortune. It's my reward money for capturing Day, and it should be enough payment for your assistance." My voice lowers. "I've also included an electro-bomb. Level three. Worth six thousand Notes. It'll disable guns for two minutes in a half-mile radius. I'm sure you know how difficult it can be to get one on the black market."

Kaede unzips the backpack and sorts through the contents. She doesn't say anything, but I can see the pleasure in her body language, the way she hunches hungrily over the bills and runs her good hand across their crisp surfaces. She lets out a grunt of delight when she reaches the electro-bomb, and her eyes widen when she holds up the metallic sphere to inspect it. Tess watches her with hopeful eyes.

"This is pocket change to the Patriots," she says after she finishes. "But you're right—it might be enough to convince my boss to let me help you out. But how can we be sure this isn't a trap? You sold Day to the Republic. What if you're lying to me too?"

Pocket change? The Patriots must have deep pockets. But I just nod. "You have a right to be suspicious of me," I say. "But think of it this way. You can walk away right now, with two hundred thousand Notes and a rather handy weapon, and never lift a finger to help me. I'm putting my trust in you and in the Patriots. I'm begging you to put your trust in me."

Kaede takes a deep breath. I can tell she's still not convinced. "Well, what did you have in mind?"

My heart skips a beat. I smile genuinely at her. "First things first. Day's brother John. I plan to help him escape tomorrow night. No earlier than eleven P.M., no later than eleven thirty." Kaede gives me an incredulous look, but I ignore her. "A fake death—a claim that John's infected with the plague. If I can help him escape from Batalla Hall tomorrow night, I'll need you and a couple of Patriots to get him out of the sector. Keep him safe."

"We'll be there, if you can make it."

"Good. Now, Day is obviously going to be trickier. His execution happens two evenings from now, at exactly six P.M. Ten minutes before that, I'll be the first person leading him to the firing squad yard. I have a secure access ID—I should be able to get Day out through one of the east hall's six back exits. Have some Patriots wait for us there. I expect a crowd of at least two thousand to show up for the execution, which means a crew of at least eighty security guards. The back exits need to be as sparsely guarded as possible. Do something—anything—to make sure most of the soldiers have to go help there. If the first block past Batalla Hall doesn't have a lot of security, you'll have enough of a head start to escape."

Kaede raises an eyebrow. "You're suicidal. You know how impossible this sounds?"

"Yes." I pause. "But I don't really have much choice."

"Well, go on. What about the square?"

"Diversion." My eyes lock onto Kaede's. "Create chaos in Batalla Square, as much chaos as you can manage. Enough chaos to force most of the soldiers guarding the back exits to enter the square and help contain the crowd—if only for a couple of minutes. That's what the electro-bomb might help you with. Set it off in the air, and it'll shake up the ground in Batalla Hall and around it. It shouldn't hurt anyone, but it'll definitely stir up some panic. And if the guns in the vicinity are disabled, they can't shoot at Day even if they see him escaping along a rooftop. They'll have to chase him or try their luck with less accurate stun guns."

"Okay, genius." Kaede laughs, a little too sarcastically. "Let me ask you this, though. How the *hell* are you going to get Day out of the building at all? You think you're going to be the *only* soldier escorting him to the firing squad? Other soldiers will probably flank you. Hell, a whole patrol might join you."

I smile at her. "There *will* be other soldiers. But who says they can't be Patriots in disguise?"

She doesn't answer me, not in words. But I can see the grin spreading on her face, and I realize that even though she thinks I'm crazy, she has also agreed to help.

TWO NIGHTS BEFORE MY EXECUTION DATE, I HAVE a slew of dreams while trying to sleep against my cell's wall. I can't remember the first few. They mix together into a confusing sludge of familiar and strange faces, something that sounds like Tess's laughter, something else that sounds like June's voice. They're all trying to talk to me, but I can't understand any of them.

I remember the last dream I have before I wake up, though.

A bright afternoon in Lake sector. I'm nine. John is thirteen, just barely starting his growth spurt. Eden is only four and sits on our front door's steps, looking on as John and I play a game of street hockey. Even at this age, Eden is the most intelligent of us, and instead of joining in, he chooses to sit there tinkering with parts of an old turbine engine.

John hits a crumpled ball of paper toward me. I barely catch it with the butt of my broom. "You hit it too far," I protest.

John just grins. "You'll need better reflexes than that if you want to pass your Trial's physical tier."

I hit the paper ball back as hard as I can. It whizzes past John and hits the wall behind him. "You managed to pass *your* Trial," I say. "Despite your reflexes."

"I missed that ball on purpose." John laughs as he turns and jogs over to the ball. He catches it before the breeze can blow it away. Several passersby almost step on it. "Didn't want to completely crush your ego."

It's a good day. John had recently been assigned to work at our local steam plant. To celebrate, Mom sold one of her two dresses and an assortment of old pots, and spent all last week taking over shifts from her coworkers. The extra money was enough to buy a whole chicken. She's inside preparing it—and the smell of meat and broth is so good that we keep the door propped open a little so we can catch a whiff of it out here, too. John isn't usually in such a great mood. I plan to take advantage of it as much as I can.

John hits the ball to me. I catch it with my broom and knock it back. We play fast and furious for several minutes, neither of us missing, sometimes making such ridiculous jumps to get the ball that Eden falls over laughing. The smell of chicken fills the air. It's not even a hot day today—it's perfect, in fact. I pause for a second as John runs to fetch the ball again. I try to take a mental snapshot of this day.

We hit the ball some more. Then, I make a mistake.

A street policeman wanders through our alley as I'm getting ready to hit the ball back to John. From the corner of my eye, I see Eden stand up on the steps. Even John sees him coming before I do, and he holds out one hand to stop me. But it's too late. I'm already in mid-swing, and I hit the ball straight into the policeman's face.

It bounces right off, of course—harmless paper—but it's enough to make the policeman stop in his tracks. His eyes dart to me. I freeze.

Before any of us can move, the policeman pulls a knife from his boot and marches over to me. "Think you can get away with something like that, boy?" he shouts. He lifts the knife and gets ready to hit me across the face with its handle. Instead of cringing, I give him a nasty stare and hold my ground.

John reaches the policeman before he can reach me. "Sir! Sir!" John darts in front of me and holds his hands out to the policeman. "I'm so sorry for that," he says. "This is Daniel, my little brother. He didn't mean it."

The policeman shoves John out of his way. The knife handle whips me across the face. I collapse on the ground. Eden screams and runs inside. I cough, trying to spit out the dirt that fills my mouth. I can't speak. The policeman walks over and kicks me in my side. My eyes bulge out. I curl up in a fetal position.

"Stop, please!" John rushes back to the policeman and stands firmly between the two of us. I catch a glimpse of our porch from where I lie on the ground. My mother has rushed out to the entrance, with Eden hidden behind her. She calls out desperately to the policeman. John continues pleading with him. "I—I can pay you. We don't have much, but you can take whatever you want. Please." John's hand comes down and grabs my arm. He helps me to my feet.

The policeman pauses to consider John's offer. Then he looks up at my mother. "You, there," he calls out. "Fetch me what you have. And see if you can raise a better brat."

John pushes me farther behind himself. "He didn't mean

it, sir," John repeats. "My mother will punish him for his behavior. He's young and doesn't know any better."

My mother rushes out a few seconds later with a cloth bundle. The policeman opens it and checks each Note. I can tell that it's almost all our money. John stays silent. After a while, the policeman rewraps the money and tucks it into his vest pocket. He looks at my mother again. "Are you cooking a chicken in there?" he says. "Kind of a luxury for a family of your type. You like wasting money often?"

"No, sir."

"Then fetch me that chicken too," the policeman says.

Mom hurries back inside. She comes out with a tightly tied bag of chicken meat lined with cloth rags. The policeman takes it, slings it over his shoulder, and casts me one more disgusted look. "Street brats," he mutters. Then he leaves us behind. The alley turns quiet again.

John tries to say something comforting to Mom, but she just brushes it off and apologizes to John for our lost meal. She doesn't look at me. After a while, she hurries back inside to tend to Eden, who has started to cry.

John whirls to face me when Mom is gone. He grabs my shoulders, then shakes me hard. "Don't *ever* do that again, you hear me? Don't you *dare*."

"I didn't mean to hit him!" I yell back.

John makes an angry sound. "Not that. The way you looked at him. Don't you have any brains at all? You *never* look at an officer like that, do you understand? You want to get us all killed?"

My cheek still stings from the knife handle, and my stomach burns from the policeman's kick. I twist out of John's grasp. "You didn't have to stand up for me," I snap. "I could've taken it. I'll fight back."

John grabs me again. "You're completely cracked. Listen to me, and listen to me good. All right? *You never fight back.* Ever. You do what the officers tell you, and you don't argue with them." Some of the anger fades from his eyes. "I would rather die than see them hurt you. Understand?"

I struggle for something smart to say in return, but to my embarrassment, I feel tears well up in my eyes. "Well, I'm sorry you lost your chicken," I blurt out.

My words force a little smile out of John. "Come here, boy." He sighs, then envelops me in a hug. Tears spill down my cheeks. I'm ashamed of them, and I try not to make a sound.

I'm not a superstitious person, but when I wake up from this dream, this painfully clear memory of John, I have the most horrible feeling in my chest.

I would rather die than see them hurt you.

And I have a sudden fear that somehow, some way, what he said in the dream will come true.

JUNE

0800 HOURS. RUBY SECTOR.
64°F OUTSIDE.

DAY WILL BE EXECUTED TOMORROW EVENING.

Thomas shows up at my door. He invites me to an early movie showing before we have to report to Batalla Hall. *The Glory of the Flag*, he tells me. *I've heard good reviews.* It's about a Republic girl who captures a Colonies spy.

I say yes. If I'm going to help John escape tonight, I'd better make sure I keep Thomas feeling good about our relationship. No need for him to get suspicious.

The oncoming hurricane (fifth one this year) shows its first signs as soon as Thomas and I step out onto the streets—an ominous gale, a gust of ice-cold wind, startling in the otherwise humid air. Birds are uneasy. Stray dogs take shelter instead of wandering. Fewer motorcycles and cars pass by on the streets. Trucks deliver extra jugs of drinking water and canned food to the high-rise residents. Sandbags, lamps, and portable radios are rationed out too. Even the Trial stadiums have postponed the Trials scheduled for the day the storm will arrive.

"I suppose you must be excited, what with everything that's going on," Thomas says as we file into the theater. "Won't be long now."

I nod and smile. People pack every seat in the house today, in spite of the windy weather and impending blackouts. Before us looms the theater room's giant Cube, a four-sided projector screen with one side pointed toward each block of seats. It shows a steady stream of ads and news updates while we wait.

"I don't think 'excited' is the best term for how I'm feeling," I reply. "But I have to say I am looking forward to it. Do you know the details about how it'll go?"

"Well, I know I'll be monitoring the soldiers in the square." Thomas keeps his attention on the rotating commercials (our side currently shows a bright, gaudy *Is your child's Trial coming up? Send him to Ace Trials for a free tutoring consultation!*). "Who knows what the crowd might do. They're probably already gathering. As for you—you'll probably be inside. Leading Day to the yard. Commander Jameson will tell us more when it's time."

"Very well." I let myself think over my plans again, details of which have been running through my mind ever since I met Kaede last night. I'll need time to deliver uniforms to her before the execution—time to help several of the Patriots sneak inside. Commander Jameson shouldn't need much convincing to let me escort Day out, and even Thomas sounds like he understands that I want to.

"June." Thomas's voice breaks me out of my thoughts.

"Yes?"

He gives me a curious look and frowns slightly, as if he's just remembered something. "You weren't home last night."

Stay calm. I smile a little, then glance casually back to the screen. "Why do you ask?"

"Well, I stopped by your apartment in the middle of the night. I knocked for a long time, but you didn't answer. It sounded like Ollie was there, so I knew you didn't go to the track. Where were you?"

I look back at Thomas with a steady face. "I couldn't sleep. I went up to the roof for a while and watched the streets."

"You didn't bring your earpiece with you. I tried calling you but just got static."

"Really?" I shake my head. "The reception must have been bad, because I had it on. It was pretty windy last night."

He nods. "You must be exhausted today. You'd better tell Commander Jameson, if you don't want her to work you too hard."

I give Thomas a frown this time. *Turn the questions back around.* "What were you doing at my door in the middle of the night? Was it anything urgent? I didn't miss something from Commander Jameson, did I?"

"No, no. Nothing like that." Thomas gives me a sheepish grin and runs a hand through his hair. How anyone with blood on his hands could still look so carefree is beyond me. "To be honest, I couldn't sleep either. I kept thinking how anxious you must be. Thought I'd surprise you."

I pat his arm. "Thanks. But I'll be fine. We'll execute Day tomorrow, and I'll feel much better afterward. Like you said. Won't be long now."

Thomas snaps his fingers. "Oh, that was the other reason I wanted to see you last night. I wasn't supposed to tell you—it's supposed to be a surprise."

Surprises don't sound like fun right now. But I fake some excitement. "Oh? What's that?"

"Commander Jameson suggested it, and she got the courts to approve it. I think she's still pretty mad about how hard Day bit her hand when he tried to escape."

"Got what approved?"

"Ah, there's the announcement now." Thomas glances back to the movie screen and points at the commercial that comes on. "We're moving up Day's execution time."

The commercial is nothing but a digital flyer, a single still image. It looks festive, dark blue text and photos over a white and green patterned background. I see Day's photo in the middle of it. *STANDING ROOM ONLY IN FRONT OF BATALLA HALL ON THURSDAY, DECEMBER 26, AT 1700 HOURS. FOR THE EXECUTION OF DANIEL ALTAN WING. LIMITED SPACE AVAILABLE. JUMBOTRON VIEWING ONLY.*

All the air squeezes out of my chest. I look back at Thomas. "Today?"

Thomas grins. "Tonight. Isn't it great? You won't have to agonize through another whole day."

I keep my voice upbeat. "Good. I'm glad to hear it."

But my thoughts churn into rising panic. This could mean so many things. Commander Jameson convincing the court to move his execution up a whole day is unusual in itself. Now he'll face the firing squad in only eight hours, right as the sun starts to set. I can't get John out now—the entire day will be spent preparing for Day's execution. Even the hour has changed. The Patriots might not be able to meet me today. I'll have no time to get uniforms for them.

I can't help Day escape.

But that's not all. Commander Jameson *chose* not to tell me about this. If Thomas already knew last night, that means she told him yesterday evening, at the latest, before sending him home. Why wouldn't she tell me? She should think I'd be glad to hear that Day is to die twenty-five hours earlier than planned. Unless she suspects something. Perhaps she wanted to throw me off just to test my reaction. Does Thomas know something he's keeping from me? Is all this ignorance about the plan just a mask to hide the truth—or is Commander Jameson keeping him in the dark as well?

The movie starts. I'm grateful I don't have to talk to Thomas anymore and can think in silence.

Change of plans. Otherwise, the boy who didn't kill my brother will die tonight.

DAY

MY NEW EXECUTION TIME COMES WITHOUT ANY fanfare but the occasional crack of thunder coming from outside the building. Not that I can see the storm from my cell, of course, with its empty steel walls and security cams and nervous soldiers—so I can only guess at what the sky looks like.

At 6:00 A.M., the soldiers remove my shackles and unchain me from my prison wall. It's a tradition. Before a publicized criminal goes off to face the firing squad, Batalla Hall broadcasts footage of them to all the JumboTrons in the square. They unchain you so you have the chance to do something entertaining. I've seen it in the past—and the onlookers in the square love it. Usually *something* happens: the criminal's resolve starts breaking down, and he begs and pleads with the guards or tries to cut a deal or an extension, or sometimes even tries to break out. No one ever has. They feed your image live to the square until your execution time comes, then they cut to the firing squad yard inside Batalla Hall, and then they show you marching out to face the executioners. The onlookers in the square will gasp and shriek—sometimes in delight—when the shooting happens. And the Republic will be happy that they've made an example out of another criminal.

They'll play reruns of the footage for several days afterward.

I'm free to walk around in my cell, but instead I just sit there and lean against the wall, my arms resting on my knees. I don't feel like entertaining anyone. My head pounds with excitement and dread, anticipation and worry. My pendant sits in my pocket. I can't stop thinking about John. What will they do with him? June promised to help me—she must've planned something for John, too. I hope.

If June is planning to help me escape, she sure is pushing her luck to the limits. The change in my execution date must not have helped her any, either. My chest aches at the thought of the danger she's put herself in. I wish I knew what revelations she'd had. What could hurt her so badly that she, with all her privileges, would turn against the Republic? And if she was lying . . . well, why would she lie about saving me? *Maybe she cares for me.* I have to laugh a little at myself. What a thought at a time like this. Maybe I can steal a goodbye kiss from her before I step into the yard.

One thing I do know. Even if June's plans fail, even if I'm going to be isolated and friendless when I head out to the firing squad . . . I'm going to fight. They're going to have to fill me with bullets to get me to stay still. I take a shuddering breath. Brave thoughts, but am I ready to follow through on them?

The soldiers standing in my cell have more weapons than usual, along with gas masks and protective vests. No one dares take his eyes off of me. They really think I'll do something cracked. I stare at the security cams and imagine what the square's crowd looks like.

"You guys must be loving this," I say after a while. The soldiers shift on their feet—a few raise their weapons. "Wasting a day of your life watching me sit in a cell. What fun."

Silence. The soldiers are too afraid to reply.

I imagine the crowd outside. What are they doing? Maybe some of them still pity me, would still be willing to protest for me. Maybe a few of them *are* protesting, although it can't be as serious as last time or I'd probably hear some of it from the hall. A lot of them must hate me. They must be cheering right now. And still others might just be out there because of morbid curiosity.

Hours drag by. I find myself looking forward to the execution. At least I'll get to see something other than gray cell walls, if only for a little while. Anything to stop this mind-numbing wait. Besides—if June doesn't succeed with whatever she's planning, I'll get to stop picturing John and my mother and Tess and Eden and *everyone* in my head.

Soldiers rotate in and out of my cell. I know five P.M. must be close. The square is probably filled with people by now. *Tess.* Maybe *she's* there, too afraid to see it happen and too afraid to miss it.

Footsteps out in the hall. Then, a voice I recognize. June's. I lift my head and look toward the door. Is this it? Time for my escape—or my death?

The door swings open. My guards make room as June enters the cell in full uniform, flanked by Commander Jameson and several other soldiers. I suck in my breath at the sight of her. I haven't seen June in such clothes before. Shining, luxurious epaulettes draping from each of her shoulders. A thick, full-length cape made from some sort of rich velvet. Scarlet waist-coat and elaborate, belted boots. A standard-issue military cap. Simple makeup adorns her face, and her hair is flawless in its high ponytail. This must be standard agent dress code for special events.

June stops some distance away from me and, as I struggle to my feet, she looks down at her watch. "Four forty-five P.M.," she says. She looks back up at me. I try to read her eyes, to see if I can guess what her plans are. "Any final requests? If you wish a last look at your brother or a last prayer, you'd better let us know now. It's the only privilege you'll get before you die."

Of course. Final requests. I stare at her and keep my expression carefully blank. What does she want me to say? June's eyes are intense, burning.

"I—" I begin. All eyes are on me.

I see June make the most subtle movement with her lips. *John,* she mouths. I glance at Commander Jameson.

"I want to see my brother John," I say. "One last time. Please."

The commander gives me an impatient nod and snaps her fingers, then mutters something to the soldier that approaches her. He salutes, then leaves. She looks back at me. "Granted." My heart pounds harder. June exchanges the briefest look with me, but before I can focus on her, she turns away to ask Commander Jameson something.

"Everything is in place, Iparis," the commander replies. "Now stop nagging me."

We wait in silence for several minutes until I hear footsteps come down the hall again. This time, there's a dragging sound mixed in with the crisp march of the soldiers. It must be John. I swallow hard. June doesn't look at me again.

And then John's in the cell, flanked by two guards. He looks thinner and paler than he did before. His long, white-blond hair hangs in dirty strings, and he doesn't even seem to notice that some of it is plastered across his face. Must be what my hair looks like too. He smiles at the sight of me, although there's little joy in it. I try to smile back.

"Hey," I say.

"Hey," he replies.

June crosses her arms. "Five minutes. Say what you want and be done with it." I nod wordlessly.

Commander Jameson glances at June, but makes no motion to leave. "Make sure it's exactly five minutes, not a second more." Then she presses a hand to her ear and starts barking out more orders. Her eyes stay fixed on me.

For several seconds, John and I just stare at each other. I try to speak, but something lodges in my throat, and my words don't come out. Things shouldn't be like this for John. Maybe for me, but not him. I'm an outcast. A criminal, a fugitive. I've broken the law over and over again. But John's done nothing wrong. He passed his Trial fair and square. He's caring, responsible. Nothing like me.

"Do you know where Eden is?" John finally breaks the silence. "Is he alive?"

I shake my head. "I don't know, but I think so."

"When you stand out there," John continues in a hoarse voice, "keep your chin up, all right? Don't let them get to you."

"I won't."

"Make them work for it. Punch someone if you have to." John gives me a sad, crooked smile. "You're a scary kid. So scare them. Okay? All the way until the end."

For the first time in a long time, I feel like a little brother. I have to swallow hard to keep my eyes dry. "Okay," I whisper.

Our time ends all too quickly. We exchange good-byes, and John's two guards grab his arms to lead him out of my cell and back into his own. Commander Jameson seems to relax a little, obviously relieved that my request is finished. She motions at the other soldiers. "Form up," she says. "Iparis, accompany the guards back to this boy's cell. I'll return shortly." June salutes, then follows John out of the cell while soldiers approach me and tie my hands behind my back. Commander Jameson disappears out the door.

I take a deep breath. I need a miracle now.

Several minutes later, they lead me out. I do what John says and keep my chin up, my eyes blank. Now I can hear the crowd. The sound of them rises and falls, a steady tide of human voices. My eyes skim the flat-screen panels lining the hall as we pass by—the people in the square look restless, shifting like waves on a stormy day, and I pick out the lines of soldiers fencing them in. Now and then, I see people who have a bright scarlet streak painted into their hair. Soldiers are going through the crowd and rounding them up for arrest—but they don't seem to care.

At some point, June joins us and falls into step near the back of the soldiers. I glance behind me, but can't see her face. The seconds drag on. What will happen when we reach the yard?

Finally, we arrive at the halls that lead into the firing squad yard.

That's when I hear Thomas, the young captain, say, "Ms. Iparis."

"What is it?" June replies.

Then, words that seize my heart. I doubt she planned for this.

"Ms. Iparis," he says, "you're under investigation. Follow me."

JUNE

MY FIRST INSTINCT IS TO ATTACK THOMAS. THAT'S WHAT I would have done if he'd caught me without so many soldiers around. Lunge at him with everything I've got, knock him unconscious, then reach Day and make a run for the exits. I already have John. Somewhere in the halls that lead back to his old cells lie two guards passed out on the floor. I pointed John to the ventilation shaft. He's waiting there for me to make my next move. I'll free Day, shout out a signal, then John will emerge from the wall like a ghost and escape with us. But I can't win a fight against Thomas and all these guards without the element of surprise.

So I decide to do what he says. "Investigation?" I ask him with a frown. He tips his cap politely, as if in apology, then takes one of my arms and begins leading me away from Day's soldiers.

"Commander Jameson asked me to detain you," he says. We round the corner and head for the stairwell. Two more soldiers join him. "I have a few questions for you."

I put on an air of annoyance. "Ridiculous. Couldn't the commander pick a less dramatic moment for this nonsense?"

Thomas doesn't reply.

He leads me down the stairwell, two flights down, until we enter the basement where execution rooms, electric grids, and storage chambers line the halls. (I know why we're down here now. They've discovered the missing electro-bomb that I gave to Kaede. Normally, inventory check wouldn't happen until the end of the month. But Thomas must've had it done this morning.) I keep the rising panic off my face. *Focus,* I remind myself angrily. *A panicked person is a dead person.*

Thomas stops us at the bottom of the stairs. He puts a hand on his belt, and I see the gleam of his gun's handle. "An electro-bomb's gone missing." The dangling lights overhead cast mean shadows across his face. "Found it missing in the early morning after I went knocking on your apartment door. You said you were up on the roof last night, right? Do you know anything about this?"

I keep my eyes locked steadily on his face and cross my arms. "You think I did this?"

"I'm not accusing you of anything, June." His expression turns tragic, even pleading. But his hand doesn't move away from his gun. "But I thought it was quite a coincidence. Few people have access down here, and everyone else was more or less accounted for last night."

"More or less accounted for?" I say it sarcastically enough to make him blush. "That sounds vague. Did I show up on the security cams? Did Commander Jameson put you up to this?"

"Answer the question, June."

I glare at him. He winces, but doesn't apologize for his change in tone. *This may be it for me.*

"I didn't do it," I say.

Thomas looks unconvinced. "You didn't do it," he repeats back at me.

"What else can I tell you? Did they do at least another pass on the inventory check? Are you sure something's missing?"

Thomas clears his throat. "Someone tampered with the security cams down here, so we have no footage." He taps his gun. "It was quite a precise job. And when I think of precise, I think of one person. You."

My heart starts beating faster.

"I don't want to do this." Thomas's voice grows softer. "But I did find it strange that you spent so much time questioning Day. Do you feel sorry for him now? Did you set something up to—"

He never gets to finish that sentence.

Suddenly an explosion rocks the entire corridor, throwing us against the wall. Dust rains down from the ceiling, and sparks flicker through the air. (The Patriots. The electrobomb. They've set it off in the square. They came after all, right on schedule, right before Day is to enter the firing squad yard. Which means all the guns in this building should be disabled for exactly two minutes. Thank you, Kaede.)

I shove Thomas hard against the wall before he can regain his balance. Then I yank the knife out from his belt, reach for the electric grid box, and pull it open. Behind me, Thomas reaches for his gun as if in slow motion.

"Stop her!"

I take the knife and slice through all the wires on the bottom of the electric grid.

A pop. A shower of sparks. The entire basement goes black.

I hear Thomas curse. (He's discovered his gun is useless.)

Soldiers stumble over each other. I quickly feel my way to the stairwell.

"June!" Thomas shouts from somewhere behind me. "You don't get it—it's for your own good!"

The words come spilling out of my mouth in a rage. *"Yeah, is that what you told Metias?"*

Not much time before backup power kicks in. I don't wait around to hear Thomas's reply. I reach the stairs and jump up three at a time, counting the seconds since the electro-bomb went off. (Eleven seconds so far. One hundred and nine seconds left before guns are functional again.)

I burst through the first-floor door into a sea of chaos. Soldiers rushing out to the square. Footsteps thundering everywhere. I make my way straight back toward the firing squad yard. Details zip around me like a highway of thoughts. (Ninety-seven seconds left. Thirty-three soldiers heading opposite me—twelve heading in my direction—some flat screens have gone dark—must be the power cut—others show pandemonium in the crowd outside—something's falling from the sky into the square—money! The Patriots are raining money down from the roofs. Half the crowd's fighting to get out of the square while the other half's scrambling for the Notes.)

Seventy-two seconds. I reach the firing squad hall and take in the scene in an instant: three unconscious soldiers. John and Day (with a blindfold loose around his neck, which the guards must've put over his eyes right before the bomb went off) are fighting with a fourth. The others must've been called to help contain the square—but they won't be long now. They'll come back in no time. I run up behind them and kick the soldier's feet out from under him. He tumbles to the ground. John punches him in the jaw. The soldier goes limp.

Sixty seconds. Day looks unsteady, as if he might pass out. A soldier must've hit him across the head, or maybe his leg is giving him trouble. John and I support him between us—I guide us into a narrower hall branching away from the firing squad corridors and we start making our way toward the exits. Commander Jameson's voice blares out from the intercoms a second later. She sounds furious.

"Execute him! *Kill him now! Make sure the square broadcasts it!*"

"Damn it," Day says under his breath. His head sways to one side—his bright blue eyes look dull and unfocused. I exchange a look with John and keep going. Soldiers will be on their way back now. Back to drag Day out into the yard.

Twenty-seven seconds.

We're a good 250 feet from the exits. (We're covering about 5 feet a second; 27 times 5 equals 135 feet. In 135 feet, guns will be reactivated. I can already hear soldiers' boots in the corridors adjacent to ours, pounding on the floor. Probably searching for us. We need at least 23 more seconds to get to the doors before they catch us in this hall. They'll shoot us dead long before we can get out.)

I hate my calculations.

John glances at me. "We're not going to make it." Between us, Day has faded into a semiconscious state. If the brothers continue on and I run back to fight the soldiers, I'll probably only take down a few before they overwhelm me. They'll still reach John and Day.

John stops walking, and I feel Day's weight shift over to me. "What—" I begin to say, until I see John pull the blindfold off of Day's neck. Then he turns around. My eyes widen. I know what he's going to do. "No, stay with us!"

"You need more time," John says. "They want an execution? They'll get one." He starts running away from us. Back down the hall.

Back toward the firing squad yard.

No. *No, no, John. Where are you going!* I waste a second looking back at him, torn in that instant, wondering if I should chase after him.

John's going to do it.

Then Day's head lolls against my shoulder. Six seconds. I have no choice. Even as I hear the shouts of soldiers behind us, in the hall leading to the firing squad, I force myself to turn around and keep going.

Zero seconds.

Guns are reactivated. We keep going. More seconds pass. I hear a commotion in the halls somewhere behind us. I tell myself not to look back.

Then we reach the exits, burst out into the street, and a pair of soldiers is upon us. I have no more strength to fight. But I try. Then someone's wrestling with me, and the soldiers go down, and Kaede runs past my line of vision. "They're here!" she shouts. "Move out!"

They were lurking near the back exits. Just like we agreed. *The Patriots came for us.* I want to tell them to wait for John, but I know it's no use. They grab us and lead us toward their motorcycles. I take the gun out from my belt and fling it to the ground. I can't have its tracker follow me now. Day goes on one motorcycle—I go on another. *Wait for John,* I want to say.

But then we're off. Batalla Hall moves away from us.

A CRACK OF LIGHTNING, AN EXPLOSION OF THUNDER, the sound of pounding rain. Somewhere far away, the wailing of flood sirens.

I open my eyes, then squint at the water falling into them. For an instant I can't remember anything—not even my name. Where am I? What happened? I'm sitting right next to a chimney, soaking wet. I'm on the rooftop of a high-rise tower. Rain blankets the world around me and wind whistles through my drenched shirt, threatening to lift me off my feet. I huddle against the chimney. When I look up at the sky, I see an endless field of churning clouds, jet-black and furious, illuminated by lightning.

Suddenly I remember. The firing squad, the hallway, the flat screens. John. The explosion. Soldiers everywhere. June. I should be dead right now, filled with bullets.

"You're awake."

Slouched next to me, almost invisible against the night in a black outfit, is June. She's sitting awkwardly against the wall of the chimney, oblivious to the rain that runs down her face. I shift to turn toward her. A spasm of pain shoots up my injured leg. Words stick to my tongue and refuse to come out.

"We're in Valencia. On the outskirts. The Patriots took us as far as they were willing. They've moved on to Vegas." June blinks water from her eyes. "You're free. Get out of California while you can. They'll keep hunting for us."

I open and close my mouth. Am I dreaming? I scoot closer to her. One of my hands comes up to touch her face. "What . . . what happened? Are you all right? How did you get me out of Batalla Hall? Do they know you helped me?"

June just stares at me, as if trying to decide whether or not to answer my questions. Finally, she glances over at the edge of the roof. "See for yourself."

I struggle to my feet. Now I can look over the roof at the JumboTrons lining the walls. I limp to the edge of the rooftop and stare down from the railing. We're definitely in the outskirts. I can tell now that the building we're perched on is abandoned and boarded up, and only two JumboTrons along this entire block are functional. I look at the screens.

The headline playing on them takes my breath away.

DANIEL ALTAN WING EXECUTED TODAY
BY FIRING SQUAD

A video recap plays behind the headline. I see the footage of me sitting in my cell. I look at the camera. Then the video cuts to the yard, where the firing squad lines up. Several soldiers drag a struggling boy out into the center of the yard. I remember none of this. The boy's blindfolded, with hands cuffed tightly behind him. He looks just like me.

Except for a few details that only I would notice. His shoulders are slightly broader than mine. He walks with what looks like a fake limp, and his mouth looks more like my father's than my mother's.

I squint through the rain. *It can't be . . .*

The boy stops in the center of the yard. His guards turn away and hurry back the way they came. A line of soldiers hoist their guns, then point them at the boy. There's a brief, horrible silence. And then smoke and sparks pour from the guns. I see the boy convulse with each shot. He collapses facedown in the dirt. A few more shots ring out. Then the silence returns.

The firing squad quickly files out. Two soldiers pick up the boy's body and take him away to the cremation chambers.

My hands start to shake.

The boy is John.

I whirl to face June. She watches me quietly. "That's John!" I shout over the rain. "The boy is *John!* What was he doing out there, out in the yard?"

June says nothing.

I can't catch my breath. I understand what she did now. "You didn't take him back," I manage to say. "You switched us instead."

"I didn't do it," she replies. "He did."

I limp back to her. I grab her by the shoulders and push her back against the chimney. "Tell me what happened. Why did he do it?" I shout. "It should've been me!"

June cries out in pain, and I realize that she's injured. A deep gash runs across her shoulder, staining her shirt with blood. What am I doing, yelling at her? I tear a strip of cloth from the bottom of my shirt and try to wrap her wound the way Tess would. I pull the cloth tight and tie it off. June winces.

"It's not that bad," she lies. "A bullet scraped me."

"Are you hurt anywhere else?" I run my hands down her other arm, then gently touch her waist and her legs. She's shivering.

"I don't think so," she replies. "I'm okay." When I push wet strands of her hair behind her ears, she looks up at me. "Day . . . it didn't go according to my plan. I wanted to get both of you out. I could have done it. But . . ."

The image of John's lifeless body displayed on the JumboTron makes me light-headed. I take a deep breath. "What happened?"

"There wasn't enough time." She pauses. "So John turned back. He *bought* us time and he went back to the hall. They thought he was you. He even wore your blindfold. They grabbed him and took him back to the firing squad yard." She shakes her head again. "But the Republic must know by now that they made a mistake. You have to run, Day. While you can."

Tears stream down my cheeks. I don't care. I kneel in front of June and clutch my head in both hands, then sink to the floor. Nothing makes sense anymore. My brother was probably worrying about me while I moped in my cell like a selfish brat. John put me first, always.

"He shouldn't have done it," I whisper. "I don't deserve it."

June's hand rests on my head. "He knew what he was doing, Day." Tears appear in her eyes, too. "Someone needs to save Eden. So John saved *you*. As any brother would."

Her eyes burn into mine. We stay here, unmoving, frozen in the rain. It feels like an eternity. I remember the night that set this all in motion, the night I saw the soldiers mark my mother's door. If I hadn't gone to that hospital, if I hadn't crossed paths with June's brother, if I'd found a plague cure somewhere else . . . would things be different? Would my mother and John still be alive? Would Eden be safe?

I don't know. I'm too afraid to dwell on the thought.

"You threw *everything* away." I bring a hand up to touch her face, to wipe rain from her eyelashes. "Your entire life—your beliefs . . . Why would you do that for me?"

June has never looked more beautiful than she does now, unadorned and honest, vulnerable yet invincible. When lightning streaks over the sky, her dark eyes shine like gold. "Because you were right," she whispers. "About all of it."

When I pull her into an embrace, she wipes a tear from my cheek and kisses me. Then she buries her head against my shoulder. And I let myself cry.

JUNE

THREE DAYS LATER.
BARSTOW, CALIFORNIA.
2340 HOURS. 52°F.

HURRICANE EVONIA HAS FINALLY STARTED TO CALM DOWN, but the rain, heavy and cold, continues to fall in sheets. The sky churns in fury. Under all this, Barstow's lone JumboTron broadcasts the news coming in from Los Angeles.

EVACUATIONS MANDATED FOR:
ZEIN, GRIFFITH, WINTER, FOREST.
ALL LOS ANGELES CIVILIANS REQUIRED TO
SEEK SHELTER AT FIVE STORIES OR HIGHER.

QUARANTINE LIFTED ON LAKE AND
WINTER SECTORS.

REPUBLIC WINS DECISIVE VICTORY AGAINST
COLONIES IN MADISON, DAKOTA.

LOS ANGELES DECLARES OFFICIAL HUNT
FOR PATRIOT REBELS.

DANIEL ALTAN WING EXECUTED DEC. 26
BY FIRING SQUAD.

Of course the Republic would announce Day's execution as successful. Even though Day and I know otherwise. Already the whispers have started in the streets and dark alleys, rumors that Day has cheated death once again. And that a young Republic soldier helped him do it. The whispers stay whispers, because no one wants to draw the Republic's attention. And yet. They continue to talk.

Barstow, quieter than inner Los Angeles, is still overcrowded with people. But the police here aren't looking for us in the way police back in the metropolis must be. Railroad city. Ramshackle buildings. A good place for Day and me to take shelter. I wish Ollie could have come with us too. If only Commander Jameson hadn't pushed the execution up a day. I'd wanted to let him out of the apartment, hide him in an alley and then go back for him. But it's too late now. What will they do to him? The thought of Ollie barking at soldiers breaking into my apartment, scared and alone, brings a lump to my throat. He's the only piece of Metias I have left.

Now Day and I struggle through the rain back to the rail yard where we're going to set up camp. I'm careful to stay in the shadows, even on this stormy night. Day keeps a cap on and tilted low over his eyes. I've tucked my hair inside the collar of my shirt and wrapped an old scarf—now soggy—across the lower half of my face. It's about all we can do for disguises right now. Old railway cars litter the junkyard, faded and rusted with age. Twenty-six of them, if you count a caboose missing half of one side, all Union Pacific. I have to lean into the wind to keep from falling over. The rain stings my wounded shoulder. Neither of us says a word.

When we finally reach an empty car (a 450 square foot covered hopper car with two sliding doors—one rusted shut, the other halfway open; must be designed for carrying dry bulk freight) safely tucked behind three others at the back of the yard, we climb inside and settle down in a corner. Surprisingly clean. Warm enough. Most important, dry.

Day takes off his cap and wrings out his hair. I can tell his leg is hurting. "Good to know the flood warnings are still in place."

I nod. "Should be hard for any patrol to track us in this weather." I pause to watch him. Even now, exhausted and messy and completely soaked, he has an untamed sort of grace about him.

"What?" He stops wringing out his hair.

I shrug. "You look terrible."

This makes Day smile a little—but it disappears as fast as it comes. Guilt takes its place. I fall silent. Can't blame him.

"As soon as the rain stops," he says, "I want to head out toward Vegas. I want to find Tess and make sure she's safe with the Patriots before we move on to the warfront to find Eden. I can't just leave her behind. I have to know that she's better off with them than with us." It's as if he's trying to convince me that this is the right thing to do. "You don't have to come. Take a different route to the warfront and meet me there. We can decide on a rendezvous point. Better just to risk one of us than both."

I want to tell Day that it's insane to head for a military city like Vegas. But I don't. All I can picture are Tess's hunched, narrow shoulders and wide eyes. He's already lost his mother. His brother. He can't lose Tess, too. "You *should* go find her," I say. "You don't have to talk me into it. But I'm coming with you."

Day scowls. "No, you're not."

"You need backup. Be reasonable. If something happens to you along the way, how will I know you're in trouble?"

Day looks at me. Even in this darkness, I can't take my eyes off him. The rain has washed his face clean. The scarlet stripe of blood in his hair is gone. Only a few bruises remain. He looks like an angel, if a broken one.

I look away, embarrassed. "I just don't want you to go alone."

Day sighs. "All right. We'll go to the warfront and find out where Eden is, then cross the border. The Colonies will probably welcome us—maybe even help us."

The Colonies. Not long ago they had seemed like the greatest enemy in the world. "Okay."

Day leans toward me. He reaches up to touch my face. I can tell it still hurts him to use his fingers, and his nails are dark with dried blood. "You're brilliant," he says. "But you're a fool to stay with someone like me."

I close my eyes at the touch of his hand. "Then we're both fools."

Day pulls me to him. He kisses me before I can say more. His mouth feels warm and soft, and when he kisses me harder, I wrap my arm around his neck and kiss him back. In this moment, I don't care about the pain in my shoulder. I don't care if soldiers find us in this railway car and drag us away. I don't want to be anywhere else. I just want to be here, safe against Day's body, wrapped in his tight embrace.

"It's strange," I say to Day later, as we both curl up on the floor. Outside, the hurricane rages on. In a few hours we'll need to head out. "It's strange being here with you. I hardly know you. But . . . sometimes it feels like we're the same person born into two different worlds."

He stays quiet for a moment, one hand absently playing with my hair. "I wonder what we would've been like if I'd been born into a life more like yours, and you had been born into mine. Would we be just like we are now? Would I be one of the Republic's top soldiers? And would you be a famous criminal?"

I lift my head off his shoulder and look at him. "I never did ask you about your street name. Why 'Day'?"

"Each day means a new twenty-four hours. Each day means everything's possible again. You live in the moment, you die in the moment, you take it all one day at a time." He looks toward the railway car's open door, where streaks of dark water blanket the world. "You try to walk in the light."

I close my eyes and think of Metias, of all my favorite memories and even the ones I'd rather forget, and I picture him bathed in light. In my mind, I turn to him and give him a final farewell. Someday I'll see him again, and we'll tell our stories to each other . . . but for now I lock him safely away, in a place where I can draw on his strength. When I open my eyes, Day is watching me. He doesn't know what I'm thinking, but I know he recognizes the emotion on my face.

We lie there together, watching the lightning and listening to the thunder, and waiting for the beginning of a rainy dawn.

ACKNOWLEDGMENTS

Every time I flip through *Legend,* I am reminded of my fourteen-year-old self, writing by lamplight into the deep hours of every school night, blissfully unaware of how long the road to publication would be. Now I know how many people it takes to birth a book and how much of a difference their hard work makes. You all have my deepest gratitude:

To my literary agent, Kristin Nelson, for first taking me on for a manuscript that did not sell and then never wavering in her faith while I wrote *Legend,* and for her brilliant insights into *Legend* that made it what it is now. I would not be here without you. To the wonderful staff at the Nelson Literary Agency for making sure nothing fell through the cracks: Lindsay Mergens, Anita Mumm, Angie Rasmussen, and Sara Megibow.

To my editor extraordinaire, Jen Besser, for taking *Legend* under her care and polishing it into a story that shines far brighter than what I could have done on my own. I am so lucky to have you on my side!

To the unbelievable team at Putnam Children's and Penguin Young Readers that has embraced *Legend* so passionately and treated me like a princess—Don Weisberg, Jen Loja, Shauna Fay, Ari Lewin, Cecilia Yung, Marikka Tamura, Cindy Howle,

Rob Farren, Linda McCarthy, Theresa Evangelista, Emily Romero, Erin Dempsey, Shanta Newlin, Casey McIntyre, Erin Gallagher, Mia Garcia, Lisa Kelly, and Courtney Wood—and to all the international publishers who have taken *Legend* under their wings.

To my incredible entertainment agent, Kassie Evashevski, for finding *Legend* the best film home possible, and to Temple Hill Entertainment and CBS Films for being that aforementioned best film home. Isaac Klausner, Wyck Godfrey, Marty Bowen, Grey Munford, Ally Mielnicki, Wolfgang Hammer, Amy Baer, Jonathan Levine, Andrew Barrer, and Gabe Ferrari, you guys are amazing. Special thanks to Wayne Alexander for lending his brilliant contract expertise to *Legend*.

To Kami Garcia and Sarah Rees Brennan for taking time out of their enormously busy and talented lives to offer a n00b writer two incredible blurbs, and to JJ, Cindy Pon, Malinda Lo, and Ellen Oh for your invaluable advice, kind words, and Twitter entertainment.

To Paul Gregory for working his magic to make me look presentable in my author photo. To my deviantArt folks, who helped nurture my creativity since 2002 with their helpful and encouraging words. To the fam bam for always being there for me (and for all the delicious food).

And most importantly, to Primo Gallanosa, who saw *Legend* in its earliest form (a two-sentence ramble), let me borrow his personality for Day and his name for the Republic's evil dictator, suggested that June should be a girl, and listened to me day and night, through all my fear, excitement, sadness, and joy. Love you.

TURN THE PAGE
FOR A CLASSIFIED
FIRST LOOK AT THE SEQUEL:

PRODIGY

PRODIGY

PRODIGY

JUNE

PRODIGY

Jan. 4. 1932 Hours.
Ocean Standard Time.
Thirty-five days after Metias's death.

Day jolts awake beside me. His brow is covered with sweat, and his cheeks are wet with tears. He's breathing heavily.

I lean over him and brush a wet strand of hair out of his face. The scrape on my shoulder has scabbed over already, but my movement makes it throb again. Day sits up, rubs a hand wearily across his eyes, and glances around our swaying railcar as if searching for something. He looks first at the stacks of crates in one dark corner, then at the burlap lining the floor and the little sack of food and water sitting between us. It takes him a minute to reorient himself, to remember that we're hitching a ride on a train bound for Vegas. A few seconds pass before he releases his rigid posture and lets himself sag back against the wall.

I gently tap his hand. "Are you okay?" That's become my constant question.

Day shrugs. "Yeah," he mutters. "Nightmare."

Nine days have passed since we broke out of Batalla Hall and escaped Los Angeles. Since then, Day has had nightmares every time he's closed his eyes. When we first got away and were able to catch a few hours of rest in an abandoned train yard, Day bolted awake screaming. We were lucky no soldiers or street police heard him. After that, I developed the habit of stroking his hair right after he falls asleep, of kissing his cheeks and forehead and eyelids. He still wakes up gasping with tears, his eyes hunting frantically for all the things he's lost. But at least he does this silently.

Sometimes, when Day is quiet like this, I wonder how well he's hanging on to his sanity. The thought scares me. I can't afford to lose him. I keep telling myself it's for practical reasons: we'd have little chance of surviving alone at this point, and his skills complement mine. Besides . . . I have no one left to protect. I've had my share of tears too, although I always wait until he's asleep to cry. I cried for Ollie last night. I feel a little silly crying for my dog when the Republic killed our families, but I can't help myself. Metias was the one who'd brought him home, a white ball of giant paws and floppy ears and warm brown eyes, the sweetest, clumsiest creature I'd ever seen. Ollie was my boy, and I'd left him behind.

"What'd you dream?" I whisper to Day.

"Nothing memorable." Day shifts, then winces as he accidentally scrapes his wounded leg against the floor. His body tenses up from the pain, and I can tell how stiff his arms are beneath his shirt, knots of lean muscle earned from the streets. A labored breath escapes his lips. *The way he'd pushed me against that alley wall, the hunger in his first kiss.* I stop focusing on his mouth and shake off the memory, embarrassed.

He nods toward the railcar doors. "Where are we now? We should be getting close, right?"

I get up, glad for the distraction, and brace myself against the rocking wall as I peer out the railcar's tiny window. The landscape hasn't changed much—endless rows of apartment towers and factories, chimneys and old arching highways, all washed into blues and grayish purples by the afternoon rain. We're still passing through slum sectors. They look almost identical to the slums in Los Angeles. Off in the distance, an enormous dam stretches halfway across my line of vision. I wait until a JumboTron flashes by, then squint to see the small letters on the bottom corner of the screen. "Boulder City, Nevada," I say. "Really close now. The train will probably stop here for a while, but afterward it shouldn't take more than thirty-five minutes to arrive in Vegas."

Day nods. He leans over, unties our food sack, and searches for something to eat. "Good. Sooner we get there, sooner we'll find the Patriots."

He seems distant. Sometimes Day tells me what his nightmares are about—failing his Trial or losing Tess on the streets or running away from plague patrols. Nightmares about being the Republic's most wanted criminal. Other times, when he's like this and keeps his dreams to himself, I know they must be about his family—his mother's death, or John's. Maybe it's better that he doesn't tell me about those. I have enough of my own dreams to haunt me, and I'm not sure I have the courage to know about his.

"You're really set on finding the Patriots, aren't you?" I say as Day pulls out a stale hunk of fried dough from the food sack. This isn't the first time I've questioned his insistence on coming to Vegas, and I'm careful about the way I approach the topic. The last thing I want Day to think is that I don't care about Tess, or that I'm afraid to meet up with the Republic's notorious rebel group. "Tess went with them willingly. Are we putting her in danger by trying to get her back?"

Day doesn't answer right away. He tears the fried dough in half and offers me a piece. "Take some, yeah? You haven't eaten in a while."

I hold a hand up politely. "No, thanks," I reply. "I don't like fried dough."

Instantly I wish I could stuff the words back in my mouth. Day lowers his eyes and puts the second half back into the food sack, then quietly starts eating his share. What a stupid, stupid thing for me to say. *I don't like fried dough.* I can practically hear what's going through his head.

Poor little rich girl, with her posh manners. She can afford to dislike *food.* I scold myself in silence, then make a mental note to tread more carefully next time.

After a few mouthfuls, Day finally responds, "I'm not just going to leave Tess behind without knowing she's okay."

Of course he wouldn't. Day would never leave anyone he cares about behind, especially not the orphan girl he's grown up with on the streets. I understand the potential value of meeting the Patriots too—after all, those rebels *had* helped Day and me escape Los Angeles. They're large and well organized. Maybe they have information about what the Republic is doing with Day's little brother, Eden. Maybe they can even help heal Day's festering leg wound—ever since that fateful morning when Commander Jameson shot him in the leg and arrested him, his wound has been on a roller coaster of getting better and then worse. Now his left leg is a mass of broken, bleeding flesh. He needs medical attention.

Still, we have one problem.

"The Patriots won't help us without some sort of payment," I say. "What can we give them?" For emphasis, I reach into my pockets and dig out our meager stash of money. Four thousand Notes. All I had on me before we made a run for it. I can't believe how much I miss the luxury of my old life. There are *millions* of Notes under my family name, Notes that I'll never be able to access again.

Day polishes off the dough and considers my words with his lips pressed together. "Yeah, I know," he says, running a hand through his tangled blond hair. "But what do you suggest we do? Who else can we go to?"

I shake my head helplessly. Day is right about that—as little as I'd like to see the Patriots again, our choices are pretty limited. Back when the Patriots had first helped us escape from Batalla Hall, when Day was still unconscious and I was wounded in the shoulder, I'd asked the Patriots to let us go with them to Vegas. I'd hoped they would continue to help us.

They'd refused.

"You paid us to get Day out of his execution. You *didn't* pay us to carry your wounded asses all the way to Vegas," Kaede had said to me. "Republic soldiers are hot on your trail, for crying out loud. We're not a full-service soup kitchen. I'm not risking my neck for you two again unless there's money involved."

Up until that point, I'd almost believed that the Patriots cared about us. But Kaede's words had brought me back to reality. They'd helped us because I'd paid Kaede 200,000 Republic Notes, the money I'd received as a reward for Day's capture. Even then, it had taken some persuasion before she sent her Patriot comrades in to help us.

Allowing Day to see Tess. Helping Day fix his bad leg. Giving us info about the whereabouts of Day's brother. All these things will require bribes. If only I'd had the chance to grab more money before we left.

"Vegas is the worst possible city for us to wander into by ourselves," I say to Day as I gingerly rub my healing shoulder. "And the Patriots might not even give us an audience. I'm just trying to make sure we think this through."

"June, I know you're not used to thinking of the Patriots as allies," Day replies. "You were trained to hate them. But they *are* a potential ally. I trust them more than I trust the Republic. Don't you?"

I don't know if he means for his words to sound insulting. Day has missed the point I'm trying to make: that the Patriots probably won't help us and then we'll be stuck in a military city. But Day thinks I'm hesitating because I don't trust the Patriots. That, deep down, I'm still June Iparis, the Republic's most celebrated prodigy . . . that I'm still loyal to this country. *Well, is that true?* I'm a criminal now, and I'll never be able to go back to the comforts of my old life. The thought leaves a sick, empty feeling in my stomach, as if I miss being the Republic's darling. Maybe I do.

If I'm not the Republic's darling anymore, then who am I?

"Okay. We'll try to find the Patriots," I say. It's clear that I won't be able to coax him into doing anything else.

Day nods. "Thanks," he whispers. The hint of a smile appears on his lovely face, pulling me in with its irresistible warmth, but he doesn't try to hug me. He doesn't reach for my hand. He doesn't scoot closer to let our shoulders touch, he doesn't stroke my hair, he doesn't whisper reassuringly into my ear or rest his head against mine. I hadn't realized how much I've grown to crave these little gestures. Somehow, in this moment, we feel very separate.

Maybe his nightmare had been about me.

It happens right after we reach the main strip of Las Vegas. The announcement.

First of all, if there's one place in Vegas that we shouldn't be, it's the main strip. JumboTrons (six packed into each block) line both sides of the city's busiest street, their screens playing an endless stream of news. Blinding clusters of searchlights sweep obsessively along the walls. The buildings here must be twice as large as the ones in Los Angeles. The downtown is dominated by towering skyscrapers and enormous pyramid-shaped landing docks (eight of them, square bases, equilateral triangle sides) with bright lights beaming from their tips. The desert air reeks of smoke and feels painfully dry; no thirst-quenching hurricanes here, no waterfronts or lakes. Troops make their way up and down the street (in oblong square formations, typical of Vegas), dressed in the black, navy-striped uniforms of soldiers rotating out to and back from the warfront. Farther out, past this main street of skyscrapers, are rows of fighter jets, all rolling into position on a wide strip of airfield. Airships glide overhead.

This is a military city, a world of soldiers.

The sun has just set when Day and I make our way out onto the main strip and head toward the other end of the street. Day leans heavily on my shoulder as we try to blend in with the crowds, his breath shallow and his face drawn with pain. I try my best to support him without looking out of place, but his weight makes me walk in an unbalanced line, as if I'd had too much to drink. "How are we doing?" he murmurs into my ear, his lips hot against my skin. I'm not sure if he's half-delirious from the pain or if it's my outfit, but I can't say I mind his blatant flirtation tonight. It's a nice change from our awkward train ride. He's careful to keep his head down, his eyes hidden under long lashes and tilted away from the soldiers bustling back and forth along the sidewalks. He shifts uncomfortably in his military jacket and pants. A black soldier's cap hides his white-blond hair and blocks a good portion of his face.

"Well enough," I reply. "Remember, you're drunk. And happy. You're supposed to be lusting over your escort. Try smiling a little more."

Day plasters a giant artificial smile on his face. As charming as ever. "Aw, come on, sweetheart. I thought I was doing a pretty good job. I got my arm around the prettiest escort on this block—how could I *not* be lusting over you? Don't I *look* like I'm lusting? This is me, lusting." His lashes flutter at me.

He looks so ridiculous that I can't help laughing. Another passerby glances at me. "*Much* better." I shiver when he nudges his face into the hollow of my neck. *Stay in character. Concentrate.* The gold trinkets lining my waist and ankles jingle as we walk. "How's your leg?"

Day pulls away a little. "Was doing fine until you brought it up," he whispers, then winces as he trips over a crack in the sidewalk. I tighten my grip around him. "I'll make it to our next rest stop."

"Remember, two fingers against your brow if you need to stop."

"Yeah, yeah. I'll let you know if I'm in trouble."

Another pair of soldiers pushes past us with their own escorts, grinning girls decked out in sparkling eye shadow and elegantly painted face tattoos, their bodies covered thinly by dancer costumes and fake red feathers. One of the soldiers catches sight of me, laughs, and widens his glazed eyes.

"What club you from, gorgeous?" he slurs. "Don't remember your face around here." His hand goes for my exposed waist, hungering for skin. Before he can reach me, Day's arm whips out and shoves the soldier roughly away.

"Don't touch her." Day grins and winks at the soldier, keeping up his carefree demeanor, but the warning in his eyes and voice makes the other man back off. He blinks at both of us, mumbles something under his breath, and staggers away with his friends.

I try to imitate the way those escorts giggle, then give my hair a toss. "Next time, just go with it," I hiss in Day's ear even as I kiss him on the cheek, as if he were the best customer ever. "Last thing we need is a fight."

"What?" Day shrugs and returns to his painful walk. "It'd be a pretty pathetic fight. He could barely stand."

I shake my head and decide not to point out the irony.

A third group of soldiers stumbles past us in a loud, drunken daze. (Seven cadets, two lieutenants, gold armbands with Dakota insignias, which means they just arrived here from the north and haven't yet exchanged their armbands for new ones with their warfront battalions.) They have their arms wrapped around escorts from the Bellagio clubs—glittering girls with scarlet chokers and *B* arm tattoos. These soldiers are probably stationed in the barracks above the clubs.

I check my own costume again. Stolen from the dressing rooms of the Sun Palace. On the surface, I seem like any other escort. Gold chains and trinkets around my waist and ankles. Feathers and gold ribbons pinned into my scarlet (spray-painted), braided hair. Smoky eye shadow coated with glitter.

A ferocious phoenix tattoo painted across my upper cheek and eyelid. Red silks leave my arms and waist exposed, and dark laces line my boots.

But there's one thing on my costume that the other girls don't wear.

A chain of thirteen little glittering mirrors. They're partially hidden amongst the other ornaments wrapped around my ankle, and from a distance it would seem like another decoration. Completely forgettable. But every now and then, when streetlights catch it, it becomes a row of brilliant, sparkling lights. Thirteen, the Patriots' unofficial number. This is our signal to them. They must be watching the main Vegas strip all the time, so I know they'll at least notice a row of flashing lights on me. And when they do, they'll recognize us as the same pair they helped rescue in Los Angeles.

The JumboTrons lining the street crackle for a second. The pledge should start again any minute now. Unlike Los Angeles, Vegas runs the national pledge five times a day—all the JumboTrons will pause in whatever ads or news they're showing, replace them with enormous images of the Elector Primo, and then play the following on the city's speaker system: *I pledge allegiance to the flag of the great Republic of America, to our Elector Primo, to our glorious states, to unity against the Colonies, to our impending victory!*

Not long ago, I used to recite that pledge every morning and afternoon with the same enthusiasm as anyone else, determined to keep the east coast Colonies from taking control of our precious west coast land. That was before I knew about the Republic's role in my family's deaths. I'm not sure what I think now. Let the Colonies win?

The JumboTrons start broadcasting a newsreel. Weekly recap. Day and I watch the headlines zip by on the screens:

REPUBLIC TRIUMPHANTLY TAKES OVER MILES OF COLONIES' LAND IN BATTLE FOR AMARILLO, EAST TEXAS

FLOOD WARNING CANCELLED FOR SACRAMENTO, CALIFORNIA

ELECTOR VISITS TROOPS ON NORTHERN WARFRONT, BOOSTS MORALE

Most of them are fairly uninteresting—the usual headlines coming in from the warfront, updates on weather and laws, quarantine notices for Vegas.

Then Day taps my shoulder and gestures at one of the screens.

QUARANTINE IN LOS ANGELES EXTENDED TO EMERALD, OPAL SECTORS

"Gem sectors?" Day whispers. My eyes are still fixed on the screen, even though the headline has passed. "Don't rich folks live there?"

I'm not sure what to say in return because I'm still trying to process the information myself. Emerald and Opal sectors . . . Is this a mistake? Or have the plagues in LA gotten serious enough to be broadcast on *Vegas* JumboTrons? I've never, *ever* seen quarantines extended into the upper-class sectors. Emerald sector borders Ruby—does that mean my home sector is going to be quarantined too? What about our vaccinations? Aren't they supposed to prevent things like this? I think back on Metias's journal entries. *One of these days,* he'd said, *there will be a virus unleashed that none of us will be able to stop.* I remember the things Metias had unveiled, the underground factories, the rampant diseases . . . the systematic plagues. A shiver runs through me. Los Angeles will quell it, I tell myself. The plague will die down, just like it always does.

"DOESN'T MERELY SURVIVE THE HYPE, IT DESERVES IT."
—THE NEW YORK TIMES
MARIE LU
LEGEND
NEW YORK TIMES BESTSELLER

NEW YORK TIMES BESTSELLING AUTHOR
MARIE LU
A LEGEND NOVEL
PRODIGY

NEW YORK TIMES BESTSELLING AUTHOR
MARIE LU
A LEGEND NOVEL
CHAMPION

Keep reading for an excerpt from

THE YOUNG ELITES

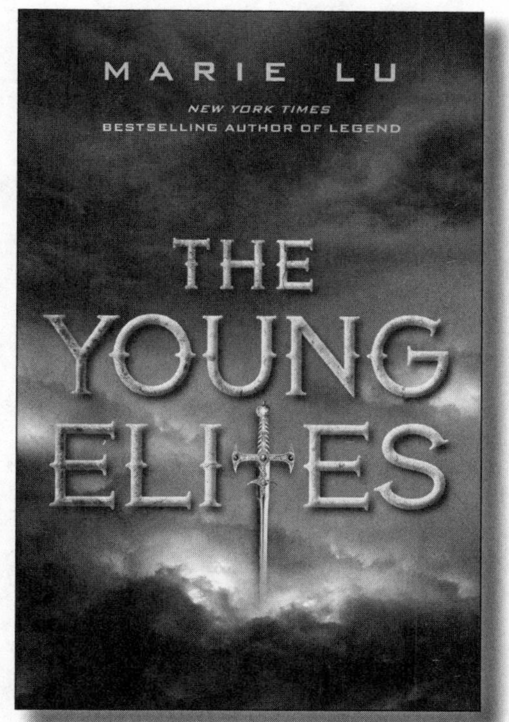

The first book in another thrilling series by Marie Lu

Some hate us, think us outlaws to hang at the gallows.
Some fear us, think us demons to burn at the stake.
Some worship us, think us children of the gods.
But *all* know us.

—Unknown source on the Young Elites

Adelina Amouteru

I'm going to die tomorrow morning.

That's what the Inquisitors tell me, anyway, when they visit my cell. I've been in here for weeks—I know this only because I've been counting the number of times my meals come.

One day. Two days.

Four days. A week.

Two weeks.

Three.

I stopped counting after that. The hours run together, an endless train of nothingness, filled with different slants of light and the shiver of cold, wet stone, the pieces of my sanity, the disjointed whispers of my thoughts.

But tomorrow, my time ends. They're going to burn me at the stake in the central market square, for all to see. The Inquisitors tell me a crowd has already begun to gather outside.

I sit straight, the way I was always taught. My shoulders don't touch the wall. It takes me a while to realize that I'm rocking back and forth, perhaps to stay sane, perhaps just to keep warm. I hum an old lullaby too, one my mother used to sing to me when I was very little. I do my best to imitate her voice, a sweet and delicate sound, but my notes come out cracked and hoarse, nothing like what I remember. I stop trying.

It's so damp down here. Water trickles from above my door and has painted a groove into the stone wall, discolored green and black with grime. My hair is matted, and my nails are caked with blood and dirt. I want to scrub them clean. Is it strange that all I can think about on my last day is how filthy I am? If my little sister were here, she'd murmur something reassuring and soak my hands in warm water.

I can't stop wondering if she's okay. She hasn't come to see me.

I lower my head into my hands. How did I end up like this?

But I know how, of course. It's because I'm a murderer.

It happened several weeks earlier, on a stormy night at my father's villa. I couldn't sleep. Rain fell and lightning reflected off the window of my bedchamber. But even the storm couldn't drown out the conversation from downstairs. My father and his guest were talking about me, of course. My father's late-night conversations were always about me.

I was the talk of my family's eastern Dalia district. *Adelina Amouteru?* they all said. *Oh, she's one of those who survived the fever a decade ago. Poor thing. Her father will have a hard time marrying her off.*

No one meant because I wasn't *beautiful.* I'm not being arrogant, only honest. My nursemaid once told me that any man who'd ever laid eyes on my late mother was now waiting curiously to see how her two daughters would blossom into women. My younger sister, Violetta, was only fourteen and already the budding image of perfection. Unlike me, Violetta had inherited our mother's rosy temperament and innocent charm. She'd kiss my cheeks and laugh and twirl and dream. When we were very small, we'd sit together in the garden and she would braid periwinkles into my hair. I would sing to her. She would make up games.

We loved each other, once.

My father would bring Violetta jewels and watch her clap her hands in delight as he strung them around her neck. He would buy her exquisite dresses that arrived in port from the farthest ends of the world. He would tell her stories and kiss her good night. He would remind her how beautiful she was, how far she would raise our family's standing with a good marriage, how she could attract princes and kings if she desired. Violetta already had a line of suitors eager to secure her hand, and my father would tell each of them to be patient, that they could not marry her until she turned seventeen. *What a caring father,* everyone thought.

Of course, Violetta didn't escape *all* of my father's cruelty. He purposely bought her dresses that were tight and painful. He enjoyed seeing her feet bleed from the hard, jeweled shoes he encouraged her to wear.

Still. He loved her, in his own way. It's different, you see, because she was his investment.

I was another story. Unlike my sister, blessed with shining black hair to complement her dark eyes and rich olive skin, I am flawed. And by flawed, I mean this: When I was four years old, the blood fever reached its peak and everyone in Kenettra barred their homes in a state of panic. No use. My mother, sister, and I all came down with the fever. You could always tell who was infected—strange, mottled patterns showed up on our skin, our hair and lashes flitted from one color to another, and pink, blood-tinged tears ran from our eyes. I still remember the smell of sickness in our house, the burn of brandy on my lips. My left eye became so swollen that a doctor had to remove it. He did it with a red-hot knife and a pair of burning tongs.

So, yes. You could say I am flawed.

Marked. A *malfetto.*

While my sister emerged from the fever unscathed, I now have only a scar where my left eye used to be. While my sister's hair remained a glossy black, the strands of *my* hair and lashes turned a strange, ever-shifting silver, so that in the sunlight they look close to white, like a winter moon, and in the dark they change to a deep gray, shimmering silk spun from metal.

At least I fared better than Mother did. Mother, like every infected adult, died. I remember crying in her empty bedchamber each night, wishing the fever had taken Father instead.

My father and his mysterious guest were still talking downstairs. My curiosity got the best of me and I swung my legs over the side of my bed, crept toward my chamber door on light feet, and opened it a crack. Dim candlelight illuminated the hall outside. Below, my father sat across from a tall, broad-shouldered man with graying hair at his temples, his hair tied back at the nape of his neck in a short, customary tail, the velvet of his coat shining black and orange in the light. My father's coat was velvet too, but the material was worn thin. Before the blood fever crippled our country, his clothes would have been as luxurious as his guest's. But now? It's hard to keep good trade relations when you have a *malfetto* daughter tainting your family's name.

Both men drank wine. Father must be in a negotiating mood tonight, I thought, to have tapped one of our last good casks.

I opened the door a little wider, crept out into the hall, and sat, knees to my chin, along the stairs. My favorite spot. Sometimes I'd pretend I was a queen, and that I stood here on a palace balcony looking down at my groveling subjects. Now I took up my usual crouch and listened closely to the conversation downstairs. As always, I made sure my hair covered my scar. My hand rested awkwardly on the staircase. My father had broken my fourth finger, and it never healed straight. Even now, I could not curl it properly around the railing.

"I don't mean to insult you, Master Amouteru," the man said to my father. "You were a merchant of good reputation. But that was a long time ago. I don't want to be seen doing business with a *malfetto* family—bad luck, you know. There's little you can offer me."

My father kept a smile on his face. The forced smile of a business transaction. "There are still lenders in town who work with me. I can pay you back as soon as the port traffic picks up. Tamouran silks and spices are in high demand this year—"

The man looked unimpressed. "The king's dumb as a dog," he replied. "And dogs are no good at running countries. The ports will be slow for years to come, I'm afraid, and with the new tax laws, your debts will only grow. How can you possibly repay me?"

My father leaned back in his chair, sipped his wine, and sighed. "There must be something I can offer you."

The man studied his glass of wine thoughtfully. The harsh lines of his face made me shiver. "Tell me about Adelina. How many offers have you received?"

My father blushed. As if the wine hadn't left him red

enough already. "Offers for Adelina's hand have been slow to come."

The man smiled. "None for your little abomination, then."

My father's lips tightened. "Not as many as I'd like," he admitted.

"What do the others say about her?"

"The other suitors?" My father rubbed a hand across his face. Admitting all my flaws embarrassed him. "They say the same thing. It always comes back to her . . . markings. What can I tell you, sir? No one wants a *malfetto* bearing his children."

The man listened, making sympathetic sounds.

"Haven't you heard the latest news from Estenzia? Two noblemen walking home from the opera were found burned to a crisp." My father had quickly changed tack, hoping now that the stranger would take pity on him. "Scorch marks on the wall, their bodies melted from the inside out. Everyone is frightened of *malfettos,* sir. Even *you* are reluctant to do business with me. Please. I'm helpless."

I knew what my father spoke of. He was referring to very specific *malfettos*—a rare handful of children who came out of the blood fever with scars far darker than mine, frightening abilities that don't belong in this world. Everyone talked about these *malfettos* in hushed whispers; most feared them and called them demons. But *I* secretly held them in awe. People said they could conjure fire out of thin air. Could call the wind. Could control beasts. Could disappear. Could kill in the blink of an eye.

If you searched the black market, you'd find flat wooden engravings for sale, elaborately carved with their names, forbidden collectibles that supposedly meant *they* would protect you—or, at the least, that they would not hurt you. No matter the opinion, everyone knew their names. *The Reaper. Magiano. The Windwalker. The Alchemist.*

The Young Elites.

The man shook his head. "I've heard that even the suitors who refuse Adelina still gape at her, sick with desire." He paused. "True, her markings are . . . unfortunate. But a beautiful girl is a beautiful girl." Something strange glinted in his eyes. My stomach twisted at the sight, and I tucked my chin tighter against my knees, as if for protection.

My father looked confused. He sat up taller in his chair and pointed his wineglass at the man. "Are you making me an offer for Adelina's hand?"

The man reached into his coat to produce a small brown pouch, then tossed it onto the table. It landed with a heavy clink. As a merchant's daughter, one becomes well acquainted with money—and I could tell from the sound and from the size of the coins that the purse was filled to the brim with gold talents. I stifled a gasp.

As my father gaped at the contents, the man leaned back and thoughtfully sipped his wine. "I know of the estate taxes you haven't yet paid to the crown. I know of your new debts. And I will cover all of them in exchange for your daughter Adelina."

My father frowned. "But you have a wife."

"I do, yes." The man paused, then added, "I never said I wanted to *marry* her. I am merely proposing to take her off your hands."

I felt the blood drain from my face. "You . . . want her as your mistress, then?" Father asked.

The man shrugged. "No nobleman in his right mind would make a wife of such a marked girl—she could not possibly attend public affairs on my arm. I have a reputation to uphold, Master Amouteru. But I think we can work this out. She will have a home, and you will have your gold." He raised a hand. "One condition. I want her *now,* not in a year. I've no patience to wait until she turns seventeen."

A strange buzzing filled my ears. *No* boy or girl was allowed to give themselves to another until they turned seventeen. This man was asking my father to break the law. To defy the gods.

My father raised an eyebrow, but he didn't argue. "A mistress," he finally said. "Sir, you must know what this will do to my reputation. I might as well sell her to a brothel."

"And how is your reputation faring now? How much damage has she already done to your professional name?" He leaned forward. "Surely you're not insinuating my home is nothing more than a common brothel. At least your Adelina would belong to a noble household."

As I watched my father sip his wine, my hands began to tremble. "A mistress," he repeated.

"Think quickly, Master Amouteru. I won't offer this again."

"Give me a moment," my father anxiously reassured him.

I don't know how long the silence lasted, but when he finally spoke again, I jumped at the sound. "Adelina could be a good match for you. You're wise to see it. She is lovely, even with her markings, and . . . spirited."

The man swirled his wine. "And I will tame her. Do we have a deal?"

I closed my eye. My world swam in darkness—I imagined the man's face against my own, his hand on my waist, his sickening smile. Not even a wife. A *mistress*. The thought made me shrink from the stairs. Through a haze of numbness, I watched my father shake hands and clink wineglasses with the man. "A deal, then," he said to the man. He looked relieved of a great burden. "Tomorrow, she's yours. Just . . . keep this private. I don't want Inquisitors knocking on my door and fining me for giving her away too young."

"She's a *malfetto,*" the man replied. "No one will care." He tightened his gloves and rose from his chair in one elegant move. My father bowed his head. "I'll send a carriage for her in the morning."

As my father escorted him to our door, I stole away into my bedchamber and stood there in the darkness, shaking. Why did my father's words still stab me in the heart? I should be used to it by now. What had he once told me? *My poor Adelina,* he'd said, caressing my cheek with a thumb.

It's a shame. Look at you. Who will ever want a malfetto *like you?*

It will be all right, I tried telling myself. *At least you can leave your father behind. It won't be so bad.* But even as I thought this, I felt a weight settle in my chest. I knew the truth. *Malfettos* were unwanted. Bad luck. And now more than ever, feared. I would be tossed aside the instant the man tired of me.

My gaze wandered around my bedchamber, settling finally on my window. My heartbeat stilled for a moment. Rain drew angry lines down the glass, but through it I could still see the deep blue cityscape of Dalia, the rows of domed brick towers and cobblestone alleys, the marble temples, the docks where the edge of the city sloped gently into the sea, where on clear nights gondolas with golden lanterns would glide across the water, where the waterfalls that bordered southern Kenettra thundered. Tonight, the ocean churned in fury, and white foam crashed against the city's horizon, flooding the canals.

I continued staring out the rain-slashed window for a long while.

Tonight. Tonight was the night.

I hurried to my bed, bent down, and dragged out a sack I'd made with a bedsheet. Inside it were fine silverware, forks and knives, candelabras, engraved plates, anything I could sell for food and shelter. That's another thing to love about me. I steal. I'd been stealing from around our house for months, stashing things under my bed in preparation for the day when I couldn't stand to live with my father any longer. It wasn't much, but I calculated that if I sold all of it to the right dealers, I might end up with a few gold talents. Enough to get by, at least, for several months.

Then I rushed to my chest of clothes, pulled out an armful of silks, and hurried about my chamber to collect any jewelry I could find. My silver bracelets. A pearl necklace inherited from my mother that my sister did not want. A pair of sapphire earrings. I grabbed two long strips of silk cloth that make up a Tamouran headwrap. I would need to cover up my silver hair while on the run. I worked in feverish concentration. I added the jewelry and clothes carefully into the sack, hid it behind my bed, and pulled on my soft leather riding boots.

I settled down to wait.

An hour later, when my father retired to bed and the house stilled, I grabbed the sack. I hurried to my window and pressed my hand against it. Gingerly, I pushed the left pane aside and propped it open. The storm had calmed some, but rain still came down steadily enough to mute the sound of my footsteps. I looked over my shoulder one last time at my bedchamber door, as if I expected my father to walk in. *Where are you going, Adelina?* he'd say. *There's nothing out there for a girl like you.*

I shook his voice from my head. Let him find me gone in the morning, his best chance at settling his debts. I took a deep breath, then began to climb through the open window. Cold rain lashed at my arms, prickling my skin.

"Adelina?"

I whirled around at the voice. Behind me, the silhouette of a girl stood in my doorway—my sister, Violetta, still rubbing sleep from her eyes. She stared at the open window and the sack on my shoulders, and for a terrifying moment, I thought she might raise her voice and shout for Father.

But Violetta watched me quietly. I felt a pang of guilt, even as the sight of her sent a flash of resentment through my heart. Fool. Why should I have felt sorry for someone who had watched me suffer so many times before? *I love you, Adelina,* she used to say, when we were small. *Papa loves you too. He just doesn't know how to show it.* Why did I pity the sister who was valued?

Still, I found myself rushing to her on silent feet, taking one of her hands in mine, and putting a slender finger up to her lips. She gave me a worried look. "You should go back to bed," she whispered. In the dim glow of night, I could see the gloss of her dark, marble eyes, the thinness of her delicate skin. Her beauty was so pure. "You'll get in trouble if Father finds you."

I squeezed her hand tighter, then let our foreheads touch. We stayed still for a long moment, and it seemed as if we were children again, each leaning against the other. Usually Violetta would pull away from me, knowing that Father did not like to see us close. This time, though, she clung to me. As if she knew that tonight was something different. "Violetta," I whispered, "do you remember the time you lied to Father about who broke one of his best vases?"

My sister nodded against my shoulder.

"I need you to do that for me again." I pulled far away enough to tuck her hair behind her ear. "Don't say a word."

She didn't reply; instead, she swallowed and looked down the hall toward our father's chambers. She did not hate him in the same way that I did, and the thought of going against his teaching—that she was too good for me, that to love me was a foolish thing—filled her eyes with guilt. Finally, she nodded. I felt as if a mantle had been lifted from my shoulders, like she was letting go of me. "Be careful out there. Stay safe. Good luck."

We exchanged a final look. *You could come with me,* I thought. *But I know you won't. You're too scared. Go back to smiling at the dresses that Father buys for you.* Still, my heart softened for a moment. Violetta was always the good girl. She didn't choose any of this. *I do wish you a happy life. I hope you fall in love and marry well. Good-bye, sister.* I didn't dare wait for her to say anything else. Instead I turned away, walked to the window, and stepped onto the second-floor ledge.

I nearly slipped. The rain had turned everything slick, and my riding boots fought for grip against the narrow ledge. Some silverware fell out of my sack, clattering on the ground below. *Don't look down.* I made my way along the ledge until I reached a balcony, and there I slid down until I dangled with nothing but my trembling hands holding me in place. I closed my eye and let go.

RAVES FOR LEGEND

"A fine example of commercial fiction with razor-sharp plotting, depth of character and emotional arc, *Legend* doesn't merely survive the hype, it deserves it."
—*The New York Times*

"Marie Lu's dystopian novel is a *Legend* in the making."
—*USA Today*

"Taut and exciting." —*Los Angeles Times*

"Smart, sharp, fast-paced." —*Entertainment Weekly*

★ "A gripping thriller in dystopic future Los Angeles . . . a cinematic adventure." —*Kirkus Reviews*, starred review

★ "A well-written, emotionally satisfying read. A fast-paced blend of action and science fiction." —*VOYA*, starred review

★ "The delicious details keep pages turning. . . . You've got the makings for a potent sequel." —*Booklist*, starred review

★ "Utterly satisfying . . . Lu's debut is a stunner."
—*Publishers Weekly*, starred review

★ "Many dystopian books are filling the shelves, but this book stands out." —*Library Media Connection*, starred review

"A romantic thriller set in a post-apocalyptic world where nothing is what it seems—*Legend* is impossible to put down and even harder to forget." —Kami Garcia, *New York Times* bestselling coauthor of *Beautiful Creatures* and *Beautiful Darkness*